MOSQUITO BEACH

D1566012

MOSQUITO BEACH

A Folly Beach Mystery

BILL NOEL

Other Folly Beach Mysteries by Bill Noel

Folly

The Pier

Washout

The Edge

The Marsh

Ghosts

Missing

Final Cut

First Light

Boneyard Beach

Silent Night

Dead Center

Discord

A Folly Beach Mystery COLLECTION

Dark Horse

Joy

A Folly Beach Mystery COLLECTION II

No Joke

Relic

A Folly Beach Mystery COLLECTION III

Faith

A Folly Beach Christmas Mystery COLLECTION

Tipping Point

Sea Fog

Front cover photo and design by Bill Noel

Author photo by Susan Noel

ISBN: 978-1-942212-58-4

Enigma House Press

Goshen, Kentucky 40026

www.enigmahousepress.com

First Edition

BILL NOEL'S
FOLLY
BEACH
SOUTH CAROLINA

1 Rita's
2 Dude's surf shop *
3 Sand Dollar
4 Haunted House *
5 Loggerhead's
6 Snapper Jacks
7 St. James Gate
8 Surf Bar
9 Cal's
10 Mr. John's Beach Store
11 Landrum Gallery/Barb's Books *
12 The Crab Shack
13 City Hall/Public Safety
14 Sean Aker, Attorney *

15 Planet Follywood
16 Woody's Pizza
17 The Washout
18 Post Office
19 Pewter Hardware *
20 Lost Dog Cafe
21 Bert's Market
22 The Edge *

* From my imagination to yours.

Chris's House
Chris's apartment
Sandbar Lane
Charleston
Center Street
East Second St
West Second St
East Ashley Ave
Arctic Ave
Ashley Ave
Cooper Ave
Indian Ave
Huron Ave
Erie Ave

First Light

Boneyard Beach
Marsh to Inland Lighthouse
Washout
Folly River
Pier
Folly Beach County Park
Marsh

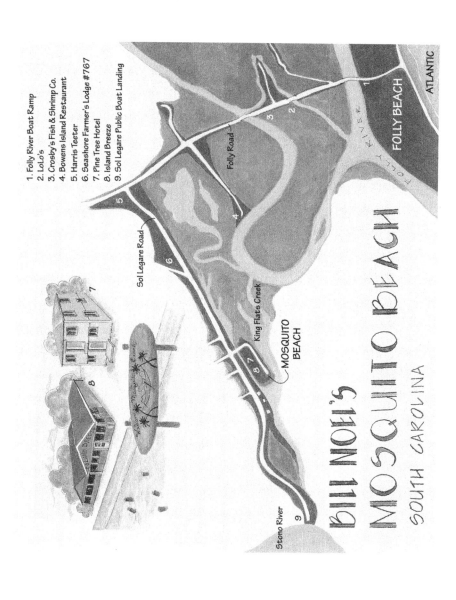

1. Folly River Boat Ramp
2. LoLo's
3. Crosby's Fish & Shrimp Co.
4. Bowens Island Restaurant
5. Harris Teeter
6. Seashore Farmer's Lodge #767
7. Pine Tree Hotel
8. Island Breeze
9. Sol Legare Public Boat Landing

BILL NOEL'S
MOSQUITO BEACH
SOUTH CAROLINA

FOLLY BEACH
ATLANTIC
FOLLY RIVER
Folly Road
Sol Legare Road
King Flats Creek
MOSQUITO BEACH
Stono River

Chapter One

"Mr. Chris, this is Al. Did I catch you at a bad time?"

I didn't tell my friend his call interrupted my exciting morning sitting on the screened-in porch watching cars speed by my cottage. What I did was ask if he was okay since during the years I'd known Al Washington, this was the first time he'd called. He also had spent much of his eighty-second year with serious health issues; for a time, it didn't look like he'd survive.

He chuckled. "Sorry to startle you. I'm fine."

I paused giving him time to elaborate but he didn't, so I said, "What do I owe the pleasure of your call?" I thought that was subtler than reminding him he'd never called before.

"Have you heard anything about a body, umm, guess more like a skeleton, found on Mosquito Beach?"

I'd never been to Mosquito Beach but knew it was a quarter-mile strip of land off Sol Legare Road about four miles from my home on Folly Beach, South Carolina.

"No, should I have?"

"Blubber Bob says you know everything bad that happens on Folly. Mosquito Beach is near there, so I figured you might've heard."

Bob Howard, occasionally called Blubber Bob or other unflattering names by Al, is a friend I'd met when I moved to Folly more than a decade ago. He was the realtor who helped me find my retirement home. He recently retired from his successful career and now owns Al's Bar and Gourmet Grill near downtown Charleston, ten miles from Folly. Al's was previously owned by and named after my caller until Bob bought it, most likely preventing Al from dying from worry, stress, fatigue, and a huge debt on the neighborhood bar.

"When do you believe everything Bob tells you?"

"Good point, but I figure he can't always be wrong."

I smiled. Bob and Al had been friends for decades, yet they were as opposite as black and white; appropriate since Al was African American, Bob was as white as an albino polar bear.

"Al, what do you know about the body, the skeleton?"

"Thought I heard something on the news. Wasn't paying attention until the news guy mentioned Mosquito Beach."

"Why'd that get your attention?"

"Spent a lot of time there in the 1950s after I got back from Korea. Mosquito was one of two or three places Negroes, as we were called back then, could go to a beach. The ocean beaches were segregated." He gave an audible sigh. "Had some good times out there, sure did."

There was another long pause which told me there was more to Al's curiosity than he'd shared.

"I don't know much about Mosquito Beach other than

seeing a sign for it on Sol Legare Road. What else did they say on the news?"

"Something about a man cutting across a field when he found bones. That's all I got."

"Want me to call Chief LaMond to see what she knows?"

Cindy LaMond was a friend who happened to be Folly Beach's Director of Public Safety, informally known as Chief. Mosquito Beach wasn't in Folly's city limits, but Cindy could use her contacts to learn what was going on.

"Oh, no. Don't bother her. Just thought you might've heard something."

"It's no bother. I'd be glad to ask."

"No need, old man's curiosity, that's all."

"You sure?"

"Yeah. Sorry to bother you. I'm sure you're busy."

"Yes, I'm so, so busy. Retirement's a full-time job, but, Al, I can always find time for you."

He laughed then repeated he was sorry to bother me. I still felt there was something on his mind about the news from Mosquito Beach.

"It's great hearing from you. Let me know if you change your mind. Be sure to say hi to Bob for me."

He laughed again; said he'd rather not incur Bob's wrath by telling him he talked to me. Before ending the call, he suggested I could tell Bob myself the next time I visited Al's.

What I didn't tell him was my next call would be to Chief LaMond.

Cindy answered the phone with, "What are you going to do to ruin my day?"

Since I'd moved to Folly after retiring from a job in the human resources department with a large healthcare company in Kentucky, I'd stumbled on a few horrific situations involving the death of acquaintances. Through luck, being at the right place at the right time, and with the help of a cadre of friends, I'd helped the police bring the murderers to justice. Cindy had more than a few times accused me of being a murder magnet, a pain in her "shapely" posterior, but in weaker moments, a good friend who helped her catch some evil people.

I asked what she knew about a body found on Mosquito Beach.

"Chris Landrum, you're going to be the death of me. Isn't it enough for you to butt in every death my highly competent department led by a more highly-competent Chief investigates, now you stick your nose in things that happened decades ago?"

"Al Washington called to ask if I knew anything about the body. I hadn't heard about it, but knew you, being highly competent, would have more information."

She sighed. "Mr. Suck-Up, why'd Al want to know?"

I explained the little he'd shared then repeated my question about what Cindy knew.

She reminded me Mosquito Beach wasn't in her jurisdiction. All she knew was what was reported in the media.

"I assume it's being investigated by your good buddies in the Charleston County Sheriff's Office. Think you could make a call and see what they have? I don't know why Al is interested, but he'd appreciate learning more."

The Sheriff's Office investigates major crimes in Charleston County which includes Folly and Mosquito Beach.

"Tell you what, I'll cut my afternoon nap short, and because I like Al, I'll call the Sheriff's Office. I'll tell you what

I learn; then you'll tell Al. Now pay close attention, you'll not, I repeat, not stick your nose where it don't belong. Deal?"

"I have no plan to get involved."

When I said it, I meant it. Honestly I did.

I hung up from my second call of the day thinking about the Yiddish proverb, "Man plans, God laughs."

Chapter Two

I spent the next hour on the computer learning about Mosquito Beach. The problem I often have when researching something on the Internet is finding too much information. That wasn't the case when it came to the small, James Island community located on the banks of a tidal creek. I was reminded that Mosquito Beach is the location of Island Breeze, a restaurant that I'd heard about after it'd been damaged by a hurricane that'd swept through the area a few years back. This might be a good chance to learn more about the nearby dining establishment.

Ten minutes later, Barb Deanelli agreed to accompany me to dinner. Three hours later, I picked her up at her oceanfront condo, and we were driving up Folly Road. Barb was three years younger than my sixty-nine years, at five-foot-ten my height, but unlike my slightly overweight body, she was paper thin.

We turned left on Sol Legare Road at the Harris Teeter grocery when Barb, who'd been unusually quiet for the two-mile ride, said, "Don't suppose Mosquito Beach was named after the Mosquito family, and not those pesky, biting troublemakers?"

It wasn't. I smiled. "That'll be a good question to ask at the restaurant."

She glanced over at me, frowned. "That means it was named after the insect most of us try to avoid."

Barb and I had dated a couple of years, so she was familiar with most of my quirky friends plus was game for most adventures. I was surprised by her reluctance to go somewhere named for mosquitos.

I patted her on the knee, smiled, then said, "Remember, you once told me you liked to try new restaurants."

She glanced at a boy riding his bicycle in a front yard, turned back to me and said, "I also would like to go to Paris. Can we do that after recuperating from mosquito bites?"

Another mile up the road, I turned left on Mosquito Beach Road marked by a surfboard with *Welcome to Mosquito Beach* painted on it. It didn't help my case that a mosquito the size of a condor was painted on the sign. A couple hundred yards farther, the pavement took a sharp right turn with the marsh and tidal creek fewer than twenty yards to our left and running parallel to the narrow road. Three small structures looking like they'd survived several hurricanes dotted the right side of the road. Small patches of grass resembled tiny islands in a sea of sand surrounded the structures. So far, the only living creature we'd seen since turning on Mosquito Beach Road was a tabby cat eyeing us with a mixture of fear and curiosity.

The lifeless landscape changed drastically as we came to a brightly painted yellow building. Island Breeze was painted on the front gable in letters large enough to be read from passing airliners. Umbrellas advertising Angry Orchard Hard Cider and Traveler Beer provided partial shade for three wooden, do-it-yourself tables made from cable spool holders. Each table was occupied. Three men leaned against the railing separating the restaurant from the screened-in patio. It was hot for mid-September, so I was surprised to see so many people outside enjoying food and drinks.

I parked across the street on a grass and sand parking area. We shared the parking area with three cars and two pickup trucks that from the dents and layers of dust and dried mud were workhorses used for what trucks were created for. Several vehicles were parked on the far side of the building. We walked across the street to the sounds of Bob Marley blaring from outdoor speakers. Animated conversations from groups seated at the tables mixed with the music. Most of the fifteen or so people appeared to pay little attention to us. A handful glanced at the newcomers. A couple of them smiled, but I didn't recognize anyone. While the Sol Legare area was predominantly African American, several of the casually dressed patrons were white. Four men wore dusty jeans and work boots, most likely having arrived in the pickup trucks.

We went inside and moved to the bar lit by colorful Christmas lights strung along the backbar reflecting in the bourbon, rum, and gin bottles where we were greeted by a woman who told us to sit anywhere. I looked around the crowded room. The walls were painted light blue and the bourbon-barrel tables covered with round pieces of wood were occupied as were the seats in front of the restaurant. We chose bar-height chairs facing the creek at the long, foot-wide wooden table nudging the screened-in porch.

A middle-aged man seated two chairs away noticed me looking around for a menu.

He pointed his beer bottle over his shoulder toward the bar. "Menu's on the chalk board."

I thanked him. Barb and I saw where oxtail headed the menu. I didn't know what that was, so I quickly skipped down the list and decided on barbecue. Barb chose the same.

"They're short on help. Order at the bar," our helpful neighbor offered.

I thanked him again then headed to the bar where the woman who first told us to sit took our order. I waited while she got a beer for Barb, a glass of house wine for me.

Before I could take a sip, the man moved one seat closer to us. "First time here?"

I said, "Yes."

He reached his coal black, thin arm my direction. "I'm Terrell Jefferson." He smiled. He wore black shorts, a black polo shirt with paint stains on the shoulder, a diamond stud earring, and a faded ARMY tattoo on his forearm.

We shook hands as I told him who we were. He said he was pleased to meet us. He glanced at my tan shorts and faded green polo shirt, then at Barb's navy shorts and red T-shirt.

He took a sip of beer, and said, "From around here?"

Barb leaned forward so she could see Terrell past my head. "We live on Folly, if you consider that from around here."

Terrell glanced around, leaned toward us. "Close enough. What brings you to Mosquito Beach?"

I had the feeling Terrell was almost irritated we were here. I shook the feeling off, reminding myself he was the one who initiated the conversation, the one who moved closer to us.

Barb nodded at me to respond.

I said, "Terrell, I've lived on Folly several years. Barb has been there a little over two years. We like visiting different restaurants, so we wanted to try Island Breeze. You from here?"

Terrell said something, but I was having trouble hearing. From the sound system, the Drifters were singing about having fun under the boardwalk. Three men standing near us were having a loud conversation about their boss who apparently was a "jerk." I asked Terrell to repeat what he'd said.

"I live off Sol Legare Road a half mile or so from here but work on Folly. Cook at Rita's. Do y'all work somewhere there?"

Rita's is one of Folly's nicer restaurants. Whenever I'm itching for a hamburger, it's my on-island go-to spot.

Barb turned to face Terrell. "I have a used bookstore on Center Street, my friend here's retired. He spends his time pestering us working folks."

"Barb's Books," Terrell said. "Never been in but have seen it. Got any history books?"

The woman who took our order brought the food in paper baskets then asked if we needed another drink. I told her not yet. She said if we did, we knew where to find her.

I took a bite while Barb said, "I have several. They're not my best sellers, but occasionally have someone looking for them. You a history buff?"

"Hang on," he said and held up his hand, palm facing Barb. "I'll be back."

We watched our new acquaintance head toward the restrooms and Barb took a bite of sandwich.

I said, "Think he'd rather talk to you than me."

Barb grinned. "Who wouldn't?"

"Funny," I said, although it was true.

"Seen any mosquitos yet?" Barb said then smacked me on the arm.

"Funny," I repeated.

Terrell returned carrying another beer. This time he took the chair beside Barb.

She winked at me.

"Started getting into history a few years back after I mustered out of the army. My grandpa got me interested," Terrell said, answering the question Barb asked ten minutes earlier.

Barb smiled, "Any particular history? US, world, ancient?"

"Never gave much thought to any of it until grandpa started telling me stories about the civil rights movement." He took another sip then slowly shook his head. "Grandpa died a year ago. I miss him a bunch."

"Sorry to hear it," I said to reenter the conversation.

"Was ninety-three, led a good life. He lived next to my parents' house, the house I inherited after they passed back before I entered the service." He shook his head. "Enough about me. Did you say if you had books about the 1960s?"

I didn't recall him asking but let Barb answer.

"I'm not sure. Next time you're nearby, stop in. I'll see what I have. Or, if you give me your number, I'll check and call you."

"That's kind of you. I'll stop by."

One of the men who'd been talking about his jerk boss apparently was tired of griping about work. He said, "Heard the body was a Civil War soldier."

His co-worker put his arm around the man's shoulder. "Nah. Wasn't buried that long." The group moved closer to the bar, farther away from us, so I couldn't hear what else they were saying.

I turned to Terrell. "I heard those guys talking about a body. Know what they're talking about?"

Terrell looked at the group, turned to me, and frowned. "A friend of mine stumbled across a body, mostly a skeleton out where the road ends." He pointed toward the far end of Mosquito Beach Road.

"Anyone know who it was?" I asked earning a dirty look from Barb, a shrug from Terrell.

"Depends on who you ask?" he said. "Somebody said it was like from the Civil War. There was a battle near here. A woman said it was a guy who died from some strange disease. People were scared of catching it, so they buried him the day he died." He paused and rubbed his chin. "One old-timer swears he remembers stories a few years back where some white guy was trying to rob a man staying in an old hotel that was here." He nodded to his left. "That's what the boarded-up building next door used to be, was named the Pine Tree Hotel, if memory serves me correct. The hotel guest shot the man as he came through the door. He was afraid the cops would arrest him if they found out, so he buried it. The old-timer said the body was buried out where the skeleton was found. I don't put much faith in that one. The old guy is known for making stuff up." He took another sip of beer then shrugged.

I said, "What do you think?"

"Hell if I know. Tell you what, though, I'd be interested in finding out."

Chapter Three

I called Al's Bar and Gourmet Grill a little before noon the next morning. The phone rang several times, so I was ready to hang up when Al answered, or I assumed it was Al. He was gasping for breath to where I had a tough time understanding what he was saying.

"Al, this is Chris. You okay?"

"Oh, hi. I'm a little out of breath. Been sweeping the sidewalk."

Even though Bob Howard owned Al's, the former owner volunteered to come in whenever his health was up to it to act like a Walmart greeter. He knew most of the patrons, had known them for years, so he could serve as a bridge between the customers and Bob, whose personality fell short on the customer service skills range. Truth be known, an alligator has more customer service skills than Bob.

"I don't know much more than I did the last time we talked. Barb and I went over to Mosquito Beach last night to eat at Island Breeze. We talked—"

"Mr. Chris, please allow me to interrupt. I hear Bob in back arguing with a supplier about the price of beef. I need to get between them before he takes hamburgers off the menu. Could you call back this afternoon?"

"Sure. Good luck playing referee."

"Don't worry, I'm getting good at it. That's a skill Bob's given me a lot of practice with. Yes, he has."

It was good Al had to go. No sooner had I set the phone on the kitchen table, Cindy called.

"This is your faithful, conscientious, I might add charming, police chief calling to let you know the latest about the skeleton that'd been hanging out on or under Mosquito Beach."

"Thanks for calling back."

"Gee, fine nosy citizen, no need to thank me. I wake up each morning thinking about what I can do to meet your countless demands."

"Thanks anyway. What'd you learn?"

"Not much. The body was found by someone named Clarence Taylor, a lifelong resident of the area. He was minding his business, walking across an area between his house and a restaurant on Mosquito Beach. Let's see." I heard papers rustling in the background. "Here it is, Island Breeze."

It wasn't the time to tell her I ate there last night.

"Anything else?"

"Give me a break. You're getting as impatient as your vagrant buddy Charles. I'm having trouble reading my hen scratches. Okay, got it. The coroner hasn't had time to do a full autopsy, but is certain the person is male, most likely African American. While he can't tell how long it'd been there, the clothing fragments appear to be 1950s vintage."

"Cause of death?"

"If I knew that, don't you think I would've told you before I told you about his taste in sartorial splendor?"

"I assume that means cause of death hasn't been determined?"

"Can't slip anything by you."

Time to fawn. "Cindy, you're wonderful. I appreciate everything you've shared. You're a good friend."

She sighed. "Are you standing in a pile of crap?"

Okay, sucking-up doesn't always work on Folly's Director of Public Safety.

"I'll stick with thanks."

"Better. Now, remind me again how you're going to stay out of whatever's going on."

"Of course, I am."

She hung up laughing.

Showers were passing through the area, so I decided to stay in, fix a peanut butter sandwich, and flip through photo magazines I'd accumulated to kill time until Al's lunch hour was over before calling.

He sounded better than last time as he thanked me for calling back. He reported he'd averted another world war, that Bob and the meat salesman were still among the living. I started to tell him about the visit to Island Breeze.

"Let me interrupt again. Could I ask a huge favor?"

"Of course."

"I've been thinking a lot about the time I spent on Mosquito. Can't get it out of my head. I haven't been there for I don't know how many years. I've wanted to drive over to see how it's changed, but doc says I shouldn't be doing much driving. Would it be too much trouble for you to take me out there? I know it's a lot to ask."

"I'd be glad to. When do you want to go?"

"How about in the morning? Tomorrow's a slow day around here. I figure Bob could probably handle everything without starting a race riot."

"Want me to pick you up there?"

"Umm, be better if you get me at the house."

———

I'd never been to Al's house, neither had my vehicle's navigation system, yet it had no difficulty directing me around the sprawling Medical University of South Carolina to Cannon Street then to his address. It was fewer than five blocks from his former bar.

The faded-green, two-story, wood structure looked as tired as did its owner. Shutters on the front windows were missing slats, several roof shingles were broken. All the windows were open. Al's gold, twenty-year-old Oldsmobile was parked in the driveway that was no more than dead weeds and ruts compressed by years of tire wear. The car was covered with a layer of dust and looked like it'd hadn't moved in weeks.

The gate on the front, waist-high iron fence squeaked so loud it rousted a black Rottweiler that'd been sleeping on the porch next door. The dog let out a series of high-pitched barks as it charged to the corner of Al's fenced-in front yard. It was making so much racket I figured I wouldn't have to knock to announce my arrival.

I was right. I walked up the three steps to the front door when Al appeared.

His serious health problems over the last year had taken a toll. His short, gray hair was lighter than the last time I'd seen him. It contrasted drastically with his dark-brown skin.

He leaned on the door frame and smiled. "Morning, Chris. I see you've met Spoiled Rotten."

I glanced at the barking dog. "Spoiled Rotten?"

Al smiled. "Ain't his real name. Gertrude named him some fancy German name I can't pronounce. He's just a baby with a big mouth. She spoils him like he's her only child. That's why I call him Spoiled Rotten. Wouldn't hurt a bug."

"What about hurting a man visiting his next-door neighbor?"

Al laughed. "Well, he hasn't eaten any visitors yet."

I wondered how many visitors Al has. I asked if he was ready to go.

"Come in while I change shirts."

I stepped in the entry and was surprised to see a neatly-made single bed in what would normally be the living room. An aluminum clothes rack was in the corner with several shirts hanging on it. The room was sweltering. Despite the windows being open, it had the musty, medicinal smell that reminded me of nursing homes.

Al saw me looking at the bed. "Bedrooms are upstairs, but doc told me with my arthritis and weak ticker I shouldn't be climbing stairs more than I have to, besides, it's cooler down here. Bob rounded up a couple of my, umm, his customers to haul the bed downstairs." He chuckled. "Bob bitched the entire time although the biggest thing he moved was that lamp." He pointed to a brass lamp on a small table on the other side of the bed. "It ain't the look you'd find in one of those fancy homes magazines, but it meets my needs. Getting old's a pain, yes, it is."

He changed shirts and turned off a portable radio that'd been playing jazz. "I'm ready."

On the painfully slow walk to the car, Al veered to the

neighbor's fence to pet Spoiled Rotten. The Rottweiler had stopped barking and leaned against the fence so Al could reach it without bending.

After saying *adieus* to Spoiled Rotten, Al joined me in the car, smiled, then said he was ready to head to the beach. It took him a few blocks before his breathing returned to normal. The weather typically began to cool by mid-September, but today was an exception. Upper eighties with bright sun were in the forecast so I was worried about Al walking around Mosquito Beach. I also knew it was best for me to keep my concerns to myself to maintain his self-esteem. I hoped it wouldn't be a mistake.

Chapter Four

Al rubbed his hand along the dashboard. "Can't tell you the last time I was in a Cadillac. Smaller than they used to be."

"It's the ATS, smallest car Cadillac makes."

"Nice, but I can remember back when they were the size of a houseboat, had those fancy tail fins. Yes, they were." He stared out the windshield. "The heyday for cars, if you ask me."

We were on Folly Road a couple of miles from the turnoff on Sol Legare Road. All Al had said since leaving his house were comments about cars. I couldn't tell if he was feeling bad or in a quiet mood, something unusual for my talkative friend.

About a mile up Sol Legare Road, Al tapped the passenger side window. "Wow."

"What?"

"Last time I saw the old Seashore Farmers' Lodge it was propped up by long pieces of wood, looked like it was ready to fall over. Hurricane Hugo nearly did it in. Glad to see someone trying to bring it back to its glory days. Looks good, don't it?"

I vaguely remember news stories from shortly after I moved to Folly. A group of locals helped by a reality TV show renovated the building, but that was all I knew about it.

"What's its story?"

He waved his arm around. "In the late 1800s, this whole area was populated by people looking like me. Mostly freed slaves. Now if you were Bob, you'd make some crack about my age. You'd say I knew because I was around back then. Thank the Lord, you're not Bob. Anyway, it was a close community. Everyone supported everyone. The Seashore Farmers' Lodge was started in the early 1900s." He smiled. "No, I still wasn't born then. White folks wouldn't sell us insurance in those days, so the locals formed the group that was sort of an insurance policy for its members. If something bad happened, house burned down, child got sick or died, someone got hurt while working on a shrimp boat, or if someone needed help with crops, everyone came together to support the family that was down."

Al became more animated the more he talked until I turned on Mosquito Beach Road. He shook his head when he noticed waist-high weeds along the side of the road. "Used to be nicer."

I drove to the end of the road so he could see what remained. Once again, he shook his head, but didn't say anything.

I pulled in the grass parking area where I parked when Barb and I were here. A man was sitting on a large slab of broken concrete at the edge of the creek. He looked to be in his seventies and wore denim bib overalls, a long-sleeve shirt despite the temperature hovering in the upper eighties.

"If you're planning on eating, you're out of luck," he said without taking his eyes off the water slowly flowing in front of him. "Don't open until three."

Al moved closer to the stranger, and said, "Thanks, my friend. We're not here to eat. Just lookin' around."

The man finally glanced over his shoulder at Al. "Not much to see."

Al laughed. "Looks that way, don't it?" He was less than a foot from the seated stranger. "I'm Al Washington."

The man stood, brushed dirt off the seat of his pants. He was at least six-foot-three and looked like he'd been a boxer in his younger days. Much of his muscle had turned to fat.

He reached to shake Al's hand. "I'm Clarence Taylor. Al, who's your chauffeur?" He pointed at me then chuckled.

I'd heard his name before but couldn't recall when or why. I stepped closer and held out my hand. "I'm Chris Landrum."

"We're good friends," Al added.

"Pleased to meet you," he said as he shook my hand with a firm grip. "From around here?"

"I live in Charleston," Al said. "Chris hangs his hat over on Folly."

Clarence nodded like that explained everything. "Why'd you choose this little corner of heaven to be looking around?"

Al could field that one.

"After I got out of the army in the early '50s, I spent a lot of weekends here. Think I was only back twice since those days. Wanted to see what it looks like."

Clarence shuffled his foot in the sandy soil. "Korea?"

"Yes, sir," Al said. "Were you there?"

"Born too late for that one," he said as he continued shuffling his foot in the soil. "Got to do my international traveling in Viet Nam." Clarence nodded, again using one of his two body movements. "Don't know about you, but I've had all the sun this old body can take. Want to join me over there in the shade?" He added a third movement when he pointed to a red picnic table beside the closed restaurant.

Al glanced at me. I gave a slight nod. He told Clarence, "Don't mind if we do."

Clarence laughed. "Then you're a heap smarter than most folks from Charleston. From my experience, they don't have enough sense to get in out of the rain or out from under the blazing sun."

Interesting, I thought since it was coming from the man wearing a long-sleeve shirt who'd been sitting in the blazing sun. Regardless, it was a wise decision to move to the shade. I let Al and Clarence take their seats before I sat beside Al.

"You live out this way?" Al said.

Clarence pointed toward the far end of the road. "Live a hop, skip, and jon boat ride that direction. Got an old house on Sol Legare Road. Got it from pop, who got it from my grandparents. I'm the only one left in these parts. Got a sister up north, somewhere in Ohio. Got herself to uppity to come back. Don't rightly know why. All she did was marry a man who owns an underwear making company. Don't reckon that'd put her up there with the Queen of Sheba. I retired from the post office, been a bum ever since." He hesitated then said, "Al, you remember the old pavilion that was out there?"

Clarence made the abrupt transition without any body movements. I waited for Al to respond.

"Spent many Saturday nights at that pavilion. Think it was the main reason I came here. I recall several fine-looking ladies I had the pleasure of dancing with."

Clarence shook his head as he nodded toward the creek in

front of us. "All that's left is them wood pilings holding up nothing."

Al and Clarence were silent, I assumed their minds were drifting back to the 1950s and dances at the pavilion.

Clarence broke the silence. "You hear about the skeleton found the other day out at the end of the road?"

That jerked Al back from the past. He shifted on the bench to face Clarence. "Sure did."

Clarence tapped his hand on the table. "I found it."

That explained why his name sounded familiar. Cindy had shared it with me.

"Had to be frightening," I said.

He sighed. "Chris, I've walked from my house, climbed in my jon boat, paddled over here, walked the rest of the way to the bars and restaurants going on fifty years. That was the first damn time I'd ever found a body. Hope it's the last. I'm not too proud to say it scared the, umm, scared me a lot."

"Clarence," I said, "you've walked from your house to here for a long time. Did you do something different that day?"

"Different. I'd say. Found a body. Ain't that different enough?"

I smiled. "True. What I meant was did you take a different path?"

He rubbed his chin. "The last hurricane did a number on the land near the water. Everything got shuffled around. Water now hangs out where it didn't before the big wind blowed through. Mushy soil makes it impossible to walk through it without stilts." He nodded. "I get your point. Yeah, I've had to change my way here since then."

"On the day you found the bones, did you walk a different path than before?"

"Now that you mention it, I suppose so. We had a big-ass rain the night before. I couldn't walk the same way I normally do."

That could explain why he stumbled on the body. Heavy rain may've uncovered some of the dirt or muck that'd covered it.

Al leaned closer to Clarence. "Any idea who he was?"

"No, but I'd say he wasn't new to the sandy dirt. He wasn't skin and bones, like they call skinny folk. He was all bones."

"Could you tell if he was black or white?" Al said.

Clarence smiled. "The bones were white, but so are mine. I haven't seen them mind you, but that's what they say. There wasn't any skin left that I saw, so I couldn't tell what color it would've been. Suppose the medical folks in Charleston will figure that out."

Al nodded. "Any idea how long it'd been there?"

"Al, my friend, from years working at the post office, I could tell you exactly how long it'd take a letter to get from downtown Charleston to Mt. Pleasant or to London, the one in England. Telling how long those bones were planted out there is outside my area of knowledge. I suspect those same folks who'll tell what color he was will answer that question." He looked down at the table and then at Al. "Bad thing about it, at least, from my way of thinking, is someone from over here might've been the one who put the poor man in the ground. I hate to think it may be someone I know, or someone who's related to someone out here."

Al rubbed his chin. "That's a bad thought, isn't it? Hope it's not true."

"Tell you one thing. It's bothering me enough to want to learn what happened."

I said, "How?"

"Don't rightly know, to tell the truth. It won't stop me asking around, especially talking to the folks who've been here forever." He wiped the sweat from his forehead, smiled at us, and said, "Now I don't know about you fellas, but all this talk about bones is giving me the heebie-jeebies. How about talking about something pleasant?"

Al must not have wanted to make his new friend uncomfortable, so he asked about the food at Island Breeze, if there was good fishing in the tidal creek, and when the other businesses that'd been here closed. The conversation slowly came to an end. Clarence said it was good meeting us. If we ever wanted to share a meal with him, he'd meet us and introduce us to the owner of the restaurant. Al thanked him for the offer. Clarence said he'd better get home in time for his afternoon nap. Al said it sounded good, he might do the same. Al's chauffeur agreed.

Chapter Five

Cindy often referred to Charles Fowler as my vagrant buddy. Through an apparent glitch in the world of logic, I call him my best friend, and he has been since I arrived on Folly. Charles moved to Folly from Detroit at age thirty-four. For the last thirty-three years, he hasn't been burdened with being on anyone's payroll. During the same period, I'd spent most of my adult life working in Kentucky. He occasionally picks up cash helping restaurants clean during busy season or delivers packages for our friend Dude Sloan's surf shop. Charles lives in a tiny apartment, remains single, and walks or rides his bike most everywhere, so his financial needs are minimal.

It'd been a few days since I'd seen my friend, so I called to ask if he wanted to meet for breakfast. He said he thought he could work it into his schedule, so we agreed to meet in the morning at the Lost Dog Cafe. I anticipated a few rough moments at breakfast, since one of his quirks—his many quirks—was giving me grief if I learned something and failed to share it with him within, oh, let's say, the blink of an eye. I wasn't certain if he'd heard about the bones, but I knew he didn't know about my visits to Mosquito Beach.

I decided to walk six blocks to the restaurant, located less than a block off Center Street, Folly's hub of commerce. The Dog was in a former laundromat, but from its colorful porches, attractive entry, and hungry customers waiting outside to be seated, you'd never guess its former life. I'd told Charles eight o'clock, so I arrived before seven-thirty, knowing he subtracts thirty minutes from whatever time we're meeting. Yes, another quirk.

I walked past three couples waiting for a table to be greeted by Amber Lewis. She'd turned fifty, looked younger, was five-foot-five, with long auburn hair pulled in a ponytail. She was my favorite server at the Dog and had worked there since before I moved to Folly. In fact, she was the first person I'd met when I arrived on the six-mile-long, half-mile-wide island. We'd dated for a while then after we decided to go separate romantic ways had remained good friends.

She gave me a high-wattage smile, glanced toward the waiting customers, then motioned me to follow. She took me to a table near the back wall where I waited while she cleared dirty plates and glasses.

"Here's a vacant table. Want it or would you prefer waiting outside until the masses ahead of you are seated."

I chose the perk Amber had reserved for her favorite people then she said she'd get me coffee. I told her Charles would be joining me. She smiled as she asked if I wanted her to tell him he'd have to wait until everyone else was seated.

"Not today."

I looked around the packed restaurant. Two city council members, Marc Salmon and Houston Bass, were in deep discussion in the center of the room. They spent most mornings at the Dog, allegedly discussing city business. Mostly they were collecting or spreading gossip about everyone and everything. I gave a slight wave to Marc who responded with a similar gesture.

I was going to walk over to say hi, when Charles entered, looked around, before heading my way. He was a couple inches shorter than I and twenty pounds lighter. He wore a long-sleeve, navy T-shirt with Penn State on the front and Nittany Lions down the sleeve, yellow shorts, a canvas Tilley hat, and was swinging his ever-present hand-made cane around like he didn't have a care in the world. He's one of the few people I know where that may be true.

He looked at his bare wrist where normal people wore a watch. Normal had never been used to describe Charles.

"Good to see you're on time," he said, then removed his Tilley, put it on the seat beside him, then propped his cane against the chair.

"Good morning."

Amber returned with my coffee plus a cup for Charles although he hadn't told her he wanted it. She had to get food for a couple seated across from us and said she'd be back.

Charles watched her go, then turned to me. "So, what did I do to deserve a breakfast invite?"

I took a sip of coffee, smiled, and said, "Nothing. It'd been a few days since we talked, so I thought we could get together."

"Hmm, if you say so."

Now, to get the thorny stuff out of the way. I told him about Al's call and our trip to Mosquito Beach. I also told him about taking Barb to eat at Island Breeze. Veins in his neck popped, his grip tightened around the mug.

Before he lambasted me for not telling him immediately after it happened, Amber returned to ask if we were ready to order. I silently thanked her, then said, "Yes, French toast."

Amber rolled her eyes. She'd been trying to no avail to get me to eat healthier. Charles said he'd have the same thing. That was a surprise since he normally chose bacon, eggs, and toast.

Amber said, "You sure?"

Charles nodded, then she went to place our orders.

I tilted my head and stared at Charles. "French toast?"

"I can't order something different?" He clunked his mug on the table. "Ronald Reagan said, 'Status quo, you know, is Latin for *the mess we're in.*'"

Add quoting US presidents to Charles's quirk pile.

"Of course, you can. It surprised me, that's all."

He took a sip and looked in his half-empty mug. Without looking up, he said, "It threw me for a loop you didn't think I was a good enough friend that you could let me know about your trip to Mosquito Beach. Oh wait, your two trips."

"You're the best friend I could ever have. Barb and I went out to eat. That happens all the time. Do I tell you about each of them? Of course not. Al and I went yesterday, now I'm telling you about it."

Charles looked up from his mug. "If that's an apology, you need to work on your delivery."

I thought it was more of an explanation, but if Charles thought it was an apology, regardless how poorly done, I'd let him take the victory. I repeated in greater detail about my trips to Mosquito.

Our dueling French toast orders arrived, and Amber refilled our coffee. She asked if we needed anything.

Charles pointed at me. "Ms. Amber, you could teach my alleged friend here how to apologize."

She patted him on the arm. "Charles, I don't do anything wrong, so I never have to apologize. You need to find another teacher. Get someone who's sorry a lot." She snapped her fingers. "Got it. Why don't you teach him?" She chuckled then rushed to a table across the room.

I shrugged then saw Chief LaMond enter. She was in her early fifties, five-foot-three, well built, with dark, curly hair, and a quick smile. She headed our way.

"Morning, thorns in my side. Either of you buying me coffee?"

"Chris is," offered my generous friend.

I motioned her to join us, and Amber set a mug of steaming coffee in front of the Chief before she was settled in the chair. Being Chief has perks.

"Cindy," I said as she took a sip, "learn more about the body?"

She glared at me. "Yep, he's dead."

Charles leaned closer to the Chief. "Learn that from the coroner?"

"I figured it out all by my lonesome. The coroner said it weighed twenty-seven pounds. Hell, my left arm weighs that much, so I figured he was dead."

Charles looked at Cindy's arm. "With or without your watch?"

"What else have you learned?" I asked before the conversation sank deeper in a pile of absurdity.

Cindy moved her arm away from Charles then turned to me. "As suspected, it was a male, African American, probably in his late teens, early twenties."

I said, "Best guess on when he died?"

"The coroner is consulting with a forensic anthropologist who'll run tests this old gal from East Tennessee is clueless about. With luck and some scientific gobbledygook, they may be able to get close to when the person died. The guesses I've heard range from a year to a hundred thousand years ago. I'm no expert, but I'd guess closer to a year than ancient times, unless cave dwellers wore black and white wingtip shoes. Mr. Skeleton dressed well."

"Glad you narrowed it down," Charles said.

Cindy took another sip and pointed her forefinger at Charles. "I know in your fantasy world, you think you're a private detective. Crap on a cucumber, in my fantasy world, I'm Charlize Theron. The point is you ain't a detective. I ain't a movie star. Wait, that was only half of my point, the rest is you and your accomplice sitting across the table need to keep your noses out of police business. Think you can do that?"

Charles gave a stage nod. "Of course we can."

What he didn't say was that we would. Cindy knew not to push.

She glanced at her watch, weight unknown, then said, "Time to go pester my officers who I'm sure are sitting around the office, drinking coffee, telling dirty jokes. My chiefly duties never get a rest.

I thanked her for letting us know what she'd learned about the skeleton.

She had Amber put her coffee in a to-go cup, headed to the exit, stopped, and returned to the table. "Oh, one other thing about the skeleton. He had a hole in his head, a hole the coroner thinks was made by a bullet." She pivoted, waved bye to us over her shoulder, and was gone.

Chapter Six

I still had the nagging feeling Al knew something about Mosquito Beach he wasn't sharing. Not only something, but something that was bothering him. Late the next morning, I had space in my stomach for one of Al's famous cheeseburgers, and for the previous owner to have another chance to share his concern.

I pulled in a vacant parking space a block off Calhoun Street and directly behind Bob Howard's dark plum PT Cruiser convertible, the un-realtor-like vehicle he'd driven since I've known him. I was a half block from Al's Bar and Gourmet Grill housed in a concrete block building. The building blended with the tired looking neighborhood of wood frame houses, plus a couple of low rent businesses. At some point in ancient history, the building had been painted white. That would be the last word to describe its color today.

I opened the door then waited for my eyes to adjust to the dark interior illuminated by neon Budweiser signs behind the bar. The sounds of Freddy Fender in his Tex-Mex country voice singing about "Wasted Days and Wasted Nights" along with the smell of frying burgers saturated the air. Motown classics and traditional country hits filled the jukebox. Bob was a huge country music fan, much to the chagrin of Al's predominantly African American customers. That was only one of the several clashing points between the customers and the bar's new owner, and the real reason Al was stationed in a chair by the front door.

"Well, Lordy," Al said as I blinked to adjust to the dark. "Look who's here."

He slowly pushed himself out of the chair to hug me. He looked as well-worn as the dilapidated furniture that populated the room. What didn't fill the room was diners. It was past the traditional lunch hour and three men were seated by the plate glass window painted black to block the interior from the street. They appeared to be finishing sandwiches. Lawrence, Al's cook, was facing the grill; the current owner, Bob Howard, was seated at his table near the back of the building.

I told Al I was glad to see him, that I woke this morning with a sudden urge for one of his cheeseburgers.

He started to say something but was interrupted by Bob's bellowing voice, "Old man, stop gabbing with the damn paying customer. Let him park his scrawny butt and order."

Calling my ample posterior scrawny should tell you something about Bob. If it didn't, let me say the seventy-eight-year-old bar owner is six feet tall carrying the weight of someone a foot taller. I don't recall often seeing him with less than a four-day-old scruffy beard or wearing shorts and Hawaiian flowery shirts, regardless of the weather.

I said to Al, "Guess I'd better get back to see my good friend before he runs off all the customers."

He looked at the three men at the table by the window. "Don't worry, they've learned to ignore the profane bundle of lard holding court back there."

"Good. Why don't you join us when you get a chance?"

Al laughed. "I will if there's a lull in the lunch rush."

I'm sure Bob would've stood to greet me if he hadn't been tightly wedged between his seat pushed up against the back wall and the table. Of course, that was only my wishful thinking.

"Good afternoon, Bob."

"What's so damned good about it? See those tightwads sitting over there?" He pointed to the three customers.

I nodded.

"That's today's lunch crowd. Sorry, I'm off by one. Some damned street person hobbled in saying he was starving. Can you believe he wanted me to give him a burger?"

"Did you?"

Bob mumbled, "Yes. If you tell anyone, I'll swear you're a psychopathic, mentally deficient bowl of Jell-O." His hand jerked up in the air. "Lawrence, damn it, don't you see this anorexic white guy needs food. Stop discriminating. Get your golden-brown face out here and take his order."

The three customers turned to Bob while simultaneously shaking their heads.

Bob glared at them. "Lawrence, while you're on your way, take those troublemakers another beer. On me." He turned back to me. "Now, where were we? Oh yeah, you were inter-rupting meditation hour."

Lawrence dropped off the beers at the other table, then asked what I wanted to order. Al's cheeseburgers were, in the view of Bob, "The best damned cheeseburger in the world," so how could I resist.

"Cheeseburger," I said.

Lawrence nodded. "Good choice."

"Only damn choice," Bob said. "And don't forget to fix him fries. Need to fatten him up, get some extra cash out of him."

"Another good choice, Master Bob," Lawrence said through a smile.

It was good seeing Lawrence adjusting to Bob's charming exterior.

"Smart ass," Bob said. "And bring him a glass of that cheap, fruity, white wine you hide in the refrigerator behind that green stuff you put on the cheeseburgers."

"Lettuce," Lawrence said as he rushed away before Bob could hurl more insults his way.

Bob watched him go and said, "Great guy. I'm lucky to have him."

"I can tell," I said, interjecting an order of sarcasm.

"Smart ass."

I'm sure Bob was still referring to Lawrence. Time to change the subject. "How's Al?"

Bob looked at Al seated by the door. "Glad you asked. He was doing much better with his ailing heart, his severe arthritis until some damned whippersnapper kidnapped him, dragged him out to some isolated strip of land by a creek, made him walk more than he has in the last seven years combined, then made him sit outside with the temperature pushing three-hundred degrees. Nearly did him in."

"I don't think it was that bad. Besides—"

Bob waved his meaty hand in my face. "Hold your defensive excuses. Let me finish. He's still alive, hasn't stopped talking about how much he appreciated you taking him. He said it was the highlight of the year. I thought seeing me every day would've held that honor, but I pretended like I agreed with him."

"He had an enjoyable time."

"After you nearly killed him."

Bob was back to being Bob. I started to ask more about Al's health, when I heard Willie Nelson singing his version of "Crazy" and Al scooting a chair up to the table.

"Couldn't you find anyone else to drag in off the street to spend money to keep this dump afloat?" Bob said as Al lowered himself in the chair.

Al leaned my direction and patted me on the arm. "Thought Mr. Chris needed saving from your griping."

Marvin Gaye joined in the discussion by belting out "I Heard it Through the Grapevine."

"Crap, not that again," Bob said as he put his hands over his ears in case we didn't know what he was talking about. "What happened to the good music?"

Good music equals country music, with no room for variations according to the restaurant's owner who never failed to let everyone know.

Al smiled at the three men at the other table tapping their beer bottles on the table in time to the music.

"See" Bob said and shook his head. "Your music is about to start a riot."

Al and Bob had been good friends for years, would do anything for each other.

Al ignored him, one of his techniques for keeping the friendship alive, then turned to me. "You recall that man's name we talked to at Mosquito? Been trying to remember it all morning."

"Clarence Taylor."

Al smiled. "Yeah, that's it. Bob, Clarence is the guy who found the skeleton."

On the jukebox, Johnny Horton replaced Marvin with his version of "North to Alaska." The three men at the other table joined in with a chorus of boos. Bob glared at them. They pointed their bottles at him and laughed.

Bob's glare turned to a smile. He kept looking at his customers but said to me, "See how happy my music makes customers?"

Al said, "They don't call Bob *the great peacemaker* for nothing."

"Who calls me that?"

"Nobody," Al said. "It was a joke."

A good one, I thought.

"Ha ha," Bob said. "So why does that damned place named after god-awful mosquitos mean so much to you?"

The music war was placed on hold, at least for now.

Al said, "You really want to know?"

"Crap, Al, your trip out there is about all you've been talking about. Figure anything you talk about more than telling me how great I am, must mean something powerful."

Lawrence delivered my order, Bob told him he'd better bring him another beer, saying he'd need it to put up with Al. Lawrence left without comment.

Al said, "In 1950, Communist North Korea invaded South Korea. The US of A was back at war. I'd just turned sixteen but lied about my age, said I was older so I could join up. They needed all the able-bodied men they could get so they weren't checking ages too close. I looked older than I was. Servin' my country was important to me. I was in three years —three danged rough years."

"Came back a hero," Bob added. "Modest Al don't like

talking about it, but he saved seven soldiers while he was over there."

Bob had previously shared that point of pride with me.

"Anyway," Al said and probably blushed but both he and the room were so dark I couldn't tell. "When I got back to the states in '53, I couldn't find a decent job in Charleston."

Bob interrupted. "Blacks were good enough to die for our country, but not good enough to eat in most restaurants or get good jobs. Damned segregation."

"Bob," Al said, "you forget who's telling this story?"

I smiled as Bob motioned for his friend to continue.

"I took a job downtown as a porter at the Francis Marion Hotel. I was lucky to get it. It was long hours, hard work, but it was work."

"What's that have to do with Mosquito Beach, old man?"

The phrase *the great peacemaker* popped into my head.

"I worked six days a week, so when I got time off, I wanted to get as far from town as I could. Mosquito Beach was a thriving black community in those days. Several bars, dance clubs, the pavilion were places to be. Yes, they were. Boy did I have a fine time." He closed his eyes, smiled, as he slowly nodded.

Bob remained silent, choosing wisdom rather than his normal MO. Ray Charles was singing "Hit the Road, Jack." The other customers began singing along. Bob didn't fake displeasure with the music, and I continued eating my cheeseburger.

Al's smile faded. "Can't help but wonder what happened."

One of the other customers raised his hand. Bob yelled for Lawrence to get the men their check. Al twisted around to make sure the men were being taken care of. His nostalgic mood was broken.

"Al, what were you wondering about? What happened?"

"Nothing, really," he said, as a couple entered. "Better get back to my post to greet those folks. Good seeing you again, Chris."

He grimaced as he pushed himself out of the chair then slowly moved toward the entrance.

Now, I had no doubt that there was something about Mosquito Beach that Al wasn't sharing.

Chapter Seven

I called Chief LaMond the next morning to see if she'd learned anything new about the skeleton's identity. After putting up with a litany of insults about pestering her before she'd finished her third cup of coffee, and before she'd finished yelling at two of her officers for ticketing a council member's wife's new convertible, she shared that the County Sheriff's Office seemed as interested in investigating the death as they were about learning the whereabouts of Jimmy Hoffa. In other words, it was a cold case. She hung up before I could thank her for the enlightening information.

I was one cup of coffee behind Cindy, so I refilled my cup then moved to the screened-in porch to watch the steady stream of vehicles pass my cottage carrying sad-faced, sleepy drivers on their way to work. Since retiring, watching people heading to work was one of my guilty pleasures.

The phone rang, and Charles said, "I'll pick you up this afternoon at five."

"Where're we going?" I asked, rather than saying something normal like, "Good morning. How are you today?"

"To eat, duh," he said, like who wouldn't have known.

He said he'd pick me up at five, so he'd be here at four thirty. I was ten minutes off. He pulled in my drive at four twenty to be greeted with, "Sorry, I'm almost late. Got talking with my neighbor about the weather. Couldn't get away."

"I was beginning to worry," I said with an overabundance of sarcasm. "Care to share where we're going?"

"Nope."

Five minutes later, the mysterious destination became clearer when Charles turned on Sol Legare Road.

It was Friday and the parking areas around Island Breeze were packed. Charles drove a hundred yards past the restaurant before finding a vacant spot. The temperature was cooler than during my other visits and twenty or so diners were crowded around tables in front of the building. The inside was equally crowded, I was beginning to wonder how long we'd have to wait.

My wonder ended quickly when someone tapped me on the shoulder. Terrell Jefferson was behind me dressed in all black, the same as he'd been when Barb and I met him. He had a smile on his face.

"Hi, Terrell," I said.

"You remembered. I'm impressed."

I didn't know how to respond so I introduced Charles.

"Where's the lovely lady you were with the last time?"

"He's going for brains tonight rather than beauty," Charles said even though Terrell had asked me.

Terrell, like many people who first meet Charles, didn't know how to respond, so he turned to me. "There's a long wait. I've got a table out back, want to join me?"

"That'd be great," Charles said, answering for both of us.

We weaved our way through the crowd to the back door that opened to a large area with several tables. All were occupied. We followed Terrell to a table near the back of the lot. There were three empty seats, a fourth was occupied by a heavyset man with a white curly beard. He was reading a paperback Walter Mosley novel through thick, black-rimmed glasses. Terrell motioned for us to take two of the empty seats.

"Jamal," Terrell said, "This is Chris and, umm, sorry, I didn't catch your name."

Charles said to the man who looked like a black Santa in his late-seventies or early-eighties, "I'm Charles."

"Jamal Kingsly. Pleased, I'm sure," said the reader. His eyes never left the book.

"Pay no attention to Jamal," Terrell said. "He'd rather read than eat."

Jamal looked over the top of the book at Terrell. "Food for the mind."

"I'm a big reader," Charles said.

"He's got nearly as many books as the Folly Beach Branch of the Charleston Library," I added.

That struck a chord with Jamal. He stuck a jack of hearts in the book before closing it, and said, "What do you like to read?"

"Pretty near anything. You?"

"Mysteries like this one." He held up the book he'd been reading. "Some history. These old bones have been around nearly eighty-two years, so now I've got to do most of my living through books."

Their discussion was interrupted when a server appeared

asking what we wanted to drink. Charles said beer, any kind. I said white wine.

She left to get our drinks, and Terrell said, "That's how I got to know Jamal. I'm into Civil War history. He lent me a book about it."

"You ain't given it back yet," Jamal said.

"My bad. I'll have it the next time I see you."

"Jamal," I said, "are you from around here?"

He smiled for the first time. "Born, reared, lived my entire life up until now within three miles of this spot." He tapped the table. "Where are you two from?"

I answered as our drinks arrived. The server asked if we were ready to order. Charles and I stuck with barbecue sandwiches plus at Terrell's urging, a side order of pickled cabbage and sauerkraut. Jamal told the server to throw in some Coco bread. I didn't know what it was but didn't want to question our new table mate.

"Is it always this busy?" Charles asked.

Terrell said, "Friday and Saturday."

Charles nodded. "Know who the body was someone found out here the other day?" He asked it like it was the most logical thing to ask after learning about weekend crowds.

Terrell glanced at me before turning to Charles. "Haven't heard anything. If the police know they aren't saying." He turned to Jamal. "Hear anything?"

Jamal sipped his beer, looked around the patio, before turning to Terrell. "No. Whoever it is, it's ancient history. Just what Mosquito needs is someone digging up its reputation for violence." This time he took a large swig of beer.

That got Charles attention. "Reputation for violence?"

Jamal sighed. "Started in the 1950s, around '55 as I recall.

A young guy was shot inside an old juke joint. Died smack dab on top of a pool table. Then, there was another murder three years later. Mind you, everything I got about the killings was second hand." Jamal smiled. "That was a little after the pavilion was built on stilts over the water."

Our food arrived, and Jamal told the server to bring another beer for Terrell who was holding an empty bottle.

Charles took a bite of sandwich, wiped sauce off his upper lip, then said, "Think the body they found could be someone from those days?"

Jamal said, "No. It's probably somebody's elder parent. Funerals were expensive. Many of the folk living around here weren't rolling in dough."

The late-afternoon sun peeked through the clouds; the temperature was warming to near uncomfortable levels. Charles removed his Tilley, fanned his face with it. "I hear he was shot in the head."

Jamal and Terrell turned to my friend.

"Who died?" came a voice from behind me.

Jamal looked over my shoulder. "Hi, Eugene, nobody died, not recently anyway. We're talking about the skeleton."

I twisted around in my seat and saw a man roughly six-foot-tall, white with gray hair, and eighty or so years under his belt looking down at us. He was thin with the posture of a Buckingham Palace guard. I was starting to think we were eating at a senior citizen center.

He glanced around the table. "Jamal, who're your friends?"

Since Charles wanted to know every human on earth, he stood, stuck out his hand, and told Eugene who he was as well as introducing me.

Eugene shook Charles's hand, patted me on the shoulder,

then turned back to Jamal. "No need to waste anyone's time talking about an old bag of bones that probably was buried out there for a hundred years. Probably some bum."

"Mr. Dillinger," Terrell said, "Is that any way to talk about the dead? He was someone's son, could've been a dad, could've been anyone."

Eugene, whose last name apparently was Dillinger, ignored Terrell's remark. He asked Charles where he and his friend were from. Charles told him we lived on Folly.

"I'm building a house over there. Just came from the job site."

Jamal said, "Eugene's a builder."

"Best in the area or was when I was doing much of the work myself. With my arthritis, I lean on my crew to do everything now," Eugene said. "My current project is ocean-front, on East Ashley past the Washout. You know the one I mean?"

I didn't. Neither did Charles who asked the address.

Eugene told him. Charles said it sounded interesting, that he'd look for it the next time he was out that way. Eugene smiled, the marketer in him seeping out. He probably thought Charles could use a new house. He didn't know Charles would have to rearrange his budget to buy a pencil.

There was an empty chair at the table beside us that Jamal or Terrell could've told Eugene to pull up if they wanted him to join us. Eugene glanced at the empty chair, but not hearing an invitation, said he'd better be going. He added it was nice meeting Charles and me, especially Charles, since he handed him his business card. His arthritis didn't stop him from marketing. He nodded bye to Jamal and Terrell before heading to the gate leading off the patio.

Jamal watched him go and mumbled, "Asshole."

That explained the lack of an invitation for Eugene to join us.

Charles needed a more detailed explanation. "Jamal, doesn't sound like you're buddies."

"Wouldn't trust him as far as I could throw him," Jamal said.

Terrell said, "He's not that bad."

"You're too young to know better," Jamal said. "That honky—no offense Chris and Charles—has been screwing over black folks since he started his homebuilding business in the 1950s. He was just out of high-school when his pop kicked the bucket. Eugene inherited a fledgling remodeling business, ripped off some customers before starting building houses. A lot of Negroes were desperate for work. Eugene promised jobs. Minimum wage back then was seventy-five cents an hour. Dillinger Executive Homes, the damned self-important name he called his business, came out here, picked up labor for fifty cents an hour, sometimes less. Lord, that was for fifty hours a week. We didn't have much choice back then."

Charles asked, "Does he still do that?"

Jamal chuckled. "Hell no. Now he hires guys who can't speak English so no telling how little he pays them. Let's just say that the African American community could use a lot fewer Eugene Dillingers."

Terrell said, "Aren't his foremen black?"

"Two of the four," Eugene said. "They've been with him twenty-five years or more. I suspect they make good money, but that don't make up for the years he took advantage of us."

If what Jamal said was accurate, I was surprised Eugene

showed his face on Mosquito Beach. "Where does he live? Does he come here often?"

"Hell," Jamal said, "he lives somewhere on your island. I don't go over there. Don't know where it is. He spent a lot of time in the juke joints here when he was getting his business going. He was one of the few white faces around in the '50s. He hired some of us, so we put up with him. Work was hard to come by."

I asked Terrell and Jamal if they wanted another beer. They quickly said yes, and I added it was my treat.

Charles said, "Me, too."

Jamal got the server's attention. The conversation took a kinder, gentler turn as Jamal started regaling us with stories of the bands that had performed at the pavilion and how Mosquito Beach had been such a popular gathering spot even after the Civil Rights Act of 1964 outlawed segregation.

"We were all friends, felt like we were one large family," he added.

I suspected that there was one man who didn't feel like that—the man whose bones are at the coroner's office in Charleston.

Chapter Eight

Over the next several days, in a moment of weakness, I painted the bedroom. It'd been a decade since a paintbrush touched anything in the interior of my cottage, and even then, the bedroom escaped new paint. Besides, the outside temperature hovered ten degrees above the average high for September. Staying inside was appealing; appealing until it took me two days, numerous twists of my already weakened back, and spilling nearly as much paint as made it to the walls. I hadn't given a second thought to Mosquito Beach during the painting ordeal.

I finished the arduous task, yelled, "Hallelujah!" to the empty, newly painted room, then walked to Barb's Books to see if I could elicit a modicum of sympathy and praise for my hard work.

"Hello, stranger," Barb said as I left the humid, late-summer heatwave to step in the attractive, air-conditioned bookstore. "It's been so long since I've seen you, I figured you skipped town with a young floozy."

I smiled. "You're reading too many of the romance novels you sell."

"Eww. You know I can't stand romance novels."

"They're still your best sellers, aren't they?"

"Back in the day when I was practicing law, I had a few clients I couldn't stand. They paid the bills, so I tolerated them. Same with romance novels. Want something to drink?"

I told her "yes" then followed her to the small back room. Until four years ago, I had a photo gallery in the space housing Barb's Books. In those days, the back room served as a storage room plus a gathering place for my friends. The room had been sloppy, held a yard-sale table and chairs, a refrigerator stocked with wine, beer, and soft drinks. Barb has the space looking like a professional office with a sleek, modern desk, a Bose sound system, and a Keurig coffeemaker. Fortunately, her new, black refrigerator held a six-pack of Diet Cokes. She handed me one, fixed herself a cup of coffee in the high-tech coffeemaker then pointed to one of the chairs. I sat as she pulled another chair closer to the door so she could see if customers ventured in.

I hinted for a sympathetic shoulder to lean on while telling about my painting experience.

She responded with, "It's about time."

The front door opened before she could elaborate. Barb left me at the table so she could greet the new arrival. She was gone a couple of minutes when I heard a vaguely familiar voice, so I peeked around the corner to see who it belonged to.

Barb was showing Terrell Jefferson the selection of history books. He saw me standing in the doorway. "Oh, hi, Chris. I didn't see you there."

He had traded his all-black clothes for black and white striped chef's pants plus a white chef's jacket.

"Chris," Barb said, "you remember Terrell, we sat with him when we went to Mosquito Beach."

"I do. In fact, I ate with Terrell a week ago at Island Breeze."

"You did?"

Terrell said, "With your friend, Charles, right?"

I nodded.

Terrell continued, "They were there last Friday. The place was packed. They looked lost, so I asked if they wanted to join my friend Jamal and me."

Barb smiled. "Chris and especially his friend Charles often look lost." She turned to me. "Terrell was looking for history books that cover the 1960s."

That was depressing since I didn't think the years of my late teens, early twenties should be in history books. I didn't say anything.

Terrell shared he was early for work at Rita's, so he stopped by.

Barb pulled a couple of tomes off the shelf while Terrell and I were talking. She flipped through the table of contents, shook her head, then re-shelved them.

"Terrell, I'm afraid we don't have what you're looking for. Check back in a week or so. We get new books all the time."

"I'll do that. Oh, by the way, Chris, remember how we were talking about the body found out my way?"

"Sure."

Barb stared at me, probably because I told her I wasn't getting involved.

"I gave it a lot of thought after you left. Grandpa Samson

told me stories about being around in the '50s up through the end of the civil rights movement in the '60s."

Barb ended her glare and turned to Terrell. "I remember you telling us something about him when Chris and I met you. Didn't he die a year ago?"

"Yes. If I remember it right, he told me several times about a friend, actually it was more like someone he knew, not a friend. Grandpa was in his late twenties in those days. He told about some of the young guys who were always raring for a fight. Always talking about equal rights, wanting good jobs. That was in the early '50s, before the civil rights movement. Anyway, the guy he talked about was leading other youngsters in fighting segregation. Got a bunch of folks riled up. A lot of the blacks got behind him, a few didn't like what he was doing. They said he was bringing too much attention down on them; making enemies because of it."

I said, "What happened to him?"

Terrell shook his head. "No one knows. Grandpa said he was there one day, gone the next."

"You think it's his body?"

"That came to mind after you left the other night."

"What was his name?"

Terrell rubbed his chin then looked at the floor. "All I remember is his first name was one of those old-time Bible names. Grandpa told me, but for the life of me I can't remember. Next time I'm at Island Breeze I'll ask around. A lot of old-timers hang out there and I'm certain some will remember. It's interesting. I'd like to know what happened to him." He looked at his watch. "I'd better get to work."

Terrell started toward the exit, stopped, and said, "Chris. I want to apologize for how Jamal acted. He's got a lot of anger about what happened back in the old days. Most of the time he hides it good, but as you saw, it's not far under the surface."

"It sounds like he has reason to be angry at Eugene after how he treated African Americans."

"True," Terrell said. "It's not only whites, Jamal was royally pissed—excuse me, Barb—irritated at many people of color back then."

I asked, "Why?"

"Some of them were, how shall I say it, umm, rocking the boat. They were pushing, pushing hard for things to change, like I was saying about the guy Grandpa told me about. The laws may've been changing but words on paper don't change what's in people's hearts. That brought a lot of heat down on everybody. Some cops didn't take a liking to troublemakers. The Klan was also active in the Charleston area. Was a bad time all around." He smiled. "Didn't mean to go off on a tangent." He glanced at his watch again. "Gotta go."

"I'll keep an eye out for the kind of books you're looking for," Barb said as Terrell headed out.

She turned to me as Terrell closed the door. "Anything else you'd like to share about your trip to Mosquito Beach?'

I told her about being there with Al.

"You're not going to leave the mystery alone, are you?"

I again told her I had no intention of getting involved. She shook her head, once again giving me her best skeptical look.

Perhaps I should have stayed home and painted the living room.

Chapter Nine

"Chris, I've got an idea," Charles said after his call woke me out of a sound sleep.

I glanced at the bedside clock and realized I'd slept an hour past my normal seven o'clock waking time. Painting had taken its toll.

"What is it?" I said, knowing little good could come from whatever it was.

"Over my morning cereal, I was reading an article online. It gave me a brilliant idea. Ready for it?"

I had serious doubts about its brilliance but gave the only acceptable answer. "Yes."

"DNA," he said like that explained everything.

"DNA what?"

"You still asleep? DNA. That's how they can tell who the skeleton belongs to."

"The guy's been dead a long time. Even if they checked his DNA, there wouldn't be anything to match it to. DNA databases are relatively new."

"That's where my early-morning research while you snoozed paid off. You're right, there probably isn't a way to figure out who he is by finding his DNA anywhere except on the body. This is where genealogical DNA comes in."

"Explain?"

"Okay, here goes. You awake?"

I sighed. "Yes."

"You know those TV ads where you spit in a little tube then stick it in the mailbox? They tell what country or whole bunch of countries you came from."

"I've seen them. How does that help learn the body's identity?"

"Millions of folks have used those DNA sites. When they get the skeleton's DNA, they can see if he has any genotyped relatives in the data bases. Then his kin can say who he was. Simple, right?"

My knowledge of anything scientific is slightly greater than anything a frog knows about cliodynamics.

"Doesn't sound simple to me."

"Doesn't have to. All you have to do is share the brilliant idea with Chief LaMond. Let her run with it."

"Don't you know Chief LaMond?"

"Sure."

"You have her phone number?"

"Yes."

"Why don't you call and share your *brilliant* idea?"

"Two reasons. First, she thinks I'm a moron. Second, she takes things you tell her serious. Don't know why, but she does. Like those hip dudes on TV say, you've got creds."

"I'll think about it."

"Hurry. I'm sure she's waiting for you to enlighten her so she can figure out who the poor guy is."

"I don't think there's a hurry. He's been dead decades. What difference will a few more days make?"

"Won't know until you tell her."

I did the only thing that'd get Charles off the phone short of hanging up on him.

"I'll tell her your idea."

"Not idea, brilliant idea."

———

I was in no hurry to call Cindy to share Charles's idea. An early-morning walk on Folly's Fishing Pier would be a good way to put off the call. I went next door to Bert's Market, grabbed a complimentary coffee, bought a pack of sugar-coated donuts, then headed two blocks to the Pier. The temperature was in the mid-seventies, perfect for the walk. I wasn't the only person who thought visiting the iconic location was a good idea. There must've been fifteen men, women, and a couple of teenagers dangling fishing rods over the side of the thousand-plus foot-long structure. Walkers made up the rest of the crowd. I recognized a couple of the men and shared pleasantries before continuing to the far end of the structure. I sat on a bench, looked back at the nine-story Tides Hotel and the Charleston Oceanfront Villas, a long condo complex adjacent to the hotel's parking lot, while thinking how fortunate I was to live in an area where people from all over the country vacation.

My phone rang, interrupting my feelings of contentment. For the second time in forever, it was Al.

"Chris, did I catch you at a bad time?"

"No."

"Good. I hate to call so early, but something's been bothering me since we were together. I had to get it out of my system."

"What is it?"

"I don't like talking on the phone. Never have. Could we, umm, is there a way we could talk in person? I hate to ask you to come over here, but—"

"Al," I interrupted, "what do you think about us going to Island Breeze tonight for supper?"

There was a long silence before he said, "That sounds wonderful, but I'm sort of afraid to leave Bob alone at the restaurant. You may not believe this," he hesitated then laughed. "He rubs some of my, umm, his customers the wrong way."

"Not loveable, personable, open-minded Bob?"

He chuckled. "That's the one."

"Won't Lawrence be there? He can protect your customers from you-know-who."

Again, he chuckled. "I'm more worried about Bob than I am the customers."

"He'll be fine."

"You convinced me."

We made plans. I continued to look toward shore and watched a line of surfers off the side of the Pier. Instead of thinking how fortunate I was to live here, I tried to figure out what was bothering Al. It didn't take long to realize I'd have to wait until tonight to find out. I also couldn't figure out exactly what to tell Cindy about Charles's idea, so decided that it could wait until tomorrow. Avoidance was one of my favorite activities.

Chapter Ten

During the decade I've lived on Folly, I'd never visited Mosquito Beach. In the last two weeks, I was pulling on the out-of-the-way strip of land for the fourth time, the second with Al Washington. Most of the ride we talked about our mutual friend, Bob Howard, and how much Al appreciated the blustery, obscene, overweight owner of Al's former business. Al shared a couple of humorous stories about the cultural clash between his customers and the wealthy, white owner, who couldn't let a day—correction, hour—go by without insulting someone. I shared some of my experiences with Bob, including how after the rental house I was living in was torched with me in it, Bob dragged me out of the hotel where I was staying after the fire then insisted I move to the cottage I eventually purchased. Bob swore it was so he'd make a commission on the sale. I knew better. His heart exceeded the size of his obscene vocabulary, which was gigantic.

It was Wednesday so Island Breeze wasn't nearly as

crowded as during Charles and my Friday visit. A table in front of the building was vacant, so I asked Al if he'd like to sit outside. He said it'd be a welcomed relief after spending most daylight hours in the dark confines of the bar.

A server arrived and Al told her a cold brew was what the doctor ordered. She joked saying for him to call her nurse Judy, then told him his prescription would be right out. I stuck with white wine so Judy didn't see anything to joke with me about.

Al stared across the street at the tidal creek. "I can still picture that wonderful pavilion. Folks dancing, smooching, hanging out, enjoying time away from work, worry, life's challenges."

All I could see was a handful of wood piles sticking out of the water—piles that once supported the pavilion.

Judy arrived with our drinks and asked if we wanted anything to eat. I deferred to Al who told her maybe in a little while. He said he wanted to enjoy the drink before eating.

He took two sips as he leaned back in the chair. "Chris, I appreciate you bringing me here. I don't get out often, probably don't have many years left. I suppose looking back makes me feel like time on this earth is longer than it really is."

"You've got a long life ahead of you."

Al smiled. "Bob lies to me all the time. I expect it. Don't make me start putting you in that boat."

I returned the smile. "That hurt. Besides, there isn't enough room for anyone else in a boat Bob's in."

"True." He took another sip, glanced at me, then down at the beer bottle as he peeled off the label. "Chris, you asked me a couple of times the other day if there was something bothering me. I wasn't ready to get into it. I apologize for not answering your questions."

"No need to apologize. My friends don't answer my questions all the time." I smiled, hoping to put him at ease.

He nodded. "Back when I was spending weekends here, must've been the summer of '53, I made friends with Elijah Duncan. We hit it off, but Elijah was a hell raiser, a trouble-maker." Al smiled, as he pointed to the piles. "I see him as clear as day. He'd be out there leaning on the railing like he owned the place. He was a sharp dresser, even wore one of those stylish double-breasted suits that were big back then. Everyone else was dressed for the weekend, casual like, then there was Elijah lookin' like he was headed uptown."

"He sounds like a character."

Al turned back toward the water, took another sip, and slumped down in the chair. "He was that, my friend. He sure was. Chris, I think the reason we became friends was before I went off to Korea, I was Elijah."

"In what way?"

"The problem with youngsters today is when they see old folks, they think we were born old. They can't see past the gray hair, wrinkled face, stooped shoulders. No, they can't."

I was tempted to say something, but knew Al wanted to make a point but was having a hard time with it. I sipped my drink.

"I haven't told anyone this," he said, hesitated, then continued, "ever. Hell, I can't tell any of my kids. Heaven forbid I say anything to Bob, or I'd never hear the end of it." He took a deep breath before continuing, "Before I went off to Korea, I was as big or bigger hell raiser than Elijah. In school, I drove my poor teachers nuts. I was a pistol." He chuckled at the memory. "Chris, I smoked cigarettes, umm, and pot. I drank too much." He took another sip of beer then glanced up from the bottle at me. "One of my friends was a little slow at thinking things. Know what I mean?"

"Yes."

"We were out one night, ran into his two older brothers. Those boys were trouble with a capital T. My friend, Benjamin was his name, and I were out walking. His brothers pulled up in a shiny green, 1948 Buick Roadmaster Sedanet." He shook his head. "I remember that car like it was yesterday. They waved us over. Benjamin begged them to take us for a ride. We hopped in the back seat. The driver peeled out like we were at a drag strip. I tell you, that car could move. Yes, it could."

Judy returned to ask if we were ready to order. That shook Al out of his ride in the Buick. I said another drink first. She said our wish was her command.

"Where was I?" Al said.

"Riding in the Buick."

"Did I mention it was stolen?"

"No."

"Benjamin's brothers had scrapes with the law for as long as I knew them. I didn't recognize the car but figured they must have bought it since I'd seen them last. That's what I told myself. I knew better. We weren't zipping around the city more than a few minutes, when I saw a car I did recognize. I heard a siren, turned, looked out the back window. There was a black and white Ford with a big red light on top. It was after us."

"What happened?"

"Benjamin's brothers weren't as slow in the head as he was but not far from it. The one behind the wheel stomped on the gas. The Buick had a big engine. It managed to pull away from the cop car. But, like I told my boys when they were growing up, cop cars are like rabbits. Where there's one, there're more. You may outrun one, but another will catch up with you. Yes, it will."

"What happened?"

"Benjamin's brother pulled in an alley. We bailed. His brothers ran one way, Benjamin and I took off the other direction. We were lucky. The cops went after his brothers while Benjamin and I managed to hide behind a row of bushes. We were there forever before we had the nerve to come out."

"Did the police catch the brothers?"

Al shook his head. "Sort of."

"Meaning?"

"In those days, the stupidest thing a Negro could do was to run from the law. They caught one of the brothers." He hesitated. "Killed the other one." He shook his head again. "It could as easy have been me. It sure could've."

"I'm sorry."

"I knew not to get in the car. I knew Benjamin's brothers couldn't afford a car, especially one that new, that pretty. I can still hear the cop's gun. Pop! Pop! Chris, I was a fool, could've been shot as easy as my friend's brother."

"Al, you were a kid. That was nearly seventy years ago. You were lucky, but you didn't get your friend's brother killed."

"I know." He shook his head. "I know."

I wondered what his story had to do with Elijah. I was about to ask, when I saw Jamal Kingsly coming across the street. He was leaning heavily on a cane and carrying a paperback book in his other hand. He did a double take when he saw me, like he thought he might know me but wasn't certain.

I stood, smiled, and said, "Hi, Jamal. I'm Chris, we met the other night when I was here with a friend."

"Yes, sir, I remember. Your friend's a reader."

"Jamal, meet another friend, Al Washington."

Al slowly stood and shook Jamal's hand.

"Al, you live over on Folly like your friend here?"

"I live in Charleston."

"What brings you out? Sure ain't the weather."

I waited for Al's response.

He glanced at me, then turned to Jamal, "I spent time here in the '50s. Wanted to see what the old place looked like now."

Jamal pointed over his shoulder at the creek. "Guess you were here when the pavilion was hoppin'."

Al gave an exaggerated nod. "I was here most every weekend the year it was built."

Jamal stepped closer to Al then looked at him like he'd inspect a diamond ring. "We were here at the same time. You don't look familiar, but hell, I wouldn't recognize myself either since this old haggard, fat body don't look anything like it did back then."

Al looked toward where the pavilion had been. He shook his head. "Those were the days, weren't they?"

Jamal followed Al's gaze. "Al, our memories make those days better than they were. Sure, we had good times over there, but age makes us forget there was no air conditioning, no work, no respect in any store that wasn't owned by someone like us. No offense, Chris."

"None taken," I said then waited for Al to respond.

"Jamal," Al said, "were you heading here to eat?"

"No sir, just hankerin' for a beer after a long day of doing nothing."

Al pointed to an empty chair. "Care to join us?"

Motown sounds filled the humid air.

"Don't mind if I do. These old legs don't move as well as they used to," Jamal sat and put the Walter Mosley paperback in the empty chair. It was the same book he'd been reading during my previous visit.

The server appeared behind Jamal's chair.

"Nurse Judy," Al said, "get my friend here whatever he wants to drink."

Jamal twisted around. "Judy, when did you go back to school and get your nursing degree?"

She put her hand on Jamal's shoulder. "Jamal, if I was a nurse, do you think I'd be out here waiting on old farts like you and begging for measly tips?"

"Well excuse this old fart's mistake."

Judy laughed and hugged Jamal. "Al, Jamal is one of my favorite customers."

"Judy," Jamal said, "are you going to get me a beer or stand and gab all night with these newcomers?"

She continued hugging Jamal then turned to Al, "You all ready to order something?"

I felt like I was a potted plant sitting on the table.

Al pointed to the building. "You got some good wings back there?"

Jamal answered for her, "The best on Mosquito Beach."

"The only on Mosquito Beach," Judy added.

"Chris," Al said, "want to start with some?"

Thank goodness, someone noticed I was still here. "Sure."

Judy said she could round up a few in the kitchen then headed inside.

"Jamal," Al said, "did you know Elijah Duncan back in the day?"

Jamal's eyes narrowed, he tapped his fingers on the table. "Smart dresser. Chip on his shoulder the size of a damned shrimp boat. Always preachin' for Negro rights years before it was safe to do. That Elijah Duncan?"

I thought he was going to pound a hole in the thick wood tabletop.

Al nodded. "That'd be the one."

"Al, that goes back a long way. Sure, I knew him. Everyone did. Why are you asking?"

"We weren't close, but the two of us got along. I saw him on weekends so don't know what he did the rest of the time. I was wondering what happened to him."

"Depends on who you ask."

Judy returned with Jamal's beer and said the wings would be out soon.

Al waited for Jamal to set his bottle on the table then said, "What's that mean?"

"Different ideas about what happened." He blinked a few times. "Let me rewind my memory. Remember, that was about a thousand years ago. Let's see, there was a story going around that Elijah ran off with Preacher Samuel's daughter. The child was barely in her teens. Preacher Samuel left for Illinois shortly after. No one asked him about his daughter, or if they did, I didn't hear about it. Then, the story was Elijah was killed by a jealous husband who dumped his body in the ocean for shark food. None of the husbands around here took credit." He snapped his fingers. "Oh yeah, how could I forget? I heard he was hanged by a group of Klan members because he was stirring up a pot of trouble, too uppity for his own good."

I said, "Jamal, what do you think happened?"

"Course I don't know for certain. He was here one day,

then he wasn't. There were as many rumors out here as there were mosquitos. I tend to think he got tired of being here. Left on his own. Probably headed north where a lot of the younger guys went to find work, to live happily ever after."

Al said, "Down deep, he was a good kid."

"Except when he was drinking," Jamal added.

Al nodded. "Except when he was drinking."

"Which was most all the time," Jamal said, then took another drink.

"Hey, Jamal," came a voice from behind me.

"Hey, Robert," Jamal said.

I turned to see a tall, thin man with long gray hair pulled in a ponytail. He wore tan slacks, a red polo shirt, a Charleston RiverDogs gold, white, and blue ball cap, and a huge smile.

The newcomer pointed at Jamal's book. "See you're still reading. Some things never change."

"No reason to stop now," Jamal said. "Besides, these old eyes are about the only thing on me still working."

"I'm a couple of years older than you, so I know what you mean. Who're your buddies?"

Jamal pointed to Al. "This here's Al Washington." He nodded my direction. "That's Chris, umm."

"Landrum," I said.

"Yeah, Landrum," Jamal said. "Al's from Charleston, Chris from over on Folly. Guys, meet Robert Graves. Him and me go back to the '50s. He lived up by where the Harris Teeter is now and sneaked over here when musicians were playing in the pavilion."

"Best music anywhere," Robert said. "We do go back, don't we, Jamal?"

"Guys, Robert was the first white guy I ever had much dealing with."

"If it weren't for Jamal, I probably would've been run off."

"I think the only thing that kept you safe was because your dad worked for that tobacco wholesaler. You'd sneak cigarettes out here and share them around."

"That too. Those were interesting days."

"You meeting someone?" Jamal asked.

"No. Thought I'd get a drink and have an excuse to get out of the house. Gets pretty boring sitting there watching stupid television shows while listening to Sandra gripe about, well, about everything."

"Want to join us?" Jamal said.

Robert smiled as he took the remaining chair.

Judy reappeared and set our order of wings in the center of the table. "Sorry it took so long guys. The kitchen's backed up."

Al told her we weren't in a hurry. She asked Robert what he wanted to drink. He said a Budweiser. The rest of us said we were okay, for now.

Al took a bite of chicken wing and turned to Robert. "Back in my younger day, I spent some time here. If I'm not mistaken, I remember seeing you."

Jamal pointed at Robert. "Would've been hard missing him. He was one of the few white faces here."

Al smiled. "Then, Robert, it's good seeing you again."

Robert nodded, as Judy set his beer in front of him. He took a sip, looked at each of us, then said, "You guys hear who belonged to that skeleton?"

I shook my head and Jamal said, "Nothing for sure. They say it's been buried a long time. Nobody's claimed it or confessed to planting it."

"Jamal," Robert said, "I'm disappointed. You've always known what's going on."

"Those days are long gone. Hell, I have trouble knowing what's happening in my own head."

"Jamal, I don't believe that for a second. You've always known more about what's happening here than anyone else on Mosquito. I heard the poor soul had been shot. That true?"

"I heard the same thing. Enough about ancient history. Let's sit back, enjoy our new friends, and the great weather."

That wouldn't have been possible if I'd been with Charles. He'd be playing detective while asking a million questions. Al chewed on a wing, bobbed his head to the Bob Marley songs playing through the sound system, and enjoyed the easy banter between Jamal and Robert. All in all, we had a great evening.

———

Al was both hyped and exhausted by the time I pulled in front of his house. On the ride back, he'd shared memories from the dances at the pavilion, how crowded it got on Saturday nights, and how many restaurants there had been "in the day." The entire time he was talking, he leaned back against the headrest with his eyes closed, his hands unmoving from their crossed position in his lap. I wasn't certain he knew we were at his house.

Finally, he opened his eyes, looked at his house, but he made no effort to open the door. "Chris, you don't know how much it meant being there tonight. You're a loyal friend to put up with this old man."

"I enjoyed it."

He closed his eyes again. "Remember what I told you about being a hell raiser when I was young?"

"Sure."

"Korea changed all that, yes it did. I saw evil, true evil, how it hurt and changed even the best people. It wasn't that I stopped having bad thoughts, Lord knows I'm not perfect. What it made me think was what I did, what I said touched other folks." He slowly shook his head. "I know I'm not making sense. I'm trying to say when I got back from that war, I started seeing how bad folks treat other folks. My eyes were opened. Think that's why I spent time with Elijah and wanted to be his friend. Like I said at the restaurant, he was a good kid, but misguided." He hesitated, then said, "No, not misguided; was more like he wanted things to be right but didn't know how to get it across without pissing people off."

"I hope he appreciated what you were trying to do."

"I suppose he did." He sighed. "When he wasn't drinking. After a few, nothing could get through to him."

"You think the body was Elijah, don't you?"

"Hate to say it, but I truly do. Everything fits."

"You could be right. There's just as good a chance it's someone else."

"You heard what Jamal said about Elijah having a chip on his shoulder, preaching equal rights before it was a smart thing to do. Remember, he said everyone knew Elijah, knew the problems he was causing."

"I'm not saying it wasn't him, but Jamal also said there were stories about Elijah running off with a preacher's daughter. He could've left the area."

Al tilted his head my direction. "He also said there were stories about a jealous husband killing him, or he was hanged by the Klan."

I thought about Charles's idea that the bodies could be identified through familial matches with their DNA.

"Did Elijah have family?"

"Suppose he did. He never talked about kinfolk. I thought that was strange. He lived close to Mosquito, yet never mentioned kin. Why?"

I shared Charles's idea about DNA familial matching,

"Don't know about scientific stuff, but if he still has kin in the area, they might know what happened to him. Think I'll have Tanesa do one of those Google searches to see if any Duncans live nearby. That's a good thought, Chris."

Tanesa was an ER doctor in Charleston and one of Al's adopted nine children. She's his only child living in the area. She's been a tremendous help with Al's medical issues and giving him the support he needs to live alone. She also drove him to work most days.

I suspected there'd be several Duncans in the Charleston area. Al would have his hands full trying to run down relatives of Elijah. Regardless, he was enthusiastic about trying. It was great seeing Al excited about something.

He barely had strength to push the car door open, so I went around to help. The walk from the car to his door was painful to watch. He leaned on me the entire way. When we got to the door, I asked if he wanted me to help him in. He said he could make it. He reminded me that was why his bed was on the first floor.

"Thanks for one of the best days I've had in years," he said as he closed the door.

I was pleased Al had such an enjoyable time but worried it may've been too much on his deteriorating body. I also started thinking about what Jamal had said about Elijah Duncan's disappearance and the possibility the bones were his. Something else was forming in the back of my brain. What was it Terrell Jefferson had said about his grandpa talking about someone on Mosquito Beach who was always wanting to fight; someone in his early twenties; someone who got people riled? And, someone who was there one day, gone the next. Terrell speculated the skeleton was that person.

What else had Terrell said about the person who disappeared? Got it. He had an old-time Bible name; a name Terrell couldn't remember. What were the odds that name was Elijah? I wonder if he's working tomorrow? There's one way to find out. Even if he wasn't at work, it was about time to get one of Rita's great cheeseburgers.

Rather than tell Charles everything later, why not have him there to meet Terrell? I called my friend as I pulled in my drive. After asking me three times what the occasion was, my telling him three times he would have to wait until tomorrow to find out, it took him all of two-seconds to accept the invitation.

Chapter Eleven

Rita's would be busy during lunch hour, so I'd asked Charles to meet me at one-thirty, knowing he'd arrive by one o'clock. Rita's was on a prime slice of Folly Beach commercial real estate. It was across the street from the Folly Beach Fishing Pier, cattycorner from the oceanfront Tides Hotel, and across Center Street from the Sand Dollar private club.

The temperature was a comfortable seventy-five degrees, so I requested a table on the patio and had been seated when Charles entered the restaurant. He wore his Tilley hat, navy blue shorts, a long-sleeve, black and gray T-shirt, with the head of a tiger in orange on the front. He tapped his cane on the floor as he approached the table.

"Go ahead, ask," he said as he put his Tilley and cane on the corner of the table.

"Ask what?"

He pointed at his chest. "About the shirt. Duh."

Charles has one of the largest collections of T-shirts and sweatshirts, most of them sporting college and university logos and nicknames, found outside a sweatshop shirt factory in China. They were interesting but I tried to ignore the shirts to avoid a lengthy monologue about them.

"Okay, what about it?"

He smiled. "That's better. Idaho State University, they're the Bengals."

"Why do I want to know that?"

"You don't. Just wanted to say it's in Pocatello, Idaho. I love saying Pocatello."

See why I avoid asking about his shirts?

Britany, one of Rita's personable servers, arrived at the table. I ordered a Diet Pepsi, Charles said the same. We told her we'd wait to order food when the drinks arrived.

"Okay," Charles said. "I have a hunch you didn't ask me here so I could tell you about Pocatello. What's up?"

"Last night I was at Island Breeze with Al when—"

Charles's hand flew my direction and stopped a couple of inches from my face. "Whoa! You didn't think to invite me?"

I explained that Al had asked me to take him. I didn't think he needed anyone else going. Charles huffed another minute before asking what the trip had to do with lunch.

Drinks arrived before I shared the connection. I asked Britany if Terrell Jefferson was working. He was, so I asked if she could tell him Chris Landrum was here and wanted to have a word with him when he had a chance. We ordered cheeseburgers and Britany said she'd relay the message.

Charles said, "Who's Terrell Jefferson? Why do we want to talk to him?"

I explained how I'd met Terrell when I was at Island Breeze with Barb, saw him again in the bookstore, how he'd told us about his grandfather telling him about a man who disappeared from Mosquito Beach in the 1950s.

Britany returned and said Terrell was busy but would get a break in an hour if we wanted to wait. I told her we would.

Charles spotted Chief LaMond walking by the patio. He waved then pointed to the empty chairs at our table. She rolled her eyes, but instead of continuing her walk, opened the patio gate, talked to a couple seated near the entry, then made her way to our table.

"You two vagrants planning a crime?"

I smiled.

Charles said, "Not now that you're here."

Britany returned to ask Cindy if she wanted anything. She looked at Charles. "You buying?"

He nodded my direction. "Chris is."

Cindy laughed. "I'll have a Pepsi and whatever food they ordered."

"Excellent choice," Charles said as Britany headed to the kitchen.

Charles took a sip, and said, "Chief, Chris wanted to talk to you about a new scientific breakthrough he was reading about. Tell her, Chris."

Revisionist history was another of Charles's "endearing" quirks.

I explained the breakthrough *I'd been reading about* the best I could considering I'd heard all of it through Charles's filter, plus I'm scientifically challenged.

After my enlightening explanation about something I knew next to nothing about, Cindy took a sip of Pepsi Britany had delivered during my lecture on biochemistry, rolled her eyes for the second time in five minutes, and said, "First, I didn't know you could read so your statement you were reading about whatever that was, struck me as absurd. Second, many of the words you just spouted sound surprisingly like something that'd be coming from the mouth of someone else at this table—hint, not me. Third, you probably won't believe this, but I, an old country girl from the mountains, actually know what you were talking about."

"You're not that old," Charles said.

"Compared to you and Chris, coal ain't that old. May I continue?"

Charles motioned her to continue.

"Whenever I get tired of hubby reading me 'fascinating' specs on the latest sump pumps and fiberglass insulation, I actually read police journals."

Cindy's husband Larry owns Pewter Hardware, Folly's tiny hardware store.

Charles leaned forward. "Can I have them when you're finished?"

"No. May I make my point?"

"Of course, Chief," I said.

"Using DNA if there isn't any on file for the bad guys by comparing it to family members is used in twelve states. Guess what, South Carolina isn't among them."

Charles said, "Why not?"

"It gets into those pesky concerns about privacy. You know how much easier my life would be if we didn't have to worry about privacy, or those danged amendments giving bad folks all those rights? And don't get me started on that Ernesto Miranda fella who got a warning named after him. If it wasn't for all that, we could beat confessions out of bad guys, knock doors down anytime we want, arrest you and your buddy Chris and charge you with giving me hemorrhoids." She leaned back in her chair. "Oh, the good old days."

I smiled, knowing she didn't mean any of it, except maybe the part about arresting Charles and me.

Before Charles hijacked the conversation further, I told Cindy about taking Al to Mosquito Beach and his theory a friend of his from the 1950s was the skeleton. Charles stared at me. I knew he was fuming because this was the first he was hearing it. The Chief asked a few questions then said she'd let Detective Callahan know.

Charles said, "Learn anything new about the body?"

It was as if what I'd told her wasn't enough.

Our food arrived, Cindy took a bite, then said, "Remind me again why it's any of your business?"

Charles looked at me, and turned to Cindy, "Because Chris's good friend Al is worried sick. He thinks it could be someone he knew back in the day. Cindy, how could you possibly deprive the poor old man of learning if it was his friend? You know he doesn't have many years left on this earth. Poor Al." He bowed his head.

I stifled a chuckle before turning to Cindy.

"Charles," the Chief said, "remember me mentioning a few minutes ago that I'm an old country girl?"

"You're not that old," Charles repeated.

"Not the point. Know what there wasn't a shortage of when I was growing up?"

Charles tilted his head. "Do I need to take notes?"

Cindy sighed. "There was no shortage of cow manure, horse manure, and chicken manure."

"Eww," Charles said.

"I thought I'd never come close to being around that much crap after I moved here. I was wrong. You spew more bullshit than I thought possible."

"I don't—"

"Charles, I'm not done. Eat your burger, keep you trap shut."

"Can't do both."

"Eat, don't talk."

He took a bite.

"Chris, not Charles, you can tell Al the experts are saying the skeleton belonged to a black male, height, five-foot-seven or eight, probably younger than twenty-one, and yes, probable cause of death, a gunshot wound to the head, or he could've died of a heart attack watching the bullet heading toward his head. No way of knowing for sure."

So far, it was consistent with Al's theory.

I asked, "Any idea when he died?"

"That gets harder. From what he was wearing, they guessed sometime in the 1950s, or he could've been going to a Halloween party in the '60s or '70s dressed like a pimp from the '50s."

"If he died in the 1950s, it matches what folks are saying about Elijah Duncan's disappearance."

"That's what the Sheriff's Office is looking at. Al might be right."

"Cindy," I said, "how hard are they looking? You said before you didn't think they were taking it seriously."

"If you ask the Sheriff Office's public relations hack, she'll say they're not letting any stone go unturned, pun intended. Will spew they're following all leads."

Charles tapped her on the arm. "Chris asked you, not a PR hack."

"Charleston records more than four hundred violent crimes a year. How much time do you think they'll spend chasing down a murderer from 1950-whatever? They'll send someone to Mosquito Beach, he or she will interview everyone who happened to be in the area during that time frame and will come back with no hot leads. End of investigation."

I shook my head. "Perhaps Al will get some solace knowing what happened to his friend."

Cindy took the last bite of her cheeseburger then glanced at her watch. "Sorry I don't have better news for Al. Now I need to get to City Hall and act like I'm doing chiefly stuff."

She left the patio after I thanked her for the information, she thanked me for the food.

Charles watched her go and said, "Wow, did you hear that?"

"What?"

"She said since the cops weren't going to, we have to find out who killed Al's friend."

Before I could remind Charles he wasn't a private detective and I wasn't one with a death wish, Britany returned with the check. She also said Terrell would meet us behind the building.

Chapter Twelve

Rita's backed up to a large, gravel public parking lot that during vacation season overflowed with vehicles most every day. Terrell was seated on an overturned milk crate near the back door talking with another employee. The men were puffing on cigarettes while waving their hands in animated conversation.

Terrell stood when he saw me, told his colleague he'd see him inside, and greeted us. I introduced Charles. Terrell wiped his hand on his food-splotched shirt, dropped his cigarette on the ground, putting the burning tobacco out with his foot, before shaking Charles's hand.

He looked around. "Let's go behind the dumpster where we can talk. It gets busy here with employees coming and going through the door."

We were shaded from the sun by the dumpster enclosure and stood close to each other to stay shaded.

"Thanks for meeting us," I said.

"What's up?" Terrell asked then lit another cigarette.

"When we talked in Barb's Books, you said your grandpa told you stories about someone who was missing? You thought that person could be the skeleton."

"Sure. What about him?"

"You couldn't remember his name, but it was something out of the Bible."

Terrell nodded.

"Could it be Elijah Duncan?"

Terrell snapped his fingers. "That's it. How'd you know?"

I told him a little about Al's experiences on Mosquito Beach in the 1950s.

"Did your friend know what happened to Elijah?" Terrell said before taking another drag on his cigarette.

"Nothing other than he had a reputation as a trouble-maker, then disappeared."

Charles couldn't stand being left out of a conversation. He stepped closer to Terrell. "Chris and I are going to figure out what happened and who killed him."

Terrell's head jerked back. "What makes you think so?"

Good question, I thought.

"Terrell," Charles said, "I've helped the police a few times catch bad guys. I'm known over here as a private detective. Got a pretty good success rate. Chris has helped me a time or two."

Charles has a tough time keeping his fantasy world to himself.

"We've been fortunate," I added.

Terrell took another puff, looked down at the gravel by his feet, and turned to me. "Gentlemen, I've lived on Sol Legare all my life. Heard about all the good that's happened out there. Heard about all the bad. Know pretty much everyone.

No offense, but you two have a big handicap when it comes to getting close to folks out there."

"We're white," I said.

He nodded. "That's part of it, but the main reason is people don't know you. Don't matter what color you are, you're outsiders. I'd have a much better chance learning what happened. Grandpa talked a lot about Elijah. I knew it bothered him when he disappeared without anyone knowing what happened." He took another puff. "I owe about everything I have, everything I know to him. After we talked the other night, I told myself I owed it to grandpa to solve the mystery of his missing friend. Don't mean to offend you, but for the life of me I can't see how you could figure any of it out. I think I can."

Charles took a step closer to Terrell. "Chris and I've solved harder problems than this one. You don't know—"

"Terrell," I interrupted, "you're probably right. We don't know what happened sixty or more years ago, probably wouldn't be able to. There's one thing we've learned over the years, people who kill won't hesitate to do it again, especially if they're cornered. If the body belongs to Elijah, the reappearance of his bones changes things. Not only were his bones brought to the surface, but so was the fact he was murdered. Whoever did it thought he's gotten away with it, has for decades. From what everyone says, Mosquito Beach is a tight-knit community with everyone knowing everyone."

"Chris," Charles said, "what's your point?"

"My point, Terrell, is if the killer is still alive and in the area, he's a danger to anyone snooping around. You need to be careful."

"I appreciate your concern, but like I said, I owe it to

Grandpa to find out what happened. Don't worry, I'll be careful."

The restaurant's back door opened, and someone yelled for Terrell.

"Guys, I've got to get back to work. Let me have your phone numbers in case I learn anything." He handed me a pen and a Rita's bar napkin.

I wrote both numbers on it. He said it was nice talking to us, for me to say hi to Barb.

"He's an interesting fellow," Charles said as we headed to the sidewalk in front of Rita's. "Let's go to Barb's Books to tell the lovely owner that Terrell said hi."

"Yes, and okay."

"Yes, and okay, what?"

"One of these days you're going to listen to what you say. I was responding to you."

"Ye of little faith, I suppose the 'yes' was to me saying he was interesting, the 'okay' was for going to the bookstore."

Maybe it was only other people Charles didn't listen to. We were two blocks from Barb's when a silver Range Rover with a Dillinger Executive Homes logo on the front passenger door honked its horn. It parallel parked a half block in front of us where Eugene Dillinger got out and waited for us.

He was dressed in what must be the uniform of builders. He had on a light blue shirt, khaki slacks and boat shoes.

"I thought that was you, Charles and, umm, Chris. I was thinking about you yesterday Charles. I remembered you were interested in the house I'm building out East Ashley."

"Good to see you again," Charles said. "The house is oceanfront, right? It sounds great."

"Tell you what, I have some free time. Hop in, I'll give you a tour."

"That's okay," I said. "We don't want to take your valuable time."

Clearly, the "we" didn't include Charles. He moved toward the Range Rover and waited for Eugene to unlock the door.

"Nonsense," Eugene said, "I always have time to show my houses."

Three minutes later, we were enjoying an extraordinarily smooth ride on East Ashley Avenue, Folly's longest street, heading away from the center of town. Charles had already commented how much he enjoyed the comfortable seats, bragged on the infotainment screen, and the vehicle's new car smell. Eugene soaked it all in, certain, I'm sure, he had a potential homebuyer sharing the front seat with him. It took all my willpower to keep from laughing.

We passed the Washout, the narrowest part of the island, a place where surfers swear they could find "boss waves," when Eugene pointed to a mustard-colored, wood-frame house on the right. A construction trailer in the drive featured the same Dillinger Executive Homes logo that was on the Range Rover.

Eugene pointed to the house that appeared nearing completion. "We tore down a pre-Hugo tiny concrete block house to make room for this magnificent structure."

He should've added *if I say so myself*.

"Nice," Charles said, one of his few understatements.

"It's sold, but I have another lot a little farther up the road. I could build you a home like this one for a mere 1.9 million."

Charles couldn't have afforded the tiny concrete block teardown even if it had been in, well, been anywhere.

"Something to think about," Charles said as Eugene pulled in the drive and ushered us toward the front door.

Eugene said something to a rebar-thin African American gentleman in work clothes, a white hard hat, and carrying himself with the confidence of someone in charge. After a brief conference, the man headed to a couple of Hispanic men working on one of the windows, barked orders in Spanish, then saluted in Eugene's direction signaling whatever Eugene told him to do had been accomplished.

"He's my foreman. A good man," Eugene said before continuing his sales pitch.

Somewhere around the time he was telling Charles about the hardwood floors, granite countertops in the kitchen, the six-person jacuzzi on the patio, I'd heard all I wanted to about the *magnificent structure*. "Eugene, Jamal told me you've been in this business since the 1950s. You must've seen countless changes."

His eyes narrowed as he glanced at me. He wasn't fond of me interrupting his sales pitch.

"I've been fortunate. Homebuilding has had peaks and valleys over the years, but I've managed to keep the quality up, kept customers clamoring for my homes."

Another *if I say so myself* moment.

"Jamal also said many of your employees came from the Sol Legare community."

"Some of my best workers came from there. That's why I go back whenever possible. Many of the residents consider me a friend. Some of their family members were on my earlier crews."

That wasn't the impression Jamal had given, but Eugene was telling the story, so I didn't see reason to challenge him.

Charles said, "did you know the person whose bones were discovered the other day?"

Eugene stopped and stared at Charles. "I haven't heard who it was. Do you know?"

"I haven't heard either. I figured since you know so many people out there you may've heard."

Eugene moved a piece of paneling from the floor, yelled to get his foreman's attention, and walked toward him. He was back in less than a minute.

"Guys, I'd love to show you more, but there are a couple of things I need to do at the office. Unless you have specific questions, let's head out."

He dropped us where we'd met him then sped off to his office to get a couple of things done.

Charles watched the Range Rover speed away, and said, "I sure know how to break up a great sales pitch. I was getting ready to write him a check for a deposit on the other house."

I said, "Unless you're in medical school, talking about skeletons will dampen most conversations."

"I think it was more than that, don't you?"

"Yes."

Chapter Thirteen

One of the first people I met on my initial visit to Folly Beach was William Hansel who lived next door to the house I'd rented. He'd greeted me in the drive before I carried my suitcase into the house. William teaches in the hospitality and tourism program at the College of Charleston and has been a Folly resident for nearly thirty years, a widower for twenty. His graduate education and teaching experience were in travel and tourism, but his true passion was history. He's been a dedicated member of a group raising funds to preserve the historic Morris Island Lighthouse visible from the east end of Folly. In recent years, he's become interested in the Civil War and its impact on South Carolina.

It'd been several weeks since we'd talked, so I thought it was time to right that wrong. Besides, I'd be interested in what, if anything, he knew about Mosquito Beach. Most late afternoons he could be found in his garden. He took it as a personal affront if a weed had the audacity to pop its head out of the soil in proximity to his vegetables. A low cloud cover and a temperature in the upper 70s encouraged me to walk instead of driving—that combined with the fact it was only three blocks away.

As I guessed, my friend was standing in his garden, leaning on a hoe, staring at something growing. My knowledge of gardening exceeded my knowledge of stratigraphy, but not by much, so I had no idea what he was focused on. I figured since he wasn't decapitating it with the hoe, it was something that was supposed to be there.

"You look busy," I joked.

"Ah, my friend," he said in his bass voice, "you've come to rescue me from laboring over my cool-season vegetables."

William is three years younger than I, my height, although thinner, and African American. He also has a way of speaking that takes getting used to. It often resembles a professor giving a lecture rather than a conversation.

"I have no idea what that means, but if my presence rescued you from anything, I'm glad to help."

He took off his gloves, dust flying as he tapped them together, leaned the hoe against a nearby tree, then neatly placed the gloves on the ground beside the implement.

"Shall I prepare us a glass of tea?"

I'm not a tea drinker, but William's hospitality made consuming the drink tolerable.

"That would be great. Can I help?"

"Absolutely not, you are my guest." He pointed to two chairs under the oak tree in the corner of the yard. "Repose thyself. I shall return shortly."

What'd I tell you about his speech?

Ten minutes later, William returned. He'd exchanged his sweaty shirt for a short-sleeve, white polo shirt. He was carrying a silver platter holding two tall drink glasses, a white ceramic sugar bowl, and napkins. Cloth, of course.

We each took a sip before he said, "What brings you out this fine day? I surmise it isn't to watch me eradicate weeds."

"As exciting as that may be to watch, I did have something to ask."

He laughed. "Then don't hold back."

"Are you familiar with Mosquito Beach?"

William took another sip of tea and nodded. "Familiar, slightly, although I've never been there. Most of my knowledge about the predominantly African American enclave comes from a gentleman I met a few years ago. He's worked at several jobs around town." William chuckled, "James Brown is his name; he lives off Sol Legare Road. To hear him talk, he's spent a lot of time at Mosquito Beach. When I feel industrious electing to walk around Folly, I occasionally run into him. As you know, I'm reserved. Mr. Brown isn't. To anyone who knows both of us, we would appear to be strange acquaintances. Ah, neither here nor there. What precipitated your inquiry?"

"Have you heard anything about a body found out there?"

William's eyes narrowed; his head tilted. "Christopher, please don't tell me you're embarking upon another quest into areas better relegated to the police."

The year I retired to Folly, a friend of William drowned; the police thought it was a suicide. William convinced me his friend had a fear of water. Even if he'd been intent on taking his life, he wouldn't have chosen drowning. He was convinced his friend was murdered. To make a long story much shorter, I, along with Charles, managed to catch the murderer. William was also familiar with other times I'd stuck my nose where it has no business venturing.

I told him I wasn't and shared some about Al's and my visit to Mosquito Beach.

"Enlightening," he said.

"You have an interest in the history of the area, so I thought you might've heard stories about those living in the Sol Legare community."

"I'm familiar with how segregated the beaches had been, including here." He waved his hand around to let me know he was describing Folly. "If African Americans wished to be near water for a respite, they were limited to places like Mosquito or Riverside Beach on the Wando River near Mt. Pleasant. Neither location had what we now would call a beach but were the best available locations for African Americans to gather near water."

"Anything else?"

"I'm afraid not. Certainly, the times prior to the passing of the Civil Rights Act in 1964 were extraordinarily difficult for citizens of African descent." He shook his head. "Even then, things didn't change quickly."

"I appreciate you sharing."

"I'm afraid I didn't share much beyond a glass of tea."

"Spending time with you is always a delight. The tea and information about the beaches were bonuses."

"And you accuse me of speaking professorially."

I laughed.

After fifteen more minutes of discussing everything from the weather to how difficult today's college students are to communicate with, William said he'd better get back to weed eradication.

I thanked him for the tea and conversation.

"Chris," he said as I started to leave, "you've piqued my interest in Mosquito Beach. James has said if I ever want to go to the restaurant there for supper to let him know. He'd meet me there. I think I'll take him up on the offer."

I told him it was a good idea then headed home. My phone rang as I was crossing Center Street.

"Chris, this is Cindy, have a minute?"

She was never that courteous, normally started a conversation with an insult, so I knew something was wrong.

"Yes," I said and moved to the alley behind Snapper Jack's Seafood Restaurant so I could hear better.

"Thought I'd tell you before you heard it from someone else and you called pestering me about it."

That had my attention. "What?"

"There's been a murder on Sol Legare Road, just past the turnoff to Mosquito Beach."

"Who?"

"Clarence Taylor."

I closed my eyes. "What happened?"

"You know about as much as I do. Detective Callahan's caught the case. Because Folly's so close to Sol Legare he called to tell me. He said a neighbor found the body in the vics yard early this morning. That would be a neighbor who didn't see or hear anything unusual next door, well, except finding Taylor with two bullet holes in his chest."

I've known Detective Michael Callahan for three years. He was the detective on the murder on Folly where he'd accused one of my friends of committing the crime, a crime he hadn't committed.

"Anything else?"

"I had a bagel for breakfast," Cindy said.

"About the murder."

"If there was, wouldn't I have shared it before telling you about breakfast?"

"I know. It's just I'm shocked. I met Clarence when I took Al to Mosquito Beach. He seemed like a nice man." I paused waiting for Cindy to respond. She didn't. "Who'd want him dead?"

"No idea. I'm glad it's not up to me to figure out. Now I must go play nice with the Mayor. Seems my department has blown the top off its budget. The way things are going with the price of gas, I'm afraid my folks will have to start chasing speeding cars on skateboards."

It took me a few seconds to shake that image out of my head, before responding. "Thanks for letting me know. If it'll help, you can tell the Mayor you were on the phone with a citizen who called to tell you how great a job you're doing."

She laughed and hung up. I leaned against the fence behind the restaurant, took a deep breath, and continued home.

———

I spent the next hour slowly sipping a glass of Chardonnay, watching a steady line of traffic drive past my cottage, while trying to figure a connection between Clarence and the skeleton. Knowing near nothing about Clarence didn't help. My only contact had been during the trip to Mosquito Beach with Al. If the skeleton belonged to Elijah Duncan and if he died in the early 1950s, Clarence would've been a child, not yet a teenager. On the other hand, hadn't Clarence said his family lived on Sol Legare Road for several generations? Even if he didn't know Elijah, his family would have. Now that the skeleton had been uncovered, could that have reminded

Clarence of something a family member told him leading to whoever committed the murder? Did yesterday's murder indicate whoever killed the person whose remains Clarence found was still around. And, was that who killed my new acquaintance? If it was, why now? The original crime happened decades ago. Had Clarence told Al and me anything indicating he knew something that'd be a problem for the murderer now that the bones had been discovered? Not really.

After an hour asking myself questions, questions I had no answers for, all I concluded was I hated someone I knew, albeit slightly, had been murdered. The identity of the murderer and why were unknown.

Should I call Al to see if he'd heard about Clarence's death? I'd rather he learned it from a friend rather than being shocked via television.

I picked up the phone to call, when it rang. It startled me so much I dropped the device. I picked it up and saw a number I didn't recognize displayed on the screen. Great, another robocall.

It wasn't. I was surprised to hear a vaguely familiar voice say, "Is this Chris Landrum?"

I said it was.

"Chris, this is Terrell Jefferson. Is it okay if I called? You gave me your number when I met you and your friend behind Rita's."

I told him it was good hearing from him. I didn't know if it was or not, but I wanted him to feel comfortable calling.

"Good, I don't know if you've heard, but there's been a murder out here. You're interested in the skeleton and this is weird, so weird. I hope it's okay for me to tell you."

I told him it was.

"You're not going to believe this. Clarence Taylor, the man that found the body, was shot in his yard last night or early this morning. His neighbor found the body. Is that weird or what?"

I didn't tell him Cindy already shared the information.

"Any idea what happened or who did it?"

"Hell if I know. It's scary. This is a tiny community. We all know each other. I don't know who did it but seems to me it must've been someone that knew him."

"Why?"

"I hear he was shot in the chest at close range. That says he knew and trusted the killer. Folks out here don't take too kindly to strangers. Old Clarence wouldn't have let someone he didn't know get close enough to stick a gun in his chest."

I didn't tell him Clarence hadn't hesitated to talk to Al and me or get close enough to invite us to sit in the shade with him.

"Any other reason you think he knew the person?"

"Chris, I'm working an early shift tomorrow. Should get off by four. Think you could meet me somewhere? There's something else, you should know."

"Why don't you let me buy you a drink after work?"

"Sounds good." He chuckled. "Anywhere but Rita's."

That I understood. "How about Pier 101?"

"Sounds even better. Let's say four-thirty."

I told him I'd see him there. Now there was one more thing I needed to do, to do quickly. I called Charles to invite him to Pier 101. He asked why. I told him if he'd show up, he'd find out. Of course, he said he would.

With tomorrow afternoon planned, I made one more call, the one I'd planned to make before Terrell's call.

Al answered, and I heard Conway Twitty in the background singing about what happened "Fifteen Years Ago."

"Al, this is Chris. You at work?"

"No, I love to put old Conway on my record player at the house. Makes me think of Bob."

I laughed and reminded myself how funny Al could be when he wasn't dodging Bob's insults.

"I was wondering if you'd heard news today about what happened on Sol Legare Road?"

"Unless Hank Williams Senior sang about it, I ain't heard it today. I've been here since ten this morning listening to Bob wail along with his country friends on the jukebox and some of my, umm, his, regulars bitching about the music."

I told him what'd happened. He didn't respond for so long that I thought something had happened to him.

Finally, he said, "Oh, my Lord. He was such a nice man. Who would've had anything against him?"

I said I didn't know, and heard Bob's booming voice in the background yell, "Al, damnit, get off that freakin' phone. Smile at that handsome couple who just stepped in. Where're your customer service skills?"

Another textbook example of the pot calling the kettle black.

"You heard the boss," Al said. "Better go. I'd hate to get fired from this job that pays nothing, although Bob makes up for it with his love for his employees, paid or otherwise."

I told him we'd talk later.

Chapter Fourteen

Pier 101 was on the Folly Pier with a panoramic view of the beach and the Atlantic. In addition to the views, it had a varied menu plus a well-stocked bar. What more could one ask for in a restaurant? There was a low cloud cover with the temperature hovering in the low eighties.

I figured Terrell who'd been cooped up in Rita's kitchen all day would prefer sitting outdoors, so I requested a patio table. Two young women pushed strollers along the Pier, three men stared at their fishing poles waiting for an elusive bite, and a dozen walkers added colorful shirts, blouses, and bathing suits to the mix.

Charles peeked his head around the corner. He wore a long-sleeve, navy blue T-shirt with Xavier University proudly displayed on the front, tan shorts, and a wide smile.

"What's the smile about?" I said as he put his Tilley on the adjacent chair before leaning his cane against his chair. The brisk breeze off the ocean mussed his already unruly hair.

"Glad you're outside. I was afraid you'd wimp out, want to be in the air conditioning. I've been stuck in the apartment most of the day."

"Stuck doing what?"

"Google stuff."

He never hesitated to share his never-ending fount of trivia, so I figured he'd eventually tell me what *stuff* he'd been Googling.

I'd have to wait. Terrell came around the corner of the building and saw us. He smiled then headed to the table. He'd changed out of his chef's coat and was wearing a black T-shirt with a large Nike swoosh on the front. He still had on chef pants.

"Aha!" Charles said. "I'm beginning to see why you invited me. Knew you wanted to catch the skeleton killer."

"He called, wanted to meet. I don't know if it had anything to do with the murders."

"Murders? Like more than one?"

I didn't have time to tell him about Clarence before Terrell took the remaining seat and made the mistake many who don't know Charles make when he said, "You go to Xavier?"

"Nope. Like the big X on the front."

"Oh," Terrell said, a common reaction to my friend.

A server arrived before Charles told Terrell all the other schools he didn't attend. She told us her name was Shelly then asked what we wanted to drink.

Terrell looked at me before turning to Shelly. He told her a Budweiser would be nice. Charles said the same, I stuck with white wine.

Terrell's eyes hopped from Charles to me to the surrounding tables. His fingers tapped on the table.

"First time here?" Charles said, noticing how nervous Terrell appeared.

"Yeah. Guys at work talk about how good the food is, but most of the time when I get off work, I want to get as far from restaurants as I can."

Terrell looked at two grackles fighting over a French fry one of them grabbed off the floor after a giggling young girl "accidentally" dropped it. Drinks arrived, and Shelly asked if we were ready to order. Terrell grabbed the menu and scanned the offerings. He looked at me and shrugged, so I told her to give us a few minutes.

Terrell had called, so I didn't want to distract him from saying whatever he had to say. I took a sip of wine.

Charles, who had the patience of a chipmunk, said, "Chris tells me you called."

Terrell turned to Charles. "Yes. Do you know about the man killed yesterday near my house?"

Charles shot me a dirty look before turning to Terrell. "What man?"

Terrell said, "Clarence Taylor, he was—"

"Whoa," Charles said as his head jerked in my direction. "Isn't that the guy you and Al talked to, the one who found the skeleton?"

I told him it was which earned me another evil look.

"Sorry to interrupt," Charles said. "My friend must've forgotten to tell me. What were you saying?"

"I was going to say Clarence was shot in his yard, shot twice. No one knows who did it."

I said, "Were you close?"

"We weren't best bros, but close. I've known him forever. I can see his house from mine. He was a lot older than me. I liked it when he'd talk about the old days."

Charles said, "You have any idea who might've killed him?"

He shook his head. "Everybody liked Clarence. He didn't have kin in the area, so he spent most nights at Island Breeze talking to everyone." He shook his head again. "Everybody liked Clarence."

One person didn't, but I didn't remind Terrell of the obvious.

"I Get Around," the Beach Boys classic, played from the speakers along the restaurant's pergola.

Charles was more focused on Clarence's demise. "If everyone liked him, why do you think someone shot him?"

Shelly returned to the table to ask if we were ready to order. I motioned for Terrell to go ahead.

He pointed to an item on the menu. "I'll have the smoked jumbo wings."

Charles went with a fried grouper sandwich; I said the same.

As soon as our server left, Charles returned to his question. "Why do you think he was killed?"

Terrell took another sip. "That's why I called Chris. I think it has to do with the body Clarence found."

"But why kill him?" I said. "All he did was stumble on the remains."

Terrell shook his head. "If that's all he did, I think he'd still be alive."

Charles said, "What's that mean?"

Terrell ignored Charles's question. He was staring at two men being seated three tables away. He then lowered his eyes and whispered, "Crap."

Charles turned in the direction Terrell had been staring. "What?"

"See the fat guy with black hair?"

I slowly turned, trying to get a better look at the men without being conspicuous. One was thin, wore a short-sleeve white T-shirt with Def Leppard in red on the front. The other man was obese, with long black hair, wearing a black T-shirt. Both appeared in their sixties.

Charles said, "What about him?"

"Name's Andrew Delaney. He's in the KKK."

Charles said, "Ku Klux Klan?"

"Yeah, but they're trying to sound classier. His group's called the Loyal White Knights of the Ku Klux Klan." He mumbled something I couldn't understand.

I said, "How do you know?"

"A white guy I work with knows him. Says he's trouble. Told me I'd do myself a favor if I stayed clear of him. I've seen him in Rita's a couple of times. Rumor is he and his buddies have been cruisin' Sol Legare, but I've never seen him there."

The breeze had picked up. It may've been my imagination, but I felt a chill in the air.

Charles glanced toward the men. "Why would he be on Sol Legare?"

"Only reason I think of is to cause trouble. My friend that told me he saw him out there said Delaney was in a pickup truck with two other white dudes. They were driving slow. My friend was walking along the road when the pickup sped up and passed real close. Said the truck nearly hit him."

"Was that the only time your friend saw them?" I asked.

"Yes, but he told me another guy saw two other trucks a couple of days earlier. Delaney was in one of them."

Charles glanced at the men again. "How do you know his name?"

Good question, I thought.

"A few months ago, there was a picture in the Charleston paper showing three guys waving a big Confederate flag down at the Battery. One of them was named Andrew Delaney. The day before the picture was in the paper, he was in Rita's; got in an argument with the server. Something stupid about his credit card. It really shook the server. She told all of us in the kitchen about it, kept repeating his name." Terrell smiled. "Course she surrounded it with profanities. We all looked to see who she was talking about. It was the guy over there." He nodded his head in the direction of the other table. "My friend on Sol Legare also saw the picture in the paper. That's how he knew the guy in the truck and told me about it."

Charles said, "Know who the other man is?"

"No, he wasn't with Mr. White Knight in Rita's."

Our food arrived, the Byrds version of "Mr. Tambourine Man" filled the air, and immersed in silence, we each took a bite.

A few awkward minutes later, Terrell said, "Sorry to change the subject, let me get back to Clarence. I was saying if all he did was find the skeleton, things might've turned out different."

Charles said, "How?"

"Clarence was a talker. Suppose after spending all that time in his house by himself, he had to say a lot of words to catch up. When he was in Island Breeze or at any of the picnics folks had on Mosquito, Clarence talked up a storm. Not only talking."

I waited for Charles to repeat, "What's that mean?" Instead, he said, "Talking about the skeleton?"

Terrell nodded. "Nearly every second since he found it.

He wasn't just talking, he more like was quizzing everyone old enough to be around Mosquito in the 1950s, early '60s. He wouldn't let anyone off the hook. Asked them if they knew Elijah, if they hung with him, if they knew if he had enemies, on and on."

"Terrell," Charles said, "do you think he was killed because he was asking too many questions?"

"No," Terrell said, and looked around at the nearby tables. "Think he was killed because he got answers."

"Elaborate," I said.

"Clarence didn't look like much in his tattered bib overalls, his wrinkled face, but I'll tell you one thing, he was smart. He was a sharp old man." He chuckled.

Charles said, "What's funny?"

"I remember Clarence once told me old-timers said the way to find out if someone was lying, they'd get a Bible, open it up and have the person tell the story again. Said if the person was lying, the pages would flip without anyone touching them. He said it'd scare the shi—umm, scare them enough to tell the truth. Wouldn't be surprised if he didn't try that trick on people he suspected of the killing."

"Terrell," I said, "think he figured out who killed the man?"

"Yes sir."

I said, "Did he tell you that?"

"No, but that's why I'm telling you. Like I told you before, with you being outsiders, I doubt you could get close enough to folks to learn much, but you never know. You said you were good at helping the police. Figured you could help again."

I didn't remind him Charles had said it, not me. I didn't have to, Charles said, "We'll do our best."

Terrell took another bite, watched a dozen or so seagulls off the edge of the Pier squawking about something, looked at me, then turned to Charles. "Don't know what you can do, but I'll tell you what I'm going to do. Clarence was more like my pop than a friend. He didn't deserve to die for asking questions. Fellas, if it's the death of me, I'm going to find out who killed Clarence, maybe who killed the buried body."

I was afraid that was where he was going with the conversation.

"Terrell, like I told you before, whoever killed Clarence won't hesitate to kill again if he feels someone is getting close to finding out what happened. It could be dangerous. You need to stay out of it, leave it to the police."

He said he'd think about it. I wasn't convinced. Now to change the subject. "Have plans been made for his funeral?"

Terrell looked out to sea and I wondered if he'd heard my question. Finally, he said, "No funeral. Police found a note on my friend's bulletin board. One of the cops I know let me copy it." He took a folded piece of paper out of his pocket, unfolded it, and handed it to me. Charles leaned over to read it along with me.

This here's my final request. Pay attention, I mean it. I've been to too many funerals in my life. I don't want to go to another one, especially with me in the box. I want someone to take what money I have left in my checking account and have me cremated. You all can spread it anywhere you want. I don't care. What I do want is for you all to throw a big celebration of my life. Hold it at Island Breeze. If I had any money left in my account, buy the drinks. If not, sorry, you're on your own. If there are any tears, I'll come back and haunt you. This is a party, a celebration.

Charles said, "When's the party?"

"It'll be in a few days. No one wants to celebrate yet. I'll let you know."

From the restaurant's speakers, Jan and Dean harmonized on "Dead Man's Curve."

Chapter Fifteen

The next morning, I woke up thinking about Terrell's theory on why Clarence Taylor was murdered, also how Terrell was determined to uncover who killed him. I was also thinking about how good French toast sounded for breakfast. I couldn't do anything about Terrell, but a walk to the Lost Dog Cafe would meet my breakfast need. It wasn't yet seven-thirty so there were several vacant tables. Amber was behind the counter waving for me to sit anywhere. I headed for my favorite booth along the back wall when I noticed Marc Salmon at a table in the center of the room. He was often seated where he could be the center of attention along with Houston, his fellow council member.

I smiled at Marc. "Where's your buddy?"

"Running late. He called a plumber last night, something about a leak in the kitchen." He glanced at his watch. "The plumber's there now."

The last time I needed a plumber, it took three days then

was a given a four-hour window for him to arrive. "How'd he get a plumber to his house this early?"

"Played the council member card. It doesn't work as good as playing the mayor card, but it beats being Joe Average Citizen."

Whatever, I thought. "I'll let you get back to eating."

"Why don't you join me? It'll be a while before he gets here. He and I've got important business to discuss. You know, we're looking at new regulations on property owners who rent houses to vacationers. The question being, does the city need to inspect them? We're also hot and heavy in trying to stop building close to the shore. For some reason a few of our citizens think if they build a house near the beach, it'll be there forever. Mother Nature has a way," he chuckled, "or wave, of proving them wrong."

Those were hot-button topics the council had been grappling with, but I suspected most of Marc and Houston's restaurant conversations centered on the latest rumors and gossip swirling around Folly.

"Why not."

Amber was quick to the table. She looked at my normal booth then at Marc. "Morning Chris. You lost?"

"Miss Amber," Marc pointed at me. "I thought Chris here needs to learn more about the governance of our city."

She shook her head. "You mean you want to see if he has any gossip."

Marc patted her arm. "You know me well."

Chris," she said, ignoring his comment. "Can I recommend our fresh fruit parfait?"

"Of course you may. I'll have French toast."

She put her hand over her chest. "Bring out the defibrillator. I think my heart's done stopped."

Marc held up his coffee mug. "Amber, don't die before you get me a refill."

She smiled at the council member. "Here are two rumors for you. Marc Salmon is an idiot. The guy sitting with him is going to be the death of me yet."

Marc laughed. "Amber, say it all again slower so I can take notes." He pretended he was writing on the table.

She rolled her eyes then left us to discuss city business or the latest rumors. I didn't have to wait long for Marc's preference.

"So," he said, "what's new?"

"Not much. I heard about someone getting killed on Sol Legare Road. Know anything about it?"

"I didn't hear about it until Mrs. B. came home from the beauty shop."

Mrs. B., for Bridget, was Marc's wife and angel-in-training to put up with him.

"What'd she say?"

"Nothing more than a man was found shot dead in his yard. Why?"

I didn't want to get in a long discussion about the murder, the skeleton, or the people I'd met at Mosquito Beach. I limited my answer to, "I'd recently met the man who was killed."

I was being overly optimistic if I thought that would end it with Marc.

"Where'd you meet him?"

I told Marc I took a friend to Mosquito Beach after he told me he'd spent time there in the 1950s. He wanted to see the place again, and we'd met Clarence Taylor on our visit. The best way to slow Marc's questioning was to give him a chance to expound on something he knew.

"Marc, you know Eugene Dillinger?"

"Sure. Big time builder. Built some of the larger houses over here. In fact, he's building one out East Ashley. Why?"

"Somebody told me he had less than a stellar reputation. I figured if anyone knew anything about him, it'd be you."

A little sucking-up goes a long way with Marc.

He looked around to see if anyone was listening before turning to me. "These are only rumors, mind you. I heard a few years ago, maybe more than a few. I think it was in the 1970s." He shook his head. "Time flies, doesn't it?" He didn't wait for a reply. "Dillinger got in trouble with our friends at the Internal Revenue Service."

"What happened?"

"Don't know for certain but heard it was a big stink. The feds don't take kindly to people not paying taxes. Go figure. He paid a large fine, they confiscated some of his properties. He was building a strip center, also some cheap houses in North Charleston in those days. Heard he lost it all. Now I don't know that for a fact. Rumor, you know."

"Isn't he—"

Marc snapped his fingers. "There's more. Another story going around was he got in trouble with the Department of Labor. Minimum wage in the '70s was a hair over two bucks an hour. Dillinger was paying his workers fifty-cents less."

That was consistent with what I'd heard about him under-paying the employees he got from the Sol Legare area.

"How'd he get from all those problems to building upscale houses at the beach?"

Amber returned with my breakfast, a coffee refill for Marc. He told her he was glad she was still alive. She told him I wouldn't be for long if I kept eating French toast every meal. Marc said that wasn't his problem. All he cared about was her remaining among the living to keep his coffee flowing. She left on that high—low—note.

Marc took a sip then pointed his mug at me. "Chris, I've known you ever since you moved here back in the dark ages. I've known your buddy Charles since prehistoric times. The only time you two ask questions like the ones you've been laying on me is when you're nosing in police business. Do these questions about Eugene Dillinger have something to do with the murder on Sol Legare?"

"Marc, I'm curious. I heard he hired a lot of his workers in the 1950s and '60s from the African American community on Sol Legere. I met him one night when I was over there eating. That's all."

"Hmm."

I escaped having to answer more questions when Houston arrived at the table saying, "Have I been replaced?"

I grinned. "You're irreplaceable."

I'll let him figure out how I meant it. My regular table was still vacant, so I started to take my breakfast to it.

"One more rumor," Marc said. "Hear he also got in trouble for using substandard building materials. I wouldn't trust him as far as I could heave Houston."

———

After my life-threatening French toast, I stopped by Barb's Books to see how the owner's morning was going.

I was greeted with, "You again."

I assumed it to be a term of endearment, so I smiled. "Good morning my favorite bookstore owner."

Fortunately, she returned my smile. "I assume you're not here to buy anything, so can I interest you in coffee?"

I'd reached my limit but didn't want to appear unappreciative. "Sure." I followed her to the back room where she fixed each of us a cup.

"Your friend Terrell was in yesterday."

"Why?"

"Unlike some people, he actually likes books rather than simply drinking my coffee."

Of course, she wasn't referring to me. "Did he buy anything?"

"Yes. I called him a couple of days ago to tell him I got a book in about the Civil War in South Carolina. He asked if I'd hold it for him, said he'd get it on his way to work"

"What'd he have to say?"

"You mean after he thanked me profusely for holding the book?"

I rolled my eyes. "Yes."

She smiled. "I didn't tell him the only other customer who has any interest in the Civil War is your friend William. Terrell didn't say much since he was running late for work. He did say one thing that bothered me. He's looking into who killed the man the other day. Suppose the decedent was Terrell's neighbor."

I told her about my conversation with Terrell at Rita's and how he said the victim was a friend, or more like a father figure since he was much older than Terrell.

"I hope he has enough sense to leave police work to the police." She tilted her head as she glared at me. "I wish everyone I know had that much sense."

"I do, too."

My phone rang before Barb asked if that included me. Charles's name appeared on the screen.

"I've got a hankering for chicken wings, maybe a barbecue sandwich for supper. Want to go with me tonight?"

I didn't have to ask Charles where.

I told him it sounded good then was surprised when he said he'd drive, would buy, and would pick me up at the house at five o'clock.

Barb either knew it'd be futile trying to discourage me from getting involved in things that were none of my business or had forgotten what we'd been talking about before Charles's interruption. She asked if I wanted to go with her Monday afternoon to an art gallery in Charleston. She said she needed to get out of the store and Mondays were slow. It wouldn't have been on my list of things I wanted to do, but the chance to spend time with Barb trumped my lack of desire to see paintings. I said I'd love to.

Chapter Sixteen

The temperature was in the upper 70s, and combined with the low humidity, it felt great outside. I was waiting for Charles on my front step when he arrived thirty minutes before the time he said he'd be here.

"On time, great," he said as I slipped in the passenger seat.

Charles was wearing his ratty, tan shorts, and a navy blue, long-sleeve T-shirt with *Fisk Bulldogs 1866* on the front.

I didn't comment on the shirt or his on-time remark. As if I didn't know, I said, "Where're we going, if it's not too much to ask?"

"Not too much to ask," he said and pulled out of the drive, turned on Center Street to head off-island. I sat back in the seat enjoying not having to drive for a change. It wasn't too much to ask but appeared to be too much to answer.

"Aren't you going to ask again where we're headed?"

"Nope."

He turned on Sol Legare Road, reinforcing what I suspected.

I wasn't the only person who thought it felt good outside. Cars were parked across the street from Island Breeze, and for a hundred yards on either side of the lively dining spot. All the tables in front were taken plus several customers standing nearby. We stepped in the crowded restaurant where there wasn't a vacant table to be had. I suspected the area out back was equally crowded.

Jamal Kingsly and Robert Graves were leaning against the bar with a beer bottle in front of each.

Jamal waved me over. "Chris, it is Chris?"

I smiled and told him it was.

"And Charles."

Charles said, "Right again."

"Guys, there's an hour wait. We've been here near that long, so we should have a table soon. If you want, you can join us." He shrugged. "If not, no hard feelings."

Charles moved beside me, smiled, and said, "We'd love to."

Jamal introduced Robert to Charles then asked where the man I'd been with the last time was. I told him about Al's Walmart-greeter-like job in Charleston and that he doesn't often get away from the bar. Robert said he enjoyed talking to Al, said not many old-timers are left. I told him I'd try to bring Al the next time.

A college-age employee came over to Jamal to say his table was ready. She had a diamond stud in her nose and was wearing a white T-shirt with a large C on the front with the word *Charleston* through it. We followed her out the back door to a table along the side of the property.

Charles pointed to her shirt. "College of Charleston?"

She gave him a wide smile. "I'm a junior." She pointed at his shirt. "You go to Fisk?"

He smiled. "No."

She started to respond, but like many who encounter Charles for the first time, didn't know what to say. She retorted with, "A server will be with you shortly."

"Ain't Fisk a black school in Tennessee?" Jamal said.

Charles smiled. He could spew trivia to a new audience. "Yes, Nashville. Founded in 1866 as an all-black school. Its student population is now about eighty-percent African American."

"Interesting," Robert said with as much enthusiasm as Mick Jagger at a ballet.

We were saved from an extended history lesson about Fisk when a tall, middle-aged gentleman with a goatee and a full head of stringy black hair arrived. He announced he was Isaac and would be serving us. I silently thanked him for the interruption as we ordered drinks.

The bubbly reggae beat of Bob Marley's "Waiting in Vain" bounced from the sound system mixing with the conversations from the crowded dining area. Jamal leaned forward so we could hear him over the music. "What brings you to our hotbed of ethnic culture?"

Charles looked around the patio. "President Gerald Ford once said, 'The three-martini lunch is the epitome of American efficiency. Where else can you get an earful, a bellyful, and a snootful at the same time?' We wanted to savor some of the best Caribbean cuisine in Charleston County, imbibe in beer, meet new friends."

Jamal stared at him with a look created by awe, or gas.

Robert smiled at Charles. "My wife Sandra looked at me a couple of months ago. She said, 'Robert, you can't shit a bullshitter.' Charles, I think she was talking about the wrong man."

Jamal laughed so loud that the couple at the neighboring table turned to look at him. Robert joined in the laughter. To Charles's credit, so did he. I never thought Charles was that funny but to maintain peace at the table, I laughed along with them.

Isaac returned with our drinks and asked Robert what was so funny.

Robert tipped his RiverDogs hat to the server and said, "Politics."

Isaac set a new beer in front of Robert and said, "Ain't that the truth?"

Instead of responding to Isaac, Robert took a long draw out of the bottle while Isaac gave each of us our drinks then asked if we wanted to order.

Jamal asserted himself as the king of the table when he said, "How about bringing a couple orders of wings?"

Isaac told us he knew where he could find some and headed out on the quest. Bob Marley continued working his way through his greatest hits with "Three Little Birds," as the chatter from diners increased in volume.

For the next few minutes, the conversation covered the typical talking points when strangers were thrown together. The weather, size of the crowd, how we liked the music, and more talk about the weather filled time until Isaac returned with our wings.

Charles's true reason for wanting to visit Mosquito Beach began to emerge when he said, "Did I hear something about a man getting killed somewhere over this way?"

"Clarence Taylor," Robert said as he shook his head. "He was one of the nicest people you'd want to meet."

"Was everyone's friend," Jamal added.

Charles said, "Anyone know what happened?"

"Suppose the person that shot him knows," Jamal said.

"Jamal," Robert said, "you know everyone better than I do. Anybody have an idea who did it?"

Jamal shook his head. "Don't know about the police, but nobody I talk to is sharing names."

Charles snapped his fingers as he turned to me. "Chris, didn't you tell me it was Clarence Taylor who found that skeleton?"

Since that was the reason Charles wanted to come tonight, I didn't think he deserved an answer. For our new friends benefit, I said, "Yes."

"Wow," Charles said in the direction of our table mates. "Think finding the skeleton had anything to do with someone shooting him?"

"Don't see how it could," Robert said. "I was talking to Clarence a couple of days before he died." He bit his lower lip. "We were right out there by the creek. Such a nice man. He didn't say anything about finding the skeleton. Nothing seemed to be bothering him." He turned to Jamal. "Do you think it had something to do with the skeleton he found?"

He shook his head. "All Clarence did was stumble on bones. How could that have anything to do with it?"

Charles bit meat off one of the wings, took a sip of beer, then said, "Chris knows this, but you fellas wouldn't. I pride myself on being a private detective. I've helped the police over the years; helped them catch bad guys. There's something I learned a long time ago, something the police taught me." He nodded and took another sip. "Know what it was?"

"I'm not good at guessing," Jamal said. "Why don't you tell us?"

Jamal didn't know he couldn't stop Charles if he'd stuck a billiard ball in his mouth.

"Guys," Charles said, "there's no such thing as a coincidence."

Of course, there was. Fortunately, neither Jamal nor Robert challenged him.

Robert said, "Are you saying Clarence was killed because he found a bunch of bones buried out there, bones that'd been buried forever?"

"Yes."

Jamal shook his head. "Man, that don't make sense."

"I agree with Jamal," Robert said. "Charles, since you're a detective, how're the two related?"

"That's a good question. I didn't know Clarence. I don't know anything about the skeleton, so it'd be hard for me to answer."

Time to move on, I thought. "I'm sure the police will figure it out."

Jamal said, "Wouldn't count on it."

"Why not?" I asked.

He pointed at Robert, then at Charles and me. "You all can't understand what it's like being black, especially in the South. It ain't your fault, you just can't. They're better now than they were in the old days, but the police still don't take crime in the black community as serious as in white places. Oh sure, they give lip-service to doing their job, investigating crimes, working on catching bad guys. Hell, sometimes they're successful." He stared at his beer bottle. "Sometimes."

Bob Marley got a break. The Four Tops were singing "It's the Same Old Song," the boisterous crowd continued to get louder. Our table fell silent.

Finally, Robert said, "Jamal, this ain't the old days, the

Klan doesn't cause trouble anymore, there are plenty of excellent white and African American cops. Don't you think they want to catch the person who shot Clarence?"

"You may be right, but I ain't holdin' my breath."

Robert mentioning the Klan reminded me of Terrell pointing out Andrew Delaney at Pier 101.

"Jamal, Robert, either of you know Andrew Delaney?"

Robert shook his head as he leaned back in the chair.

Jamal glared at me, gripped his beer bottle so hard I was afraid it would break. Through gritted teeth said, "Why?"

I took that as yes. "Robert reminded me of something I heard the other day from someone else who lives over here, Terrell Jefferson. I was talking to him when he saw Andrew Delaney. He told me Delaney was a member of the Ku Klux Klan and had been riding up and down Sol Legare Road. He didn't know why."

Jamal continued to strangle the beer bottle, then said, "How'd Terrell know the bastard?"

"He said someone at work knew him and told Terrell to stay clear. Said Delaney is bad news. Jamal, I figured since you knew everything that goes on here, you'd know him."

"The Klan has been strong in Charleston, not as much now as in the past, but still around. A few years back, they got all hot and bothered when some of the wiser politicians pushed to have Confederate monuments removed from public places. That got the Klan riled up. Hell, it probably got them more attention with more people joining. Bad always comes out of good." He chuckled. "You can probably guess we don't share afternoon tea and crumpets. Yes, I know who he is."

Isaac returned to see if we needed anything else. Again, Jamal spoke for us. He said two more orders of wings would be perfect. Marvin Gaye was singing "What's Going On," and Robert said, "Anybody have something good to say about anything?"

Charles must have a different definition of something good. He said, "Anybody know yet who the skeleton belonged to?"

"Nobody's proved it yet," Jamal said, "but I'd put money on Elijah Duncan."

That was the same thing he'd told Al and me.

"I thought he ran off with Preacher Samuel's daughter," Robert added.

Jamal said, "He was trouble around here. Let's move on. Let the past be gone."

Robert looked at his watch. "Fellas, you'll have to eat wings by yourself. If I don't get home soon, Sandra will be burying my body out here." He threw a twenty on the table saying he figured it'd cover his share of the food.

"Thought you were going to buy my beer," Jamal said.

"In your dreams, old man."

Jamal reminded Robert that he was four years older than Jamal then gave him a man hug before he headed home to Sandra.

Our wings arrived quicker than the first time. Jamal patted his stomach. "Now that Robert's gone, that's more for us. Eat up, boys."

Chapter Seventeen

We'd finished the wings and socializing with sunset still a half-hour in front of us. Charles asked if he could see where Clarence found the skeleton. He'd driven, so I didn't have much choice. I told him to drive to the end of Mosquito Beach Road. We passed a cyan-colored building and pulled in a small, rutted, sandy parking area under a large live oak. The tidal creek was on our left, a wide swath of marsh to our right. The tide was out and a couple of jon boats rested on pluff mud. It would've been difficult for a boat to dock during low tide. Roughly four hundred feet across the marsh, I saw cars on Sol Legare Road and the back of houses.

Hidden behind one of the oaks to our left, a short piece of yellow crime-scene tape was tied to the trunk of a small tree. The loose end flapped in the light breeze. Straggly grass, weeds, and sand had been trampled by what looked like a herd of buffalo or many law enforcement officials. This must be where the body had been. Charles headed to the spot where the ground had been excavated.

He looked around then said, "Chris, I can't see the other buildings from here but have a clear view of the houses across the water. There wouldn't have been much privacy to bury someone."

"True now, but I wonder how many of those houses were there when it was buried. Look how deserted it is out here now. If he was buried after dark, I doubt anyone would've been close enough to see anything."

Charles nodded toward the three houses closest to where we were standing. "Think one of those belonged to Clarence?"

"Could be. He told me he lived a short jon boat ride from where we are. Come to think of it, he said he inherited his house from his father who inherited it from his father."

"Meaning, he probably would've lived there when the guy was buried." He looked back at the houses across the water. "Young Clarence could've seen what happened."

"Maybe," I said. "If the skeleton belongs to the man Jamal and Al thinks it is, he was killed in the early 1950s, making Clarence ten or so at the time. Don't you think he would've said something then about what he saw?"

"If he understood what he was seeing. Just trying to figure it out," he said then walked around the trees, pushed some brush aside with his cane, and stared at the ground like he'd find a written confession stuck in the sandy soil. Finally, he looked up. "Don't think there's anything else to see."

———

I was scheduled to meet Barb at seven at Loggerhead's Beach Grill located directly across the street from her condo in the Charleston Oceanfront Villas. Like the night before at Island

Breeze, the weather continued its moderate temperature with low humidity, both rare for September. It was perfect for sitting outside at the restaurant's large elevated deck. On a less positive note, I knew the exceptional weather would bring out more patrons than seats at the popular venue, so I arrived forty-five minutes before Barb was to get here hoping I could get a table. Ed, the restaurant's owner along with his wife, Yvonne, said he was glad to see me as I reached the top of the stairs. I looked over the packed deck. Ed put my name on a list saying there should be something available before Barb arrived. I thanked him and managed to find a vacant stool at the outside bar when a couple was told their table was available, giving up their seats.

I ordered a glass of Chardonnay from the harried bartender and listened to my favorite island entertainer, Teresa Parrish, aka Sweet T, sing "Jolene," from the raised area in the corner of the deck. My wine arrived, and I glanced around the crowded deck and realized how fortunate I was to live where so many people from other parts of the country want to spend their hard-earned vacation time and dollars.

Teresa transitioned into "Smile, Smile, Smile," one of her self-penned songs, as a vaguely familiar man pushed his beer belly up to the bar taking the stool next to mine. It took me a few seconds to remember it was the alleged KKK member Terrell had pointed out. He wore a black T-shirt like the one he'd worn the other time I'd seen him.

I didn't see Mr. KKK order, but the bartender set a plastic cup of beer in front of him. He took a sip, turned toward the stage, and bumped my arm. Beer sloshed on my shorts.

He said, "Crap! Sorry, man."

I told him it was okay and hesitated. To talk or not to talk, that is the question. I decided to do a Charles imitation.

"Are you Andrew?"

He looked at me like he couldn't recall seeing me before, a legitimate expression since he probably hadn't.

He finally smiled. "Andrew Delaney, at your service. Let me buy you a drink to make up for my clumsiness."

I told him he didn't have to, that my shorts would dry.

"I insist." He looked at my face again. "Have we met?"

I told him who I was then added, "Someone pointed you out to me the other day at Pier 101." I didn't want to give him time to ask who, so I added, "Live over here?"

"James Island, just past Harris Teeter."

"What brings you to Loggerhead's?"

He must've thought it was a trick question. He narrowed his gaze. "Why?"

"Curious."

"A couple of friends live over here. They like to hang out at a few of the outdoor bars so I thought I might run into one of them."

"They're not here?"

"Not yet. Even if they don't show, the beer's good. Let me order that wine."

I again told him it wasn't necessary, but it didn't stop him. I hoped the bartender was slow since my glass was still half full.

"Past Harris Teeter," I said, "That's near Sol Legare Road, isn't it?"

"Close, why?"

Why must be one of his favorite words.

"Since you live out that way, I was wondering if you heard about the murder on Sol Legare Road."

I waited for why.

"Who hasn't? Why?"

I figuratively patted myself on the back.

"What'd you hear?" I asked ignoring his predictable use of the three-letter word.

"Only that it was an old black man." A frown appeared on his face. "Excuse me, I should've said African American. Got to be politically correct, you know. Heard he was shot in his yard, probably by some other, umm, African American. Black-on-black killings are the way most go down. What did you hear about it?"

It may've been in the upper-70s, but I was skating on thin ice. "Not much more than you've heard. I met him once. Seemed like a nice man."

Andrew stared at me like I'd grown horns. "Where'd you meet Clarence?"

The victim had gone from being an *old black man* to Clarence. Interesting.

"A friend and I were on Mosquito Beach a while back and met him. How'd you know him?"

My second drink arrived. I was beginning to think just in time. I watched Andrew's expression change from a frown to glimmers of anger. Had I said too much?

"I may've met him years ago. I worked for a landscape company back then. My boss hired quite a few, umm, African Americans from out Sol Legare. His name sounded familiar when I saw it in the paper." He lowered his voice. "My friends and I don't have, don't want to have, contact with black folks, if you know what I mean."

After hearing what Terrell had said about him, I suspected I knew, but he didn't need to know that. I shook my head. "I'm not sure what you mean."

His eyes shot daggers my direction. Yes, I'd gone too far.

"You a bleeding-heart liberal?"

I forced a smile. "No way," I said, hoping to lower his blood pressure, mine as well. "I was curious what you meant about you and your friends. It sounded like you might be a member of a white supremacist group. Just curious."

He returned what most likely was a forced smile. "What if I am? Have a problem with that?"

I had several but expressing any of them would surely bring an abrupt end to our conversation. I shook my head.

That appeared to appease him. He said, "I've got my own opinion about blacks, but in my line of work, have to get along with everyone. Enough said."

I thought of something the famous politician and legislator, Sam Rayburn, once said, "No one has a finer command of language than a person who keeps his mouth shut." I followed that sage advice. Charles would've been proud of me. Not for keeping my mouth shut, but for being able to quote someone, even if it wasn't a president.

He tapped his empty beer bottle on the counter then looked at his watch. "Don't look like my friends are going to show. Better head out."

His friends are probably at a Klan rally.

Andrew started to slide off the stool, turned, patted me on the back, and said, "Be careful out there. Never can tell what might happen to you out Sol Legare."

Chapter Eighteen

Barb hadn't arrived, but good to his word, Ed told me a table was ready earlier than he thought it'd be, then escorted me to a spot along the railing overlooking the street and Barb's condo building. The live music had ended, and numerous conversations floated through the air sprinkled with bursts of laughter.

I replayed my conversation with Andrew as I waited. He hadn't said much I didn't know or would've guessed. I was pleased he didn't get too defensive or angry when I asked if he was a white supremacist. It clearly irritated him, but he kept his anger under control. He also didn't deny it. One thing stuck out. He knew Clarence's name and said he may've met him years ago. He was also interested in how I knew Clarence. Did that mean anything beyond the obvious. Probably not, yet it struck me as interesting.

Barb saved me from reading more into Andrew's comments. She weaved her way around the tables. She wore a red blouse, tan shorts, and a smile that made me forget Andrew.

"Sorry I'm late," she said as she sat on the other side of the small table. "Had a rush of customers as I was locking up."

That was something I'd never experienced during the years her building housed Landrum Gallery. In fact, not only did I not have a rush of customers as I was trying to close for the day, I never had a rush of customers, period. That's a big reason why my former gallery space is now a bookstore.

"You're worth waiting for."

She pointed at my wine. "How many of those have you had? You're sounding like some of your weird friends."

"This is number two. I like to think my friends, weird or otherwise, are beginning to sound like me."

"You wish."

A server arrived before our conversation regressed further. She said she was Lorraine and asked what Barb wanted to drink. Barb told her she would have what I was having. She added she would probably need more to put up with me. Lorraine didn't offer an opinion.

"So, how've you spent another day in retirement?"

It didn't take many words to say until I arrived at Loggerhead's, I hadn't done anything since greeting the morning. I then mentioned Charles and I spent time yesterday on Mosquito Beach. Barb's wine arrived, and our conversation began to feel like an interrogation by a defense lawyer, which was what she'd been before moving to Folly. She began by asking why we had gone there. I told her it was his idea.

She stared at me. "Did Charles handcuff you, throw you in his car, force you to go with him?"

"No."

"Did he want to visit Mosquito Beach because there wasn't anywhere to eat on Folly?"

"Another no."

"Are you two playing detectives again?"

"Of course not."

Barb smiled, shook her head, then held up her wine glass before saying, "Knew I'd need more of these."

Lorraine must have seen Barb's gesture. She returned to ask if we wanted to order. Thank you, Lorraine.

Barb said, "Crab cakes plus another glass of wine."

I went with the flounder dinner but made a point of not ordering more wine.

Barb watched Lorraine go, then turned to me, "Now that you and your shadow aren't playing detective, did you learn anything out there that if you happened to be playing detective you would've found enlightening?"

"No. We talked to Jamal Kingsly and Robert Graves," I explained who they were. "They knew the man killed the other day."

"Did either of them confess to killing him or tell you who did?"

I smiled. "We must not be as good at being detectives as Charles thinks. We didn't ask. They did have something interesting to say about the skeleton. Jamal thought it was Elijah Duncan, the man Al knew back in the 1950s. He told Al and me the same thing when I took Al to Mosquito Beach."

"Why does he think it's Elijah?"

"Nothing concrete other than Elijah ruffled feathers about race relations in the days when it wasn't the wisest thing to do."

"Did they both think it was Elijah?"

"Only Jamal. Robert thought Elijah had run off with a preacher's daughter."

"What proof did Robert have?"

"None. To be honest, I don't think either man knows what happened. They're sharing stories that've been going around for decades."

"Speaking of stories going around for years, your new friend Terrell was in the store again. He's still trying to find books on the civil rights movement. The last time he was in, I told him I'd call if I got any." She chuckled. "He's as patient as Charles."

"Interesting you should mention Terrell. When Charles and I talked with him after work the other day, he pointed out a man sitting near us saying he's a member of the Ku Klux Klan. The guy's name is Andrew Delaney." I took a sip of wine.

"And?"

She also was becoming as patient as Charles. There's hope for her.

I nodded toward the bar. "Before you got here, I was waiting at the bar for the table. Guess who was sitting beside me?"

"Andrew Delaney."

"Charles needs to add you to his detective agency."

"Funny. I suppose there's a reason you're telling me."

"We started talking. He told me he lives off Folly Road near where it intersects Sol Legare. I asked if he'd heard about the man getting shot. Not only had he heard about it, he knew Clarence by name."

"Wasn't the name all over the news?"

"Yes, but he said he may've known him years ago."

"Don't tell me you're leaping from *may have known him* to killing him."

"Not necessarily. I found it interesting that a member of the KKK knew the man who was murdered."

"Did Delaney tell you he was in the Klan?"

"Not directly, but from everything he said, it was clear he either is or was a Klan sympathizer."

"You think that'd be motive enough to kill Clarence?"

"Don't know."

Our food arrived, distracting Barb for a few minutes, but not enough to change the subject.

"Chris, that's quite a stretch. I'd tear a prosecutor to shreds if he tried to convict a client of mine with that feeble evidence."

"I know it's not much, but I think I'm going to share it with Chief LaMond."

Barb smiled. "You're going to share it with the Chief then step aside?"

"Of course."

I pretended I meant it. Barb pretended she believed me.

Chapter Nineteen

The next day began with me walking next door to Bert's for coffee and a cinnamon Danish. After all, breakfast is the most important meal of the day. I then walked two blocks to the Folly Beach Fishing Pier where I ate at the far end of the structure. I remembered my promise to Barb and started to call Chief LaMond when the phone rang. I was surprised to see the Chief's name on the screen.

"Morning Cindy, how'd you know I was getting ready to call you?"

"I'm Chief. I know everything."

"Good, so you know why I was calling."

"Okay, perhaps there are a couple of things I don't know. Where are you?"

I told her. She said she'd see me in five minutes.

The sun was breaking through low, dark rain clouds off the coast and heading away from shore. Other than a few fishermen, the Pier was unusually quiet, with a handful of walkers nearby.

The Chief wasn't off much. She was headed my way, then stopped to talk to two men leaning against the railing and staring at their fishing rods. They said something, she laughed, and patted one of them on the back before continuing toward me.

She sat beside me, reached over, pulled off a corner of my Danish, put it in her mouth, then mumbled, "We meet again on the edge of the edge."

Folly was nicknamed *The Edge of America* because of its location and because so many people gravitate to it when they are at the edge of their careers, existence, or wit.

"Morning, Cindy. How's your world?"

"Gee, you can be civil when none of your weird friends are around," she said as she picked off another slice of pastry plopping it in her mouth.

"One's around now."

"Cute. Why were you going to call?"

I leaned toward the Chief. "You first. You called me, remember?"

"True. Our friend Detective Callahan called yesterday. He was full of no information."

"He must've had some or you wouldn't have called."

She held her forefinger an eighth of an inch from her thumb. "This much." She leaned back on the wooden bench.

"You waiting for me to ask what he told you?"

"Yep."

I motioned for her to continue.

"Okay, you beat the confidential information out of me. Callahan said without DNA to compare and only estimates from the forensic anthropologist, the range of time of death of the skeleton is between 1940 and 1960, give or take a few leap years. He wasn't a skeleton back then, just recently dead."

"Didn't you say they found black and white wingtip shoes with him?"

"Wow! Unlike most people I encounter, you pay attention to what I say."

"Always."

"Don't push it. Yes, the shoes were a model produced in the late 1940s. There's no way of saying when the victim wore them, but it's consistent with what Detective Callahan found from interviewing a handful of folks who would've been around in the early '50s. It's also consistent with what your friend Al said. Elijah Duncan disappeared around 1953. According to a couple of men Callahan interviewed, he was a snazzy dresser, one who'd wear two-tone wingtips."

"I don't suppose any of the folks interviewed had much insight into what happened to Elijah?"

"Nothing worth hanging a murder charge on. Seems he simply disappeared. I know that's not what your buddy wants to hear. To be honest, I'd be shocked if we ever learn if the body belongs to Mr. Duncan. He didn't put it this way, but Detective Callahan considers the case cold, from his perspective, closed. Sorry."

"That's too bad. What about Clarence Taylor's murder?"

"Technically, I suppose, the Sheriff's Office knows more about his murder than they do about the one in the '50s. They know who he was and when he was shot."

"And?"

"That's it. No suspects, no motive."

"Don't you find it strange that Taylor finds the skeleton then is murdered?"

Cindy looked toward the beach then back at me. "Strange, definitely. Connected, no clue."

"But—"

"What about *no clue* did you not grasp?"

"Sorry. I'm just frustrated. He seemed like such a nice man."

"Frustration noted. Detective Callahan shares that feeling. He's working the case. I'm hopeful he'll get to the bottom of it, but with the clue pool empty, it won't be easy." She tapped me on the leg. "Now, since you're about as old as a diamond but not nearly as valuable, I know your brain cells are dying off as we speak, so I doubt you remember you said you were going to call me. Think you can find the reason somewhere in your deteriorating gray matter?"

"What do you know about white supremacists in the Charleston area?"

"Not much. From bulletins we receive from the feds, there's an uptick of Klan and other white supremacist groups activity in a bunch of states including South Carolina. The only real contact I've had with any of them was when some white supremacists thought it was a clever idea to wave the Confederate flag around a few locations on Folly. I thought it would have been a better idea if they'd wrapped themselves in the flags and jumped in the ocean." She pointed to the railing at the end of the Pier. "But hey, free speech is a strange and powerful thing. It makes us what we are as a country. Why the interest?"

Do you know Andrew Delaney?"

"Name's not familiar. Describe him?"

I did. I also explained how he'd been pointed out to me at Pier 101 as being a member of the Ku Klux Klan, then how I happened to be seated next to him at Loggerhead's last night.

"Why are you telling me this?"

"We started talking."

"Did you ask if he was in the Klan? If he was, where he got his white robes?"

"Not directly. He didn't come out and say it but left the distinct impression he was a member of an extremist group."

"That's not illegal. What about him bothered you?"

"I've heard that Klan members have been riding up and down Sol Legare Road. It's bothering some residents."

"I can understand that but it's a free road, out of my jurisdiction, I might add. What do you want me to do about it?"

"Nothing. There's one more thing about him. I asked if he heard about the murder the other day. He brought up Clarence Taylor's name saying he may've known him years ago. Don't you find that interesting?"

"You're adding one plus one and getting three. Delaney might be a member of an extremist group; he may have known Taylor years ago; therefore, he murdered him. In my undersized brain, that doesn't compute."

"I'm not saying he did. It seems more than a coincidence."

"Tell you what. I'll pass it along to Detective Callahan. He'll probably think I'm making a big deal about nothing. When he does, I'll give you all the credit."

"That's what friends are for."

She laughed and abruptly changed the subject by telling me about one of her officers who was showing his kid how he'd skateboarded when he was young. He's no longer young. He ran off the road with the skateboard going one way, the officer going another landing on his left arm. Now instead of wearing a uniform he's wearing a cast. Cindy thought it was way funnier than she should have.

Her expression turned serious.

"How's Al doing? I know you're worried about his health."

"Thanks for asking. He's slowing quite a bit. He's eighty-two, an age I thought was ancient when I was young. I know several people his age who are in much better shape. All his years spending day and night at Al's, plus raising nine kids, has taken a toll. He's not spending nearly as much time in the bar now than he did after Bob first took over. He's also spending more time thinking about the past. I suspect that's why he wanted me to take him to where he had good memories after returning from Korea."

"He's lucky to have friends like you, even Bob. If you tell your hefty, blustery friend I said that, I'll arrest you for...hell, I'll find something."

"Your secret's good with me."

"Enough chitchat." She started to stand, then added that unless I was going to give her a recording of someone confessing to killing Clarence Taylor, she had to get to the office to pester her officers.

I had a theory but no confession, so I thanked her for listening. She said it was more fun listening to me than to the drunks and irate citizens she spends time with. I repeated that's what friends are for.

I didn't have to go to an office, pester anyone, or be pestered, so I leaned back on the bench and watched three dolphins a hundred yards off the back of the structure. I've always been amazed by how graceful the aquatic mammals glide through the water, unlike most humans who think smacking the water is swimming. It's also possible, likely, I dozed.

My phone's ringtone jarred me out of my reverie. Al Washington's name was on the screen.

"Good morning, Al. Is everything okay?"

He chuckled. "You don't have to ask that every time I call. If something isn't okay, I'll let you know."

"You're right. I'll stick with good morning."

"Good morning to you, my friend. The reason I'm calling is to ask a huge favor. If the answer is no, I certainly understand, I sure do."

"Tell you what, why don't you ask then I'll determine how big a favor it is?"

"Fair enough. Ever since we were at Island Breeze, I've had a powerful desire for more good Caribbean food. After eating them every day for let's say a hundred years, I'm tired of my burgers, yes, I am. That's even if Bob says they're the best in the galaxy."

"Al, what do you say we go back to Island Breeze?"

He laughed. "If you insist."

"When?"

"How about tonight?"

"Umm, okay. Think Bob can get along without you there?"

"Think so. He's learning how not to offend every customer coming in the door."

"That's progress."

Chapter Twenty

The weather veered from good to *good grief* as I was on the way to get Al. Waves of torrential downpours covered Charleston, flooding several streets. I detoured around barriers the closer I got to his house. Fortunately, there was a parking spot in front of his gate. He must've been watching for me. He came out, opened a large red and green golf umbrella before motioning for me to stay in the car. I leaned over to push the passenger door open while he closed the umbrella, shook water off, put it in the footwell, then slid in the seat.

"I know how to pick nights to go out eatin', I sure do," he said as a greeting. "Think we need to try another time?"

"The rain will end soon," I said like I knew what I was talking about. "Besides, there shouldn't be too big a crowd."

He smiled. "Sure wish my glass was half-full like yours, yes I do."

"Don't be silly. You're one of the most optimistic people I know."

"It's getting harder. These old bones remind me every day how they're nearing the end of their run."

I didn't respond.

We took another detour to get to Folly Road. The rain stopped as quickly as it had begun, and the rest of the ride was uneventful. When I parked, Al said he was taking his umbrella in with him in case it was raining when we were leaving.

Al's old bones must have been screaming in pain. I was afraid he wasn't going to make it across the narrow road to the restaurant's entrance. I saw the real reason he brought the umbrella when he leaned on it with every step.

I was right about rain keeping customers away. There were only five diners. I recognized two from restaurants on Folly where one was a bartender, the other a server. If they were surprised to see me, it didn't show. The woman behind the bar was the same person I'd seen on my previous visits. She pointed to three vacant tables, told us to sit wherever we wanted.

Al pointed to a table in the corner in front of a colorful tapestry adorned with Bob Marley's smiling face. Painted beside the tapestry were the words "One Love," referring to Marley's song by the same name. The sound system was quiet. The lady behind the counter pointed to the menu board as she asked what we wanted to drink. Al said Ting. I had no idea what that was, so I stuck with Diet Coke. A college age server brought our drinks and asked if we were ready to order. Al squinted at the menu board. I told the server to give us a few minutes.

Al watched her go to the next table. "Thank you. I have trouble reading the fine print this far away. Would you mind telling me what's on it?"

There were only four items. One was jerk chicken. Al said that he left the only jerk he knew minding Al's.

I smiled and he said, "Let's wait a few minutes to order. I'd like to sit and soak in the atmosphere, I sure would."

I told him to soak all he wanted. The sounds of Bob Marley singing "No Woman, No Cry" flowed out of the sound system. Al smiled as he took a sip of his drink.

The rain had returned, and two men rushed in the door, flung water off their ball caps, then moved to the table beside us. I recognized both from previous visits, Robert Graves and Eugene Dillinger. Eugene waved toward the lady behind the bar and said, "Two beers."

Robert looked at Al, then at me. "Met you two in here before, didn't I?"

Eugene snapped his fingers and reached his hand out to me. "Didn't I see you here with another guy? I remember now. You and him visited a house I'm building."

They both were right. I reminded them who I was then introduced Al to Eugene.

"You're becoming a regular," Eugene said in my direction.

I told him Al had spent time on Mosquito Beach when he got back from Korea in the early '50s.

Eugene shook his head. "Korea, one hell of a mess. Glad you made it back safe, Al."

"Eugene, were you in Korea?" Al asked. "You look about the right age."

"No, thank God."

Robert tapped Eugene's arm. "Let's let these guys drink in peace."

The server returned to ask if we were ready to order.

I started to say not yet, but Al said, "How about a couple

of orders of wings. We'll split them with my new friends here." He pointed to Robert and Eugene.

Robert said, "Al, you don't have to do that."

"Don't have to, want to."

The server left to put in our order. Al asked if Robert and Eugene were regulars.

"Eugene's in all the time," Robert said, "I'm here about once a week. Sandra says I—"

"Chris," Eugene interrupted, "while I'm thinking about it, tell your friend Charles I got an option yesterday on an oceanfront lot out West Ashley. If he's still interested in me building him a house, he'll love this one. It's going to have a fantastic Atlantic view from the deck."

I saw Al give me a strange look. He knew Charles, so I didn't blame him. I told Eugene I'd give Charles the message then changed the subject before Al commented.

"Either of you hear anything new about Clarence Taylor's murder?"

Robert glanced at Eugene and said, "It a crying shame, if you ask me. Clarence was one of the nicest men out this way. I'd known him for ages. If he had enemies, I never heard about them. How about you, Eugene?"

"I don't think I ever mentioned it to you, Robert, Clarence worked for my construction company for a few weeks back in the 1950s or the early '60s. That was before he went off to Viet Nam, then came back to get that good paying job at the Post Office." He laughed. "Old Clarence was skinny in those days."

Al said, "Did you two stay close all those years?"

"Not really. I think I pissed him off more than once when he worked for me. If he could get out of doing hard work, he would."

Our wings arrived, the server put an order on each table. I ordered another diet soda, Al, another Ting, the other guys asked for their second beer.

Al took a bite, wiped his mouth with a paper towel from the roll on the center of the table, then said, "Eugene, I think I remember Robert from over here in the 1950s. Were you here much then?"

"Not as much as my boy Robert here. I was growing my home building business. I was over occasionally trying to hire workers. Most of the time I was on James Island throwing up houses as quick as I could. Business was booming. Why?"

Al nodded. "Was wondering if either of you knew Elijah Duncan? He was here around 1952 or so."

"Elijah Duncan," Robert said and shook his head. "I recall him, but don't know much about him. How about you, Eugene?"

"Was he a sharp dresser, thought he was God's gift to woman, always itching for a fight about civil rights?"

Al laughed. "That'd be Elijah, yes it would."

"Why ask about him?" Robert said.

"We were friends about the time he disappeared. No one seems to know what happened to him."

Robert rubbed his chin. "I remember hearing about someone turning up missing. That could've been your friend. I heard he ran off with a preacher's daughter."

I said, "I heard a detective from the Sheriff's Office has been asking about Elijah. There's speculation that he could've been the body."

Eugene leaned my direction. "Where'd you hear that?"

"A friend of mine is Chief on Folly. She heard it from a Sheriff's Office detective."

Robert shook his head. "No one's talked to me, how about you Eugene?"

"Nope. No reason to, I don't know anything about it."

Robert said, "Al, if it was your friend, I'm sorry to hear what happened."

"Me too, I sure am."

"Guys," I said, "do you think Clarence's murder could have anything to do with him finding the body?"

"I heard he was asking everyone about who might've murdered the guy he stumbled on," Eugene said.

"Even if he was," Robert added, "I don't see how it could have anything to do with him getting shot. My money's on an outsider."

"Why?" I asked.

Robert looked at Eugene, turned to me, and said, "Rumors have been going around that there are some, how shall I say it, outside agitators trying to stir up race issues around here. Could easily have been one of them getting in an argument with Clarence, ending with a bullet. The Clarence I remember had a quick temper. It could've gotten him killed."

"Chris," Al said, "think I'm ready for some curry chicken."

He was done talking about murder. I motioned the server over, ordered curry chicken for Al, a barbeque sandwich for me. I asked Robert and Eugene if they wanted anything. Robert said he had to get home to Sandra, Eugene said he wanted to check on his construction site on Folly. They thanked us for the wings and conversation then headed to the bar to pay for their drinks.

Al watched them go. "Nice men."

"Compared to Bob, you're right."

Al laughed before turning serious. "Are the police really asking folks over here about knowing Elijah?"

"That's what Cindy said."

"Good."

"She also told me to say hi the next time I see you."

He smiled.

Jimmy Cliff's smooth reggae sounds of "The Harder They Come" filled the room.

Chapter Twenty-One

Barb called the next morning to remind me I'd agreed to accompany her to a gallery opening that evening. I said of course I remembered, that I was looking forward to it. The opening must have been somewhere in my memory bank, but until she called, it'd been misfiled. She said she'd pick me up at three o'clock and hinted since it was being held at one of Charleston's classy galleries it might be wise for me not to wear shorts. I asked if I should leave my chewing tobacco at home. She laughed before saying she knew I didn't chew tobacco but if I wanted to, she'd get me some so I could leave it at home. I told her it wouldn't be necessary; I'd even wash behind my ears before she picked me up. She responded with the same response I often get from Charles. She hung up.

Unlike Charles, she pulled in the drive at the time she'd designated. The temperature was in the upper 70s, so she had the retractable hardtop down on her new, cardinal red, Mercedes SLC roadster. She'd recently traded her Volvo for the Mercedes and said she wished she had more opportunities to drive. This was one of those opportunities. Who was I to argue? I slipped in the beige, soft leather passenger seat and kissed her cheek. She wore a red silk blouse, tan linen slacks, and tan open-toe sandals. I felt underdressed in my navy, short-sleeve, button-down shirt and gray slacks.

"What's the deal about the art exhibit?" I asked as she pulled out of the drive.

"It's the opening of an exhibit by a young Colorado painter. I read about it in the paper, thought it'd be a good chance to get away from the bookstore. Besides, it's a wine-and-cheese event. Hard to turn down."

We headed up Folly Road to the turn off to downtown Charleston. Her Sirius XM radio was on the '60s channel and Chubby Checker was blaring out "The Twist." I sat back enjoying the air blowing through my thinning hair. Barb's short black hair was going several directions. One of the many things I admired about the woman next to me was she didn't worry about appearances or what others thought of her. That is, except not wanting me to wear shorts tonight.

The road we were on became Broad Street and we drove several blocks through residential neighborhoods before reaching the intersection of King Street where Broad turned from primarily residential to commercial, an area dubbed gallery row because of several art galleries lining the historic street. The opening was in Mary Martin Gallery on the corner of Broad and King.

Parking is always an issue in this area, so Barb drove several more blocks before finding a spot on the street. That wasn't a problem since it was perfect walking weather, so we enjoyed gazing at some of the cities most beautiful residences on Tradd and Meeting Street before reaching King for the block-long walk to the gallery.

I didn't feel quite as underdressed when I saw the wide variety of attire of the twenty or so people milling around the room. Two men wore seersucker suits and bowties, another couple had on ironed jeans and bright red and green tops. The others wore everything in between. An attractive elderly lady met us at the door, with a British accent, welcomed us to the exhibit, handed each of us a glossy, full-color brochure highlighting the featured artist, then told us to mingle, visit the refreshment table, and meet Lawrence, the artist. The man she pointed out was at the side of the room talking to a woman about one of his paintings. He was roughly five-foot-four, thin, with short curly brown hair. Despite his diminutive height, he would've been hard to miss in his white, flowing long shirt and red slacks. We thanked her, skipped meeting the artist who continued an animated conversation with a potential buyer who had an ear-to-ear smile, then headed to the wine and cheese.

A college-age caterer greeted us at the drink table and offered us a glass of white wine. I took two glasses after slipping two dollars in a glass tip vase located by the cocktail napkins.

I handed a glass to Barb who was studying the brochure. She said, "Lawrence apparently doesn't have a last name or thinks we all know who he is like Oprah or Elvis." She pointed to one of his paintings. "The brochure says his paintings are reminiscent of works by Georgia O'Keeffe, recognized as the mother of American modernism."

"Oh," I said, not having a clue what that meant. What I did say was, "It's refreshing that most of his paintings are landscapes of mountains. So many of the paintings I see on the coast are seascapes."

Others arrived. We kept moving so we wouldn't block

Lawrence's paintings from those who were studying them like they were the most fascinating works they'd ever seen. I spent most of the time studying the price tags ranging from five to seventeen thousand dollars. I liked his work, but his mountain scapes were too steep for my budget. Barb had drifted to the other side of the gallery where she was talking to a woman about a painting with a stream in the foreground, a sun drenched mountain in the background, when someone tapped me on the shoulder. I turned to see Lawrence smiling as he pointed to the painting I was viewing.

"That's my favorite," he said. "I simply loved the light that spring morn."

"It is incredible," I said, figuring that would be the appropriate response. What I really thought was incredible was the eleven-thousand-dollar price.

"Are you a collector?" he asked with a smile.

"No, but I am a photographer, so I appreciate the challenges of light and shadows you've captured masterfully," I said, pushing my limit on sounding artistic.

His smile lessened, probably after he figured I wasn't a potential buyer. "Are your works in nearby galleries?"

"Not currently."

He looked around the crowded gallery. "I'd better continue mingling."

He could have added, *since I can't sell you anything*. I said it was nice meeting him and wished him well with his work.

As no-last-name Lawrence headed toward a couple gazing at a canvas, I noticed his black and white wingtip shoes, reminding me of the shoes found with the skeleton on Mosquito Beach. This was the first time I'd thought of it since Barb picked me up. I also realized the painting the couple was looking at was of a cow's skull over the door of a rustic cabin with a majestic mountain range towering over it, one more reminder of the murder years ago. That depressing thought combined with the realization that even if I wanted to purchase one of these paintings I'd have to sell my house to afford it, made me lose interest in the exhibit which wasn't difficult since I had little interest to begin with. Now, how do I convince Barb we should leave?

She was talking to a couple in their thirties who appeared mesmerized by Lawrence's painting of a closeup of a flower. I heard the man with a wineglass in one hand, the woman's hand in his other hand say, "Stunning, absolutely stunning." The woman with him said, "Truly." Barb nodded, turned to me as I approached, and rolled her eyes. She patted the woman on the back, whispered something, then grabbed my elbow to lead me away from the stunned couple.

"Chris, don't we have to be somewhere? Like anywhere."

I didn't have to try hard to convince her to leave.

We left the gallery, walked one block up Broad Street, then turned right on Meeting Street. I did a Charles imitation when I asked Barb if she knew why the intersection was called the "Four Corners of Law."

"Sure. After all, I'm a lawyer. I know stuff like that. Charleston's City Hall is on one corner, the County Court-house on another, then there's the Federal Courthouse." She pointed at the church at the remaining corner. "Finally, St. Michael's Episcopal Church. Four corners, four buildings representing laws, including the church representing ecclesi-astical law."

"Not bad. Now, do you know who coined that phrase?"

She looked at the buildings on each corner and shook her head. "No."

"Robert Ripley."

"The Ripley's Believe It or Not guy?"

"One and the same."

"There you go, channeling Charles again."

"Sorry, couldn't help it."

"If the trivia lesson's over, can we go?"

We started walking toward the car. I put my arm around her waist. "Do you ever miss practicing law?"

"Not for a second. Why?"

"Seeing those buildings made me think of it."

"Now I have a question. Other than being in a hurry to do your Charles imitation, why'd you want to leave the opening?"

"I started thinking about the skeleton found on Mosquito Beach, then Clarence Taylor's murder."

"Let's see," she said as she squeezed my hand, "would those be the murders you're not getting involved with, the ones you're leaving to the police?"

I returned her squeeze. "Yes."

She stopped. "You're not going to do that, are you?"

"I don't want to get involved. To tell you the truth, I don't know how I can."

"Yet that's not going to stop you."

I whispered, "No."

"What do you know for certain?"

"Clarence found the skeleton. Now he's dead. I'm fairly certain the skeleton is Elijah Duncan who went missing in 1953."

"What's the connection between Clarence and Elijah?"

"None really. Clarence was a decade younger than Elijah, so they probably weren't acquainted even though they grew up within a mile of each other."

"So, there's no connection."

"I've heard Clarence was asking questions about Elijah."

"What kind of questions?"

"Trying to learn who might've known him. There're still a few old-timers who go back that far."

"Did he learn anything?"

"Don't know."

"Are you thinking the person who killed Elijah killed Clarence?"

"Possibly."

We reached the car. Barb leaned against the fender. "Two things. First, that seems like a farfetched theory. Second, if it happens to be true, there couldn't be too many people around who might've known Elijah. Needless to say, 1953 was a long time ago, so anyone who's still around would most likely be in his or her eighties or older."

"I've met some of them."

"I suspect the police have also talked with them."

I nodded.

"You're not going to let it go."

I shook my head.

She surprised me when she stepped in front of me, kissed me, then said, "Please be careful."

Few words were said on the ride home. I was comfortable with the silence. It appeared Barb was as well.

Chapter Twenty-Two

After hanging with the upper crust, wine-and-cheese crowd last night, I wasn't ready to face another large group at a restaurant, so I headed to Bert's for breakfast. I grabbed coffee and settled for a cinnamon roll before heading to pay when someone called my name. Actually, the person said Christopher, so I knew before turning it was Virgil Debonnet. I preferred Chris for two reasons. First, it's easier to say, shorter to write. Second, I didn't like the name Christopher. Why? Just because. Virgil was slow to catch on.

I'd met Virgil six months ago a few days after Charles and I were kayaking only to be nearly decapitated by a single-engine airplane crashing in the marsh within feet of us. Four men were in the plane, two survived. The pilot had been poisoned causing the crash. To make a much longer story shorter, I met Virgil which eventually led to the two of us becoming the target of a killer. We survived, barely. Since then, Virgil and I had run across each other on several occasions.

I pivoted, smiled, and said, "Hi, Virgil. How many times do I have to tell you to call me Chris?"

He returned my smile. "I suppose more since I'm still calling you Christopher."

Virgil was in his forties, my height, with slicked-back black hair, and always wearing sunglasses.

I shook his hand while asking how he was doing.

"Amazingly well for me."

Two years ago, he owned a mansion overlooking the Charleston Harbor, a yacht, had a blue blood wife, a lifestyle bordering on one for the rich and famous. Drugs, drink, gambling, horrible stock investments combined to cost him his fortune, house, yacht, plus his wife after she told him poverty wasn't in her genes. He now lives in a small apartment on Folly. From what I could tell, he was far happier than anyone should be after his downward spiral into poverty.

"Any luck on the job search?"

He'd burned all bridges in the financial industry where he'd previously worked. To my knowledge, he spends most of his days walking around the island or frequenting bars, sharing drinks and tall tales with those around him.

"My gainful employment hiatus is still in effect, although, my landlord allows me to remain in residence if I preform maintenance tasks on the apartments in my current domicile."

"Good," I said, not knowing what else to add.

"A roof over one's head is a valuable commodity." He smiled again. "Enough about me. The rumor mill has been milling stories of one Christopher Landrum, aka Chris, who apparently is taking more than a cursory interest in a skeleton recently uncovered at a nearby venue. Care to elaborate?"

"Where'd you hear that?"

He chuckled. "Enlightening what one hears while bending elbows with some of this enchanting island's fellow imbibers."

If the answer was in there somewhere, I missed it. "Who told you?"

"Let's see," he said as he looked down at his resoled Guccis. "Oh yeah, Macy at Planet Follywood shared what he'd heard from someone who works at Rita's. Macy's acquaintance, whose name he didn't relay, said one of his fellow employees knew you, that you were helping him determine the name of the person who is now merely a skeleton. He also said in its previous life, the skeleton had been murdered. I figured you and Charles are better at catching killers than are the police, so you'd be seeking whoever murdered Mr. Skeleton."

"Have you heard anything about a more recent murder on Sol Legare Island?"

"No, but the last few days, I've been working on fixing the plumbing in two of my landlord's apartments. No time to visit my normal hangouts." He shook his head then squinched up his face. "You wouldn't believe what people flush."

I hadn't eaten, so I didn't want details. "The man who found the skeleton was murdered."

"Coincidence?"

"Don't know."

"You going to find out?"

"That's up to the police."

"I recall you saying that before. Believe it was before we had a few intimate moments with a boat hook and a bullet." He tilted his head, tapped his foot.

"Ancient history."

Virgil smiled. "You can convince some folks, but remember, I'm part of your crime-fighting trio."

When Charles and I first met Virgil, he tried to convince Charles that since he knew some of the people involved in the plane crash he could be part of my friend's private detective agency. No was a word Virgil couldn't seem to wrap his head around.

"Virgil, you do know there's not an agency outside Charles's mind?"

He smiled. "Semantics. The next time you run into Charles tell him all he has to do is call. I'll put unstopping toilets in my rear-view mirror to do whatever he needs me to do to catch the bad guys."

"I'll share that good news with him," I said, with a pinch of sarcasm.

"With that out of the way, got a question. Are you planning to head to Harris Teeter anytime soon?"

And I thought Charles was good at changing directions on the head of a pin.

"Probably. Why?"

"My scooter is under the weather, needs a part."

"They have scooter parts at Harris Teeter?"

"No, but I didn't figure you had reason to go to the cycle shop on Folly Road past Harris Teeter."

"Virgil, would you like me to take you to get the part?"

His smile widened. "Would you, fine sir?"

With my calendar blank for the next, umm, forever, I figured I could work it in.

"Yes, when?"

He looked at his watch, nodded his head left, then right. "Now?"

Five minutes later, I was munching on the roll, sipping

coffee, and steering, so I left most of the talking to Virgil who excelled at filling dead air with words. I learned more than I wanted to know about the advantages of PVC pipe over cast iron in plumbing, how he was picking up a few dollars a week dog walking two Irish setters for a lady two block from his apartment, and making serious efforts to cut back on drinking. He was cutting back because he wanted to plus lacked finances to maintain his habit. We arrived at the cycle shop before he shared more of his innermost feelings. He'd called ahead so they were holding a flywheel for his scooter. He paid, and we headed home. I asked if he knew how to install the part.

"Sure, that world-renowned scooter mechanic Mr. Greasy Hands Google said it's easy-peasy."

Fortunately, I didn't have to respond. The phone rang.

"Chris, this is Terrell, you know, from Rita's."

"Sure, Terrell, what's up?"

Virgil wasn't like Charles who'd be gesturing for me to put the phone on speaker so he could hear. He stared out the window, probably replaying Mr. Google's easy-peasy instructions.

"I know you've been over at Mosquito several times lately. Are you going to be there anytime in the next couple of days?"

"Why?"

"I've got three days off, been working on my house. I thought if you were nearby, you might stop in."

I didn't figure it was to help with the work. Did he have something important to share? "Terrell, I'm with a friend, we're on Folly Road near Harris Teeter. If it's okay with my friend, we could stop by now?"

Virgil must have started listening. He nodded.

"Umm, sure, I guess."

"If it's inconvenient, I could make it another time."

"No, that's not it. Things are a mess here. I didn't want to … never mind, now is perfect." He gave me directions and I said we'd be there in a few minutes.

I set the phone on the console and Virgil said, "What'd I agree to?"

I told him who Terrell was.

Virgil smiled. "So, meeting him doesn't have anything to do with you figuring out who killed Mr. Skeleton?"

I shrugged.

Chapter Twenty-Three

I followed Terrell's directions and turned on the first road past where Mosquito Beach Road intersects Sol Legare Road then turned in the third gravel drive. The house was a single-story wood frame structure that had withstood numerous storms and hurricanes over the years. The front porch and steps looked new and were in drastic contrast with the rest of the structure. Scrap lumber matching the porch leaned against the side of the house and a rusting, green Ford pickup truck with two pieces of lumber in the bed was parked at the far end of the drive.

Terrell was quick to the door. He had on a white, paint-splattered T-shirt and black shorts, held a paintbrush in one hand, a lit cigarette in the other. He pushed the screen door open with his elbow.

"Welcome to my humble abode." He waved us in with the paintbrush.

The living room was to the left and was obviously the canvas for his painting. Tarps covered the sofa and what appeared to be a couple of chairs or possibly a table. Blue and green flowered wall covering was still on two walls with the edge closest to the ceiling curled from age. The other two walls had been stripped of the wall covering; newly applied light-gray paint covered one of them. The walls with the flowery wall covering had a coating of nicotine stain over most of them. The spot where the sofa had been against the wall was cleaner than the rest of the wall. The ceiling which had once been white was covered with a layer of nicotine stain. The smell of cigarette smoke and paint was overwhelming.

I introduced Virgil to Terrell who suggested we move to the back porch. He said the smell of paint may be distracting. After living in the house for years, I suspected he was oblivious to the stench of cigarette smoke. I hadn't had the foresight to bring a gas mask, so I quickly agreed to go outside. We walked through the kitchen on our way to the porch. The appliances and counter were old, but clean and neat. The floor looked new.

Terrell saw me looking and said, "Installed it myself."

"Looks great," I said.

Terrell said, "Thanks. I've been saving everything I can, trying to bring this old house up to snuff."

A large cardboard crate sat in the middle of the floor with the word Wolf stenciled on each side.

Virgil wasn't looking at the floor but was rubbing his hand across the top of the crate. He said, "Had one of these bad boys in my house."

Terrell looked at him with new admiration. "Best stove anywhere. You a chef?"

Virgil smiled. "Not a chef. Heck, I'm not even a homeowner anymore."

Terrell waited for Virgil to elaborate. He didn't, so Terrell said, "I've been coveting one of those since I learned to cook. It arrived this morning."

"Need help installing it?" Virgil said.

"Nah. Thanks for asking."

I'd had enough chef talk. The smoke and paint smell still polluted the air. "Ready to head out back?"

Virgil patted the stove container one more time then followed Terrell and me outside.

The back porch was much older than the front steps and in the shade. While it was in the eighties, it was comfortable.

Terrell motioned us to sit in brown resin plastic chairs lined against the railing.

"Walmart special," he said with a smile. "You're the first to break them in."

"I'm honored," Virgil said as he rubbed his hand along the arm of the chair.

Terrell didn't appear to know how to take Virgil's comment, so he turned to me. "Thanks for coming. As you can see, I'm in the middle of stripping wallpaper and painting the living room. I should've done it when I got the house but work always got in the way." He lit another cigarette and took a long draw. Thankfully, he turned his head to blow the smoke away from his guests. "Terrible habit, I know. Tried stopping several times." He shook his head. "You can see how successful I was."

Virgil leaned forward in his chair. "Know what you mean."

Terrell said, "You smoke?"

"No," Virgil said. "My bad habits were distilled spirits and hard drugs."

"Oh," Terrell said.

He still appeared not to know how to take Virgil. He had my sympathy since I knew the feeling.

Virgil smiled. "Nice house. Lived here long?"

Terrell gave him the same story he'd shared with me about inheriting the residence. He ended by saying, "It's not much, but it's all mine. Now that I'm getting able to fix it up, it'll have the best memories from my folks, and my touch. Best part about it is no mortgage."

"I had one once—house, not mortgage," Virgil said. "Ah, those were the days."

That was the second time Virgil had mentioned his house. Again, Terrell was left without a comment.

I needed to move the conversation to why Terrell had asked me over, rather than getting into a lengthy conversation about Virgil's life, regardless how interesting I knew it to be.

"Terrell, we don't want to keep you from painting. What did you want to tell me?"

He pointed in the direction of Sol Legare Road and said, "Can't see it from back here, but from the front porch, I can see Clarence Taylor's house. Loved that man." He slowly shook his head.

"Who's Clarence Taylor?" Virgil asked.

"A friend who was recently killed."

"Oh, I'm terribly sorry. What happened, an accident?"

Terrell looked at the floor. "If two bullets in the chest is an accident, yes."

This time Virgil was without words. I gave a brief explanation about who Clarence was and about his untimely death.

"Terrell, I'm terribly sorry," Virgil said.

"Me too," Terrell said and turned to me. "I called the

number your friend Charles gave me. I didn't get an answer. Didn't want to leave a message. That's when I called you."

Other than coming in second, that didn't tell me why I was here. "I'm glad you did."

"Charles said he was a detective, that you helped him sometimes. That's why I called."

Virgil leaned forward. "They're both great detectives. Six months ago, Chris and I were in the marsh when—"

"Virgil," I interrupted before he sucked the wind out of Terrell's story. "Let's let Terrell finish."

He leaned back in the chair.

I said, "Terrell, go on."

"I haven't thought about anything but poor Elijah Duncan since Clarence found his body rotting out there in the ground. I told you before how my family goes back generations on Sol Legare Island. Grandpa Samson knew Elijah. From what he said, they were friends." Terrell pointed to the back door. "Grandpa left this house to my parents, they left it to me. I figured since it didn't cost me anything, I need to repay Grandpa. Only way I know how is to find out who killed his friend." He shook his head. "Now somebody killed my friend. I know as certain as I'm sitting here it was because Clarence figured out who murdered Elijah."

He'd shared all this earlier, so I still didn't know what precipitated a call.

Virgil didn't know any of it. "Why do you think your friend's death had something to do with the, umm, skeleton of, what's his name again?"

"Elijah Duncan," Terrell said. "You didn't know Clarence, but I did. Known him since I was a toddler. One of the best people I've ever run across. He didn't have enemies. He was loved by all, so he couldn't have been killed because someone didn't like him."

Virgil said, "What about things like him being killed for money he owed someone, or over a woman? I hear lots of murders have to do with love. I came close to that a couple of times with my ex." He stared off into space.

Terrell lit another cigarette, looked in the direction of Clarence's house, and waited for Virgil to continue. Once again, he didn't so Terrell said, "My friend didn't have more than a few dollars to his name. Before his government check came every month, he couldn't pay for anything. Was always borrowing a few dollars to buy food. And, don't even think he was killed because he didn't pay it back. He paid his debts with a smile and words of appreciation. Always."

"What about a woman?" Virgil said.

"Not Clarence."

It was time to take Virgil out of the interrogation. I said, "What're you thinking, Terrell?"

"I've been doing a lot of digging into who would've been around Mosquito when Elijah was killed. Wanted to bounce some of it off you and Charles."

"Go ahead."

"There aren't many old-timers left who were around in those days. Hell, I doubt there're over six or seven still alive who were about the same age or older than Elijah. I've talked to a few of them in the last few days." He smiled. "Most said they didn't recall much about him but the ones that did said Elijah was nothing but trouble. Said he dressed all neat and fancy, but his hell raising was anything but fancy. Boy did he stir up the race issues they faced back then."

Virgil said, "What's that mean?"

Terrell stared at him. I was afraid he wasn't going to say anything, at least, anything nice.

He took another puff on his cigarette before saying, "Elijah said, some say shouted, what other African Americans were thinking or talking quietly about among themselves. Virgil, you're younger than I am, so you weren't around during the civil rights movement in the early 1960s, much less what was going on with total segregation when Elijah was young in the 1950s. People my color were treated like second-class citizens, if that good."

"I've read about it," Virgil said.

"Virgil, it's not your fault, but you were born white, probably didn't pay much attention to what you were reading. I'd wager you didn't have many black friends, probably knew little to nothing about what was really going on back then."

"True, my friend. Sad to say, but true."

"Anyway," continued Terrell, "Elijah not only stirred up whites with his loud opinions, he bothered many blacks because they thought he'd bring bad things down on them. The less pot stirring the better."

"Did anyone say anything helpful?" I asked to redirect Terrell's comments.

"Not much. Every time I brought Elijah up, most wanted to leave it alone. What's past is past was their attitude. I don't understand. Why weren't they more interested in finding out who killed someone they knew?"

"Maybe they didn't want to relive what must've been bad times for, umm, blacks," Virgil said. "That was what, sixty or so years ago?"

"Segregation was bad but out here there was a thriving African American community," Terrell said, "Folks looked out for each other. It wasn't all bad. In some ways it was better than it is now."

"Something went bad for Elijah," Virgil said.

"Terrill," I said, "Who'd you talk to?"

"Chris, you've already met a couple of them, Jamal Kingsly and Eugene Dillinger. I saw Robert and Sandra Graves Friday and said I wanted to talk to them about Elijah but didn't have time that day. There are two other old-timers who don't spend much time here like they used to when Mosquito was in its heyday. I'll be knocking on their doors next week."

"What did you want Charles and me to do?"

"Nothing really. Figured since you're detectives you'd be able to tell me if I was barking up the wrong tree or if I was on target. Hell, I'm a cook, when I want to sound important, tell folks I'm a chef. I ain't no detective."

I didn't think it would do any good to remind him Charles and I aren't either. What I did feel the need to remind him again was the danger of asking questions.

"Terrell, you still need to be careful. Asking the wrong person questions can be dangerous. Whoever killed Elijah won't hesitate to kill again."

"Terrell," Virgil said, "seems like there's a good chance whoever killed Elijah is no longer among the living. He would be eighty or older. You may be wasting your time chasing a ghost."

Terrell glared at Virgil. "I can't prove it. Not yet anyway but I know as certain as I can be the person that killed Elijah, regardless how many years ago it was, killed Clarence."

Virgil asked, "What makes you so certain?"

"Because that's the only thing that makes sense. Clarence

was nosing around trying to find out who killed Elijah. He must've found out. It cost him his life."

I didn't know what Charles or I could do but thought a good time to be here to talk to some of the folks who were around in the 1950s would be at the party Clarence wanted.

"Terrell," I said, "has a date been set for the party Clarence requested?"

"No. Some of the guys are debating when would be the best time. My guess is that it's a few days off. I'll let you know as soon as I hear."

Terrell dropped his cigarette butt on the deck, put it out with his foot, then glanced at the door.

I took the hint; said we'd better let him get back to painting. He thanked us for coming, said it was good meeting Virgil. I wasn't certain he meant that about Virgil.

Chapter Twenty-Four

On the return trip to Folly, I said, "Virgil, what do you think?"

"I think when he gets all the nicotine off the walls and ceiling, the house might collapse."

"I was thinking more about Terrell's thoughts about the person who murdered the man in the '50s."

"I knew what you meant. I was pondering everything he said but it's easier saying something about the house collapsing. Know what I like about that boy?"

It's interesting that Virgil referred to Terrell as a boy since he was younger than Terrell. I hoped he didn't mean it as a derisive term.

"What?"

"His respect for elders. That's something in short supply these days. When he talked about his grandpa, he did it with such reverence. I could see love in his face. The love wasn't because his grandpa gave the house to his parents who gave it to Terrell."

"I agree. He talked about his relatives the same way the last time he'd mentioned them."

"And, did you hear how reverential he spoke about the man who was recently killed?"

"Clarence."

"Yeah. They weren't related but it didn't make a difference. Besides, I liked that cute little diamond earring in his left ear. He's a man after my weird heart."

I shared how Terrell had expressed interest in books about the Civil War and the civil rights movement. How the past meant something to him, how he wanted to learn as much about it as possible.

"You know I'm not a detective like you and Charles, although I suspect I'm more of one than Chef Terrell, so this question may not have anything to do with anything."

I wasn't going to argue who was or wasn't a detective. "What's the question?"

"When you two were talking about whoever murdered Mr. Skeleton, even when the recent murder was mentioned, both of you kept saying he when referring to the killer. Could it be a she? Just asking."

I hadn't thought about it that way, but Virgil had a point. Most likely, Elijah's grave wasn't dug deep or it wouldn't have been uncovered as easily if it'd been buried for decades. There's no reason why he couldn't have been shot by a woman, the same could apply for Clarence.

"Good point. Yes, it could've been a female."

"Wonder how many of those people Terrell hasn't talked to yet are women?"

He mentioned one, Sandra Graves. He still needed to talk to her and her husband. But that was all. I picked the phone off the console to redial the number Terrell's call had come from.

I didn't think he was going to answer. I pictured him on the ladder ripping paper off the wall. He sounded out of breath when he finally answered. I apologized for calling while he was working. I asked if there were any women he wanted to talk to who were around in the 1950s?

"Two, maybe three, why?"

I told him Virgil's theory. He seemed skeptical but said he'd keep it in mind when he was running down others. I encouraged him not to overlook anyone, man or woman, who might have known Elijah. He said he wouldn't.

Virgil smiled like he'd solved the mystery.

———

I dropped Virgil at his apartment after he profusely thanked me for taking him to get the flywheel. I asked if he needed help installing it but wasn't disappointed when he said he could do it himself. My mechanical skills were slightly better than my skill reading Sanskrit.

I pulled in the drive when my phone rang with William Hansel's name on the screen. I could count on one hand the number of times he'd called in the more than a decade I'd known him.

"Good afternoon, William."

"How did you know? Oh, I keep forgetting, caller identification. A good afternoon to you as well. You're probably wondering about the nature of my call. I wished to enquire if you would happen to provide an old man a respite from eradicating unwanted interlopers from his modest garden?"

It wasn't Sanskrit, so I had a vague idea what he was talking about.

"Is that an iced tea offer?"

He chuckled and said, "Correct."

"Tell you what, I don't know where I could find an old man, but if the offer of tea is from someone I know who has a garden, I'd be glad to be of assistance. Would now work?"

"That would be wonderful."

"I'll be there in ten minutes."

I wasn't a detective like Charles, but I didn't have to be to know William had something more on his mind than someone to provide a respite from weed slaughtering. I pulled in his drive and noticed that he'd started his respite. He was seated under the live oak tree and sipping from a tall drink glass. The silver platter from my earlier visit was on the chair next to him. It held a second drink glass, a sugar bowl, a spoon, and two cloth napkins.

"I see you started without me," I said as I moved the platter to the ground. I took a sip from the second glass.

"You kindly said you didn't know where you could find an old man, but I'm acutely aware one resides in this aging body. I'm getting too old to continue the never-ending battle against these insidious weeds." He sighed before taking another sip of tea.

I smiled. "Yet, you're never going to stop, are you?"

He shook his head. "No. While my muscles might disagree, the therapeutic value of this exercise exceeds its drawbacks."

William loved teaching but had often shared his occasional run-ins with his dean or the high number of mind and butt-numbing meetings drained much of his enthusiasm for the job. He used time in the garden to decompress.

"I'm sure it does."

He took another sip before turning toward me. "I've been giving a lot of thought to our recent conversations about Mosquito Beach and my experiences earlier in life with, well, the best way to say it would be growing up African American. You and I have never spent much time on the topic. As you are aware, I loathe sharing personal experiences or feelings."

He hesitated like he was waiting for a response.

"That's something we have in common."

He nodded. "As odd as it may seem, that's why I feel comfortable sharing things with you I wouldn't reveal to anyone else. Does that make sense?"

Sort of, I thought. "Yes."

"I believe I shared the last time we met under this tree that I'd become acquainted with a gentleman who works around town."

"James Brown."

"You remembered."

"An easy name to remember," I said, and motioned for him to continue.

"He's several years younger than I, but we spoke a time or two about our experiences being in the minority on Folly. He doesn't live here, but spends many hours working on Folly, has for years. I found it interesting in that when we were growing up, most of those individuals around us were of the same race that he and I share. I had surmised our experiences with others, particularly Caucasians, would've been similar. I spent my formative years north of the Mason-Dixon line; James spent his in the South. It wasn't until I moved here some thirty years ago that differences began to stand out. James reinforced that I wasn't imagining the dissimilarities."

"Like what?"

"I had the good fortune to not have been born when slavery was a legal institution in the United States. I was twelve when the Civil Rights Act was passed in 1964, nearly a hundred years after the abolition of slavery, so I have few memories of the times before that momentous event. The schools I attended were integrated by the time I started the first grade. It was much later than that in South Carolina. Even then, subtle segregation continued." He hesitated, looked at my glass, and said, "Let me go inside and get more ice."

Before I could say it wasn't necessary, he'd headed to the house leaving me to wonder where he was going with the story. He returned with a stainless ice bucket, dropped two cubes in my glass. He must've sensed my confusion about the direction of his story.

"I've gotten off track, allow me to summarize. I possibly read about it in history books during my younger days, but until I moved here, I didn't realize how a matter of a few hundred miles could render attitudes so differently. When I was growing up, I had a vague awareness of the Ku Klux Klan, but that was all. I didn't have direct contact with the organization beyond what I heard in the news. I'm not saying there weren't Klan groups where I was living, I later discovered there were. I also haven't had direct contact with any of the groups here, although I've learned there are some in nearby counties." He took another sip, smiled, and said, "I continue to drift, and appreciate you letting this old man stray from his point."

I didn't know what his point was, so I couldn't tell if he was straying. "William, I'm in no hurry. Keep plying me with tea, and I'll sit here all day."

He laughed. "That won't be necessary. Last summer I was coerced into attending a picnic at work. My preference would have been coming home and pulling weeds, so you can see how much I didn't want to attend the gathering. It was hot, a day much warmer than today. One of my students was there wearing a sleeveless shirt, something I'd never seen him do. I noticed a tattoo on his upper arm—the Odin's cross, a white supremacist symbol." He shook his head. "I wouldn't have said anything, but he saw me looking and said something to the effect that yes, it was what I thought it was." William shook his head again. "I told him it was none of my concern. It was the last day of the term, so I had little desire to converse further with the gentleman. I turned to leave, when he said, 'Not all Klan members wear sheets.' That's a direct quote."

"Why do you think he felt the need to tell you anything?"

"Excellent question, my friend. To this day, I'm not certain. I'm not naïve enough to think people who affiliate with the Klan wear distinctive garb all the time. They look like you and, well, not me, when they're at work, in stores, in restaurants, or in my class. The more I thought about what he said, I concluded he was implying it is not always possible to tell a hater from anyone else when contact is made in public."

"I agree."

"With that said, do you think the officials who are looking into the demise of the man whose skeleton was found on Mosquito Beach are considering all options, including the murderer might not have had anything personal against the poor man other than the color of his skin?"

"I hate to say this, but I don't think anyone is spending time looking for the person responsible for killing Elijah

Duncan. They're giving it lip-service, but it appears that's all."

"Elijah Duncan?"

I shared what was known about Elijah and why it was thought he was the victim. I also told him about Clarence Taylor's murder, that Clarence had been asking questions about the skeleton. He asked me again if I was sticking my nose in whatever was going on. I didn't deny it.

He said he needed to get back to his weeds he swore had grown an inch since we'd been under the tree. I thanked him for the tea and conversation.

I left to his final words, "Please be careful. Who else would shoot the breeze with this old man."

On the way home, I realized that what I failed to share was what I knew about Andrew Delaney and his affiliation with the Klan.

Chapter Twenty-Five

I answered the phone to Charles saying, "Ready to go?"

"How about a hint about where you're going?"

"Fishing."

"Then no."

"I'm not talking about fish fishing. Gotta go. I'm almost late. Be there in five."

A minute later, Charles was in my drive blowing the horn, in three more minutes we were driving out West Ashley Avenue. A block past the road that led to Sunset Cay Marina, I saw Eugene Dillinger's silver Range Rover parked in an empty oceanfront lot beside an Island Realty sign with SOLD printed diagonally on it. Charles pulled in beside the SUV and Eugene stepped out to greet us.

"Sorry we're late," Charles said as he bounded out of the car. "I had to wait for Chris."

Eugene looked at his Rolex or Rolex knock off. "You're a few minutes early."

Late in Charles time.

"Glad you could meet us," Charles said. "After Chris told me about the lot, I had to see it."

It was becoming clear what kind of fishing faux detective Charles had meant. I stood back to let him throw out the line.

"I'm glad you did," Eugene said. "It won't be long before I'm building on this slice of heaven. You're a wise man to show early interest. Shall we walk around?"

"You bet," Charles said.

As we walked, Eugene spewed facts about the size of the property, how the house on each side was owned by full-time residents, meaning they weren't on the rental rolls with a constant turnover in tenants, and how it was two miles from the center of town, the center of crowded, vacation central. In other words, we were standing on a property surrounded by peace and quiet. Charles nodded with each statement.

I followed, wondering when Charles was going to bring out the fishing gear.

Like a good salesman, Eugene saved the sizzle for last. After sharing way more than I wanted to know, he led us to the back of the property where a steep drop-off led to the beach.

He waved his hand toward the surf. "Picture the wide steps I'll build from where we're standing down to the pristine beach. Now look up and down the beach." He hesitated to give us time to follow his direction, then continued, "How many people you see cluttering the area?" He didn't wait for an answer. A mistake around Charles. "Compare that to—"

"Five," Charles interrupted.

That knocked Eugene off his sales pitch.

Eugene said, "Five?"

"Five people on the beach."

"Oh, yes, umm, think how many there'd be in the same

amount of space near the center of town around the Fishing Pier."

He didn't put it in the form of a question. Perhaps he was gaining insight about Charles.

"Eugene," Charles said, "there's no doubt that this is a perfect property. The price range you mentioned on the phone appears fair."

"Charles, will you be financing the lot or the construction?" He held his hand in front of Charles. "I ask because I have contacts with lenders, could fix you up with those having the best rates. They look favorably at my construction and, as you can see, this site is magnificent."

"No, I've been fortunate enough to have inherited, umm, enough not to need a mortgage."

Eugene's posture, already near perfect, straightened even more, a wide grin appeared on his face. I turned my head so he couldn't see my eyes roll.

"Excellent. Shall we start looking at a variety of floor plans to meet your needs? I've also got photos of houses I've built showing possible options."

"Not yet," Charles said.

Not yet, not ever, I thought.

"Oh," Eugene said, his posture slumped.

"I need to meet with my financial advisor to see what needs to happen to free up the money."

"That sounds prudent," Eugene said, then started walking toward his SUV.

"Oh, while I'm thinking of it," Charles said, "have you learned more about the skeleton found on Mosquito Beach?"

Eugene looked at Charles. "What's that have to do with this property?"

Good question, Eugene.

"Nothing," Charles said, "I remembered the first time we met, we were talking about it. You said you had friends out there, so you might know something new."

Eugene shook his head. "Not really. I think it was some old bum who died of natural causes. No one knew what to do with the body, so they stuck it in the ground. Cost, zero. Besides, that's ancient history."

"That could be it," Charles said. "I also heard a young guy out there is asking around about the body. Name's Terrell Jefferson, I believe. He's been talking to some of the old-timers who would've been there around the time the person was killed. He thinks it belongs to, umm, Chris, what's the name?"

"Elijah Duncan."

"Yeah, that's it. Has Terrell talked to you?"

"He has, couple of times in fact. He came to my East Ashley job site asking a bunch of questions. The second time was here on Folly the other day. I was heading to St. James Gate for lunch, Terrell was on his way to work at Rita's. We talked a couple of minutes, no more. He was running late."

"What'd he say?" Charles asked.

"Not much, as I recall. Same things he asked at the job site. He asked if I remembered anyone gone missing back in the 1950s. I may have but it was a long time ago. I didn't remember anyone." We were at Eugene's vehicle, where he added. "Charles, sure you don't want to look at floor plans?"

"Not yet."

Eugene nodded. "Tell you what, I have photos of other projects in here. Why don't you take them with you so you can look them over?"

"Good idea," Charles said. "You sure Terrell didn't say Elijah Duncan's name when he was talking to you?"

If Eugene got dizzy from Charles's abrupt transition, it didn't show.

"Don't recall. He may have but was in a hurry to get to work. I had a roofing issue I was trying to solve in my head, I didn't catch everything he was saying." He grabbed a large envelope from the front seat and handed it to Charles. "You can keep these, I have more. After you talk to your financial advisor, give me a call so we can get together to go over potential plans." He waved his hand in the direction of the ocean. "Picture yourself stepping on your wide deck, leaning back in a comfortable chair, sipping on a cold drink, looking at that glorious view."

Charles and I stood beside his vehicle watching the Range Rover pull off the property and head toward town.

I said, "Private detecting pay better than I thought?"

Charles smiled. "You'll have to ask my financial advisor."

"Would that be the clerk at Circle K who sells lottery tickets?"

He snapped his fingers. "I forgot to share that with Eugene."

"Get any bites on your fishing line?"

"Couple of nibbles. He said he talked with Terrell about the skeleton. From what he said, he didn't confess to Terrell he killed the man."

"I would've noticed if he had."

"Tell you one thing I figured out. Did you catch how fast the old boy decided he had to leave when I started asking questions about the skeleton?"

"Yes, it was nearly as quick as he cut the tour short of the house he was showing us when you brought it up."

Charles said, "I caught it. Don't forget, he said the body was probably some bum. He said the same thing at Island

Breeze. It's like he didn't know anything about it. I don't believe him."

"I don't either but that isn't enough to accuse him of the 1953 murder."

"I was about to ask him if he knew anything about poor old Clarence's murder."

"He probably wouldn't have confessed to that one either. Besides, I'd hate for it to be Eugene. Who would you get to build your oceanfront house if he's locked up?"

Moving away from Charles's fantasy world, I told him about Virgil and my visit to Terrell. After catching grief about not telling him sooner, he expressed the same concern I had about Terrell's safety. I told him I tried to warn the cook, but doubted it took hold. He's determined to find out what happened.

"I hope he takes your advice," Charles said. That was something that Charles had seldom done.

On that note, he dropped me at my house.

Chapter Twenty-Six

Uneventful would've been the best description of the next two days. I spent several daylight hours walking around the island taking photos of colorful houses, lawn ornaments, sea oats, and dunes. Since closing Landrum Gallery, I haven't had an outlet to sell my photos, but my love of photography, my habit of photographing places and things on Folly hadn't lessened. Many retirees gravitate to golf, some of the more fit retirees lean toward surfing to relax. I'd tried both and was as good at each as I was at swimming to Ireland. Photography was my thing.

I was sitting on the porch sipping a Diet Coke while watching traffic pass by the house when I noticed I'd missed two calls. That didn't make sense until I realized I must've accidentally muted the phone. The first call showed a number I wasn't familiar with. After a long pause on the recording the person ended the call without saying a word. The second call again popped up with the same number and came seven hours ago.

This time there was a message: "Chris, this is Terrell, you know, from Rita's. I've been talking to the old-timers that were around Mosquito in the '50s. The more I dig, the more I find that're still alive. Remember, I told you I was going to find out who killed Elijah way back then, maybe who killed my friend Clarence? Umm, since you and Charles are detectives, I need to tell you what I found. You won't believe it, but I'm pretty sure I know who it was. And get this, if I'm right, the person killed both men. If after you hear what I found and why I think I know who did it, umm, well, after that, if you think I'm right, maybe you could go with me to the police. They'd believe you before me. Give me a call when you get this. Oh yeah, before I forget, Clarence's party is Saturday night."

I called the number Terrell had given me. No luck. There was no answer, no machine to leave a message. I called Rita's and asked the woman who answered if Terrell was working. She said she could barely hear over the crowd. I repeated the question. She told me to hang on while she checked. I was beginning to wonder if she'd forgotten me, when she returned to say he was off today. I tried his number once more and received the same result. I thought about driving to his house but figured if he didn't answer his phone, he probably wasn't home. I'll try again in the morning.

Three hours later, the phone rang when I was getting ready for bed. My friends knew not to call this late and I didn't know what CCSO meant that popped up on the screen. I was ready to let it go to voicemail, when it struck me what the initials stood for. I answered.

A vaguely familiar voice said, "Mr. Landrum?"

I said it was, then realized who was on the other end. I was right about the meaning of CCSO.

"This is Detective Callahan with the Charleston County Sheriff's Office. We've crossed paths on a few occasions."

"I remember."

"Do you know Terrell Jefferson?"

I took a deep breath, barely above a whisper said, "Yes, why?"

"Could you tell me how you know him?"

I gave the detective a brief rundown of my contacts with Terrell. He asked when I talked to him last. I told him and repeated, "Why?"

"Mr. Landrum, umm, Chris, Mr. Jefferson was found dead late this afternoon. I'm sorry for your loss."

I was stunned. After catching my breath, I managed to mumble, "What happened?"

"He was murdered. Found in his house with two bullet wounds in the back."

"When?"

"The coroner's best guess is sometime early this afternoon. Why?"

I didn't answer, but said, "Why'd you call me?"

"Mr. Jefferson had paper in his pocket with your name and number on it. His phone shows he recently made two calls to your number. After that there were two calls from your number to his phone."

"Detective, Terrell left me a message earlier today."

"What did it say?"

"Rather than trying to repeat it, I think you need to hear the message."

"Are you at home?"

I told him I was and gave my address. He said he was at Terrell's house and would come over within an hour.

Our call ended, I slumped in the chair, and put my head

between my hands. I pictured my new acquaintance holding a paintbrush while getting excited about improving his house. Improvements he'll never complete.

I must've drifted longer than I thought. The next thing I remembered was Detective Callahan's unmarked Ford Explorer pulling in the drive. Callahan is in his forties, with short hair. He was wearing a navy sport coat and gray slacks. I met him at the door and motioned him in.

"We meet again, Mr. Landrum."

"Please call me Chris."

He and I had shared a few tense conversations since we'd met four years ago but had learned to trust each other as a result. He'd endeared himself to me after one lengthy discussion when he'd referred to a retired detective from his office whom I'd developed a rocky relationship with as a COF— Cranky Old Fart. He couldn't have been more accurate.

We sat at the kitchen table.

"Again, Chris, I'm sorry about Mr. Jefferson."

"Me too. He seemed like a nice man."

Callahan nodded toward my phone on the corner of the table. "The message?"

After the message played, Callahan stared at me, shook his head, and said, "I can't believe this is happening again. What in the hell are you and your friend doing playing detective? Playing detective again."

"We're not playing detective. A friend of mine, Al Washington, spent time on Mosquito Beach after he returned from Korea in the early 1950s. He asked me to take him over there since he hadn't been back in years. When we got there, we met Clarence Taylor, the man who found the skeleton, the skeleton you're investigating. Al might've known the victim, someone who disappeared decades ago. The man's name was

Elijah Duncan. It appears it was Elijah, and as you know, Clarence Taylor was recently murdered."

Callahan tapped his fingers on the table like a humming-bird with ADHD, jotted a couple of notes, then resumed staring at me. "Help me understand how you're not playing detective."

"The last two times I talked to Terrell, he said he'd been close to Clarence, had known him his whole life. Terrell was determined to find out who killed him. I told him to be care-ful, to leave it to you and others conducting the investiga-tions. If someone murdered twice, there was little to stop him from making Terrell number three."

I didn't mention I'd heard as far as Elijah's murder was concerned, it was a cold case, that Callahan was the cop who was treating it that way.

"Chris, it irritates the hell out of me that amateurs are going around acting like it's their calling to solve crimes. You know firsthand how dangerous that can be."

"I agree, but—"

"The only but is me telling you to butt out. Do you understand?"

I nodded. I understood, but it wasn't going to stop me from getting involved. I didn't know much about Elijah, but I knew Clarence and Terrell. I liked both men. Now they're dead.

"With that out of the way, I want you to do two things. First, email that voicemail to me. Second, tell me anything you know that could help me catch the person or persons responsible for the two deaths."

"Three, counting Elijah?"

He nodded. "Three."

I'd never emailed a recorded call and asked Callahan how

to do it. He took the phone and said, "And you think you're bright enough to catch a killer."

"Not if he uses a voicemail app as a murder weapon," I said, hoping to lighten the mood.

Callahan smiled, but it lacked sincerity. He tapped a few commands, typed something, then handed it back to me. "Done. Anything else I need to know?"

I told him the names of three people I'd met on Mosquito Beach who were old enough to have killed Elijah. I didn't share anything about Charles and my visit to Eugene's house under construction or the visit to the empty lot. I didn't need him scolding me again for butting in. Callahan said he'd talked to them, and to two others I didn't mention. He didn't share their names. I also told him about Andrew Delaney's connection to the Klan. He asked if Andrew was old enough to have killed Elijah. I told him no.

"You're trying to hang two murders on him because he's a member of the Klan?"

"Not really. I thought you needed to know in case you want to talk to him."

"Anything else?"

"No."

"Then once again, I'm sorry about Terrell." He hesitated. "And Clarence."

"Thank you."

"I'd tell you to be careful, but both of us know I'd be wasting my breath."

Chapter Twenty-Seven

I waited until morning to tell Charles about Terrell, the message he'd left, and Detective Callahan's visit. As I could've predicted, he gave me a hard time for not letting him know as soon as Callahan was out the door. I explained I was so shaken I couldn't talk to anyone. He said he understood, but it shouldn't have stopped me from calling. Also, and equally predictable, he asked what our next move was to find out who killed Terrell. He didn't say it, but I knew he meant find out who killed Terrell, Clarence, plus Elijah. He ended by telling me to meet him at the Lost Dog Cafe for lunch, he was buying. His uttering that rare offer told me he understood how much the murders were affecting me.

I walked to the Dog to try to clear my head of depressing thoughts about Terrell. I wasn't successful but at least got some much-needed exercise. The temperature was in the mid-seventies, so I wasn't surprised to see Charles on the front patio. He wore a long-sleeve, blue T-shirt with Peru State Bobcats in white letters on the front, tan shorts, and was sipping coffee. He saw me approach, set the coffee down, then glanced at his bare wrist to remind me I was late. Of course, I wasn't, but that had never stopped my friend's obsession with time, incorrect time.

I walked to the side entrance of the patio. As soon as I pulled out the chair opposite Charles, Amber was at the table.

"Let's see," She looked at her wrist where she actually wore a watch. "Too late for French toast," she said. "What artery clogging item do you want for lunch?"

I smiled and said, "Charles is buying. Surprise me."

"Crap, we're plum out of chocolate-covered gravel. How about a mahi salad?"

"Something cheaper," Charles said. "Didn't you hear him say I'm buying? Sure there's no more gravel?"

Amber patted Charles on the head. "How about a hot dog with home fries?"

"Perfect," I said.

After Amber headed to the kitchen, Charles looked around to see who was close enough to hear.

He leaned closer. "You okay?"

"To tell the truth, no."

"Thomas Jefferson said, 'Honesty is the first chapter in the book of wisdom.' You know Terrell's death isn't your fault."

I nodded although I wasn't sure I meant it. Would Terrell still be alive if the first time we'd met I'd discouraged him from trying to learn the identity of the skeleton? Would he be alive if he didn't talk to everyone he knew old enough to have been around when Elijah was murdered? Would he be alive if after Clarence was murdered, I'd pushed harder for him to leave it to the police?

"Earth to Chris," Charles said, tapping me on the arm. "Did you hear what I said?"

"No," I said, honestly. Thomas Jefferson would've been proud. "What?"

"Same thing I asked on the phone. What's our next step in finding the killer?"

I told him what Detective Callahan said about me, about us, staying out of police business.

"That ever stopped us?"

Amber arrived with my lunch and a refill on Charles's coffee before I responded to his question. She also arrived with a question of her own.

"Can you believe what I just heard in there?" She tilted her head in the direction of the dining room.

Charles said, "You heard Folly's two handsomest men are sitting on the patio."

She laughed, and looked around, probably to see where they were. "Don't you mean funniest?"

"Amber," I said, "what did you hear?"

Her laughter faded. "One of the cooks at Rita's was killed yesterday."

"Who told you?"

"Marc Salmon."

No surprise, I thought.

Charles said, "What else did he say?"

"Not much. Said the man was found at his house off Sol Legare Road."

I said, "Did Marc say who he was?"

"No."

"How'd he hear about it?" Charles asked.

"One of the local cops." She looked at me, her focus narrowed. "Chris, you don't look surprised. Did you know?"

I didn't want to get in a lengthy discussion, but if I didn't tell her before she found out from someone else, she'd do a Charles and be on my case.

"Yes, I met Terrell Jefferson when Barb and I were eating on Mosquito Beach. A county detective told me about the murder last evening." I hoped that was enough to prevent trouble with Amber down the road.

"Oh," she said. "I'm sorry."

Two women seated at a table at the other end of the patio motioned for Amber to bring their checks. She gave them a salute then headed inside.

Charles said, "Now that Marc knows, within hours, everyone on Folly, heck, everyone in the US, Canada, and probably Uruguay will know."

I said, "I don't know what we can do. I keep coming back to what Terrell told us. The Sol Legare community is a tight-knit group. We're outsiders."

"Terrell was from there, lived there his entire life, and that's why he thought he'd be able to discover the killer or killers."

I looked at my half-eaten plate of food, then at Charles. "Look where it got him."

"More reason for us to get involved," Charles said.

It didn't make sense, but I knew what he meant. "What do you think we should do?"

He took another sip of coffee, then said, "Wonder when his funeral will be?"

"He only died yesterday. It'll be at least a couple of days."

"You'd better find out. We don't want to miss it. What do you think will happen now to Clarence's, umm, death party?"

I could see wheels spinning in Charles's head. Where

better to nose around and talk to people who knew Terrell and Clarence. Possibly talk to a killer.

I called Al that evening. I'd hoped to catch him at home, instead I could tell from the country music in the background he was at the bar. He said there had been an unexpected late rush for beer in the neighborhood. Bob asked him to stay to handle crowd control.

Al added, "Most likely, Blubber Bob figured he was outnumbered ten to one. He needed me to keep him from getting whupped."

I had a hard time hearing him for the music and asked him to repeat what he'd said.

He did, and I said, "You've done your good deed for the day."

"I've got a suspicion you didn't call to see how business was doing."

"I'm afraid you're right. There's been another murder near Mosquito Beach."

"Oh, my Lord. Who?"

"Terrell Jefferson. He's the first person I met the night Barb and I want to supper at Island Breeze."

"Did I meet him?"

"No, he wasn't there when you were."

What happened? Did it have something to do with Clarence Taylor's death?"

"No one knows. I think it did because it's too big a coincidence both being murdered after trying to find Elijah Duncan's killer."

"What do the police think?"

"All I know is Detective Callahan caught both cases. He's good so if anyone can solve it, he can."

"Don't want to throw water on your optimism," Al said after a long pause. "Is the detective you're talking about white?"

"Yes."

"Don't know for sure about Sol Legare now, but back when I was hanging out there, it was a closed community. Didn't take kindly to outsiders. Thought it could take care of its own problems. Outside cops, especially white ones, didn't have much of a chance, even if they cared, which some didn't."

"I hope it's not as bad as it was then."

"Wouldn't put money on it."

"I hope you're wrong."

"I do too, yes I do. What'll happen to the party Clarence wanted them to hold?"

"It was scheduled for Saturday, but with Terrell's death, I don't know."

I heard voices in the background and Al's muffled voice like he'd put his hand over the phone. Finally, he said, "Chris, think I'd better go save Bob. He just told one of his best customers that if he played one more Motown song, Bob was going to throw him out on his rear. He didn't say rear."

"Sounds like you're needed."

"Yes, sir, I sure am. Will you let me know when the party will be? I'd like to be there."

"Want me to take you?"

"If you don't mind."

"I'd be honored," I said and ended the call.

I was curious if a decision had been made about Clarence's last-wish party. I didn't have phone numbers for anyone I'd talked to at Island Breeze, so I called the restaurant. A man with a Caribbean accent answered with, "Island Breeze. May I be of assistance?"

I asked about Clarence's party. He said it was still on for Saturday.

I then did the wise thing and called Charles to give him the news. For the second time tonight, there was loud background noise that made it difficult for me to hear.

"Where are you?"

"Loggerhead's. Outside bar. Why?"

"I'm having a hard time hearing you."

"You've got ancient ears. Listen gooder."

There was no future disagreeing, besides, there was some truth to his statement. I said, "I'm letting you know the party at Island Breeze is still on for Saturday."

"Say that again. It's loud here. I couldn't hear you."

No, I didn't tell him he had ancient ears. Instead, I repeated it.

"Great," he said, "I'll see if Virgil can go with us."

"Why would Virgil want to go?"

"He's with me. We've been talking about the murders. He wants to learn more about the folks out there."

"Why?" I repeated.

"It's your fault. You took him to meet Terrell before he went and got himself killed. Virgil now has a stake in finding out who killed him. Isn't that right, Virgil?"

I hadn't realized that this was a three-way conversation. I heard someone in the background. I assumed it was Virgil. Charles said, "Oh, right, I'll tell him. Chris, Virgil wanted me to remind you about a few months back when he saved your life on the boat."

That wasn't how I remembered the incident. In fact, it was

the opposite, but with Charles's alternate reality, and now I suppose with Virgil's, the best course of action was to ignore the discrepancy.

"What's his point?"

He mumbled something, I assumed to Virgil. Then I heard him say, "Virgil, you tell him."

"Yo, Chris, this is Virgil, how're you doing?"

"Fine."

"You ought to be here with us. Did you know if you tell a guy sitting next to you on a barstool, not Charles, but on the other side, how much you like his shirt, he'll buy you a beer?"

It sounded like Virgil had bragged on several shirts. "I didn't know that."

"Yessiree, it's true. Hey, thanks for letting me go with you all to that party."

How'd I miss extending the invitation?

"Glad you can go."

"I can help you two figure out who the killer is, or is that killers are? Come to think of it, there could be three killers. One guy killed Mr. Skeleton; one killed that Clarence guy. Some dirty, rotten bastard killed my new friend Terrell. Anyway, Charles, and even you, have taught me a bunch about being a detective. I'll help. Won't charge you a penny. Course, you could buy me a beer sometime. Talking about beer, Chris, I'd talk longer but my glass is empty. Gotta tell the guy next to me how much I like his shoes." He lowered his voice. "They aren't as nice as my Guccis, but hell, whose are?"

I was beginning to regret saying I'd go to the party, and it was still two days away.

"You still there?"

"Afraid so. How many beers has Virgil had?"

"Only two since I've been here. Why?"

"He sounded like he's over his limit."

"He did say he'd been here an hour before I showed up. Didn't see any iced tea glasses nearby. What time are you picking me up for the party? I'll tell Virgil, although I doubt he'll remember much about tonight when he falls out of bed tomorrow."

I told him what time then added, "You may want to make sure he makes it to his apartment tonight."

"I'll peel him off the barstool in a few minutes before Virgil tells the generous, well-dressed beer buyer that he likes his underwear. Nothing good could come from that."

I'd planned on calling Al after getting Charles off the phone, but after the three-way conversation with Charles and Virgil, my ear hurt. Al's call could wait until tomorrow.

Chapter Twenty-Eight

Al was waiting at the front door when we arrived to take him to the party. He wore black dress slacks, a purple short-sleeve dress shirt, a black driver cap, and shoes nearly as shiny as Virgil's. He also carried an equally shiny black cane. My friend was ready to party.

Charles gave up the front passenger seat so Al could have more legroom.

Al shook his head, smiled, and said, "Charles, thanks for the kind gesture, but let me sit in back. Before I meet my maker, I want to be chauffeured around in a Cadillac by a white man."

Charles held the back door open for Al and said, "Want to let the chauffeur borrow your cap?"

Al shook his head before he noticed the other passenger in the back seat. Virgil smiled. "Hi, fine sir, I'm Virgil Debonnet. I'm amazed your driver didn't bring the Rolls for someone as important as you."

Al returned Virgil's smile. "I've heard my friends in the

front seat talk about you." He laughed. "You're as full of BS as they said you were."

Virgil's smile turned serious, then back to a smile, before becoming a full-throated laugh. "My sterling reputation precedes me."

Al returned the laugh, patted Virgil on the shoulder, and turned to me, "Driver, to the gala."

Twenty minutes plus several of Virgil's jokes later, we pulled on Mosquito Beach Road to be greeted by more vehicles than I'd ever seen there. They were parked on every piece of flat ground not covered by water, trees, or a building. The temperature was in the mid-seventies with a cloudless sky. That was fortunate because there wouldn't have been room inside for the people who spilled across the front of the building. From what I could see, the crowd also filled the back-dining area. So Al wouldn't have to walk far, I let him and Charles off at the door, then drove nearly to the spot where Clarence had found the body before finding a parking spot. Virgil had refused to get out with Charles and Al saying he'd stay with me in case I needed help walking. I sarcastically thanked him.

Aretha Franklin's "Chain of Fools" blared from the outdoor speakers as we approached Island Breeze. The sounds of a loud, enthusiastic crowd greeted us as we entered the packed restaurant. I didn't see Charles or Al, but Eugene Dillinger was standing inside the back door waving in my direction. The builder wore a white shirt that looked like silk, navy slacks, and held a colorful drink.

"Your friends are at my table out back. They asked me to point you in that direction."

Great. Nothing like having to listen to a sales pitch for a beachfront property with Charles pretending to be rich. I smiled and introduced Virgil to Eugene who didn't skip a beat before asking if Virgil lived on Folly, quickly followed by asking if he was in the market for a new house. On the way to the back door, Virgil said yes, he lived on Folly but wasn't currently looking for a house. He made the mistake of mentioning he'd owned one overlooking the Battery and Charleston Harbor. Eugene put his arm around Virgil's shoulder then said, "Drinks are on me."

Virgil didn't even have to tell Eugene he liked his shirt.

Eugene's table was two large cable spools pulled together on the right side of the property near a large American flag. In addition to Charles and Al, Robert Graves and a woman I assumed to be his wife were seated closest to Charles, with Jamal Kingsly on the other side of the tables. Eugene motioned for me to take the chair beside Jamal, for Virgil to sit between Robert and Charles. Eugene took the remaining seat before sharing the names of everyone at the table. Sandra, Robert's wife, was the only person I hadn't met. It wasn't quite as loud as inside, but not much quieter. Bob Marley's heavily accented voice shared his thoughts on "Bad Boys" as two women standing across from us swayed to the music.

Robert leaned toward me to say, "Bob Marley and Aretha Franklin were Clarence's favorite singers. You'll be hearing a lot from them tonight."

A college-age server tapped me on the shoulder and asked what my friend and I wanted to drink. Charles and Al had already ordered. I said white wine, Virgil asked if they had Blue Hawaiis. She asked if it was a brand of beer. He said no, that it was a drink with light rum, blue curacao liqueur, and pineapple juice.

"Rum we got. No pineapple juice. I don't know what curacao is."

Virgil nodded at her. "How about a Budweiser?"

She smiled. "That we've got."

Charles said, "Eugene, thanks for letting us share your table. Looks like a packed house."

"Clarence had many friends." He looked around the crowd. "Most folks here wouldn't have missed it. There're some who never met Clarence. They're here because it's Saturday night with good weather."

"He was a prince," Sandra said.

Virgil said, "I didn't know Clarence. Until tonight, I didn't know anyone at this table except Charles and Chris so I'm not speaking from personal experience, but it seems not everyone thought your man Clarence was a friend or a prince."

That silenced his table mates.

Robert put his arm around his wife. "My friend, I assume you're speaking about the person who took his life."

Virgil nodded.

"The person who shot Clarence couldn't be from here. Everyone loved the man." He removed his RiverDogs cap, placed it over his heart, bowed his head, and continued, "He was one of the nicest people I ever knew. God rest his soul." He returned the cap to his head, apparently his sort-of prayer was over. "Sandra and I go way back with him."

Sandra added, "Virgil, you're right about one thing. You don't know any of us. I challenge you to find one person here who has a bad word to say about our friend Clarence."

Virgil held both hands up, palms facing Sandra. "Dear lady, I apologize if I said something that offended you. All I meant was someone shot him, shot him twice as I understand it. That's not an act associated with love."

I needed to change the subject before Virgil dug a deeper hole.

"Sandra, Al tells me there were some wonderful times out here back in the 1950s. Were you around then?"

She smiled. "Sure was. Lots of handsome men were too. Now if you ask my parents, I was never here. They said self-respecting white girls didn't hang around where there were Negroes." She leaned over and kissed Robert's cheek. "What they didn't know, didn't hurt them, or me."

"She flirted with all of those handsome men," Robert said as he squeezed her hand.

Al smiled. "Not with me. I would've remembered someone as lovely as you."

Sandra blushed. "Such a sweet talker."

Al tipped his cap in her direction.

Jamal leaned closer to Sandra and said, "Robert's wrong about one thing. Things were different back then. Most of the guys here were black. If they showed interest in a white lady like Sandra, they'd be asking for trouble. Hell, it wouldn't have had to be anything more than a smile. Sandra's parents were right about the attitudes."

The server returned to ask if we wanted anything to eat or more drinks. Eugene said another round of drinks, that it was on him. Jamal said she'd better get us a couple of servings of wings. He didn't say it was on him. She left to the sounds of Aretha Franklin singing "Natural Woman" and laughter from a nearby group.

Al, who hadn't said much, said, "Jamal, that night you and I were talking out here about Elijah Duncan, you said you thought he'd left and headed north to find work. Have you heard anything else since they're fairly certain the skeleton was his?"

Elijah's death was heavy on Al's heart, but I'd hoped he wouldn't bring it up tonight. We were here to celebrate Clarence's life.

"No. Suppose I was wrong about him leaving." Jamal looked at Robert, Sandra, and Eugene. "All you guys knew him, didn't you? What do you think happened?"

Sandra said, "I think whatever happened to him is buried just like he was. Everyone here knew he was trouble, speaking out about wanting everything us white folks had. Elijah was right, but the early '50s were the wrong time to be shaking-up the laws and those who controlled them."

Jamal nodded. "You're right. He nearly got me beat up once when we were together. He started mouthing off to a white police officer about him always stopping blacks for speeding while letting white folks speed but never doing anything about it. I thought for sure we were heading to the hospital or the cemetery."

Charles said, "What happened?"

"The officer got a radio call about a bad wreck on Folly Road. He gave us one last snarl then rushed off to the wreck." He shook his head. "Never thought I'd be happy to hear about a wreck." Jamal turned to Eugene. "Eugene, didn't Elijah work for you?"

"A little while. We're not here tonight to talk about Elijah. Clarence was one of a kind, wasn't he?"

I wasn't certain but thought that when Charles and I were touring Eugene's construction project on Folly he said he didn't know Elijah. I'll ask Charles later. Eugene was right about one thing. Tonight was about Clarence.

I said, "Jamal, why was Clarence so special?"

"Chris, I suppose everyone who knew him could tell you stories to explain it." He looked around the table, but no one offered any. "Eugene and Sandra, I don't know if you remember. Clarence worked for the Post Office. At least twice I know of, probably times I don't know about, when someone who was short on money or was having home problems brought in a package going to someone who lived in the area, instead of putting it though the system, he'd deliver it himself after work. Didn't charge the customer anything. It wouldn't have cost that much to mail, but he knew every penny counted for his customers." Jamal smiled. "He probably would've lost his job if the boss man found out."

Sandra added, "Saw him several times in our neighborhood sticking packages in mailboxes. I knew that wasn't his job. I suspected he was doing what Jamal said."

Aretha Franklin was spelling "Respect" from the sound system. Jamal pointed to the speaker and said, "Respect. That's what Clarence was all about."

Al waited for the song to end, and said, "Anyone think Clarence's death had anything to do with Elijah?"

He wasn't ready to take the discussion of his friend off the table.

"How could it?" Robert said. "It'd been what, sixty-five years between the two."

"It wasn't connected unless you believed Terrell," Jamal said.

I was surprised that it'd taken this long before Terrell was mentioned.

Charles asked, "What's that mean?"

Jamal glanced at Robert and Sandra, before saying, "Terrell had a stick up his butt about the deaths. He went around asking everyone old enough to know Elijah to tell him everything about the man. He then spewed his theory that the murders were done by the same person. He wouldn't let it go. Robert, Sandra, he talked to you, didn't he?"

Sandra said, "He ran into me at Harris Teeter, cornered me in the produce department then started asking questions about Elijah. I told him I went out with Elijah once." She smiled. "Well, we didn't go out, it was more like he stopped me one day asking if I was going to be at the pavilion that Friday night. I said yes, we met, danced a few times, that was all. He never asked again, which was okay. Robert came along a few months later and swept me off my feet." She leaned over and hugged him.

Robert said, "When I saw them talking at the store, I figured Terrell was talking to Sandra about the improvements he's making at his house. He's mighty proud of it. That new large front porch, painting all of it, that fancy new stove, adding new tile in the kitchen and bathroom. The house never looked better."

Sandra said, "I didn't think I was ever going to get out of the produce section."

Eugene laughed. "I can do one better. Terrell came out to the house I'm building on Folly, followed me around for what must've been thirty minutes. It was a hundred degrees or so. He was wearing his chef's outfit. The boy was sweating up a storm."

Charles asked, "What'd you tell him?"

Our wings arrived before Eugene answered. Everyone at the table was more hungry than curious about what Terrell said. Everyone except Charles, of course.

"Well?" He said while Eugene reached for a wing.

Bob Marley was singing "Redemption Song," a couple behind us was singing along, and Charles stared at Eugene chewing the meat off the bone.

Eugene took another bite then pointed the bone at Charles. "Told him I had no idea who killed either man but was sorry they were dead. Clarence had been asking the same kind of questions. That's all."

I doubted that was all since Terrell had been with Eugene a half hour. He hadn't said anything tonight that he hadn't mentioned when he'd taken us to see the house he was building. I doubted I'd learn more if I pressed.

Charles must've figured the same thing about Eugene. He said, "Robert, was Terrell pestering you like he pestered your wife?"

"Pestered, no. He was persistent though. I knew little about Clarence other than he was liked by all, including me. Terrell was talking to all us old-timers who might've known Elijah. You already know what I told you about Elijah."

Charles took a sip of the beer the server set in front of him, looked at Jamal then at Robert. "Did Terrell tell any of you that he knew, or thought he knew, who'd killed Clarence?"

Sandra shook her head.

Robert said, "Not to me. I wouldn't be surprised if he didn't have suspicions. He was a sharp fellow who was like a laser-guided missile once he had a target in his sights."

"I agree with Robert," Jamal said as he stuffed a wing in his mouth.

Eugene said, "I already told you what he said at the construction site."

Virgil held his new beer in the air. "I propose a toast." He waited for us to put down our food and raise our drinks. "Here's to Clarence, a friend to everyone who knew him. And take a sip for Terrell, too. May they rest in peace."

I was pleased that Virgil didn't say everyone who knew him except one.

The party was still going strong when Al said he hated to but needed to get home. I told my riders I'd get the car and pick them up in front of the building. Before I reached the car, I spotted a familiar face sitting in a blue pickup truck backed into a spot on the creek side of the road.

"Andrew, remember me, I'm Chris?"

He looked to see if anyone was nearby. Seeing no one, he stepped out of the truck, shook my hand, and chuckled, "Sure, I remember everyone I spill beer on."

"What're you doing here?"

"You mean what's a Klansman doing in this brown part of the world?"

I wouldn't have put it that way, but yes. I nodded.

"That's a good question. I heard there was going to be a party honoring Clarence Taylor. Was working up the nerve to go in to pay my respects."

"I believe you told me you may've worked with Clarence."

"You have a hell of a good memory. Yes, we worked together. Not many people know it." He rolled his eye. "Especially my Klan brothers." He looked around again. "Chris, have you ever had your friends tell you how horrible someone was, then when you got to know the person, you liked them?"

"Yes."

"I was that way with Clarence. At first, I didn't go out of my way to pay attention to him at work. He took the lead, talked to me every chance he got. Then, when he was working at the Post Office, I saw him most every time I was in there." He shook his head. "Damn, I didn't want to like him. He was a ni ... umm, black. I was a card-carrying member of the Klan. He was a nice guy who didn't deserve getting himself killed. That's why I wanted to be here."

"Are you going in?"

He shook his head. "Thought about it but couldn't bring myself to cross that racial line. I'm paying my respects out here." He looked around again to see if anyone was near. "Know what really pisses me off?"

I told him I didn't.

"I'm a member of a group that thinks blacks shouldn't have a lot of the jobs they have, stealing work from whites, a bunch of other bad things." He sighed. "Now I'm sitting out here and the person who killed my friend Clarence, my black friend, is sitting in there having a good old time."

"How do you know?"

"Don't for certain, but Clarence must've trusted the person who shot him. He never would've let someone he didn't know get that close. This is a small community where everyone knows everyone. So, I'd bet a bunch of money everyone who knew him well is in that party. Am I right, or am I right?"

He didn't wait for my answer. He said he'd better move on before word makes it to any of his Klan brothers. I said it was nice talking to him.

If he'd waited, I would've told him he was probably right about everyone who knew Clarence being at the party. The question he didn't ask, and I couldn't answer even if he'd asked was did Charles, Virgil, Al, and I just spend two hours at the same table with that person?

I picked up my friends in front of Island Breeze to the sounds of Aretha Franklin singing "Amazing Grace."

Chapter Twenty-Nine

"Okay, fellow detectives," Charles said after we dropped Al off at his house, "What'd we learn tonight?"

Virgil raised his hand like he was in school, except he didn't wait for the teacher to call on him, "That was the most fun I've had at a dead person's party."

I knew Charles wouldn't let it go. "Virgil, how many dead person's parties have you attended?"

"Went to three wakes for people who lived near me when I lived at the Battery. The wakes were for guys I don't recall ever seeing smile. To carry that through to death, the wakes were—pardon the pun—dead. Plenty of booze but none of the laughter going with it."

"Virgil," Charles said, "did you learn anything that could help us catch the killer or killers?"

"Oh, umm, let's see, everyone was friendly. Friendlier than anyone I know would be to strangers. Offering us seats at their table. That was kind. Oh yeah, Eugene is quite a salesman. I nearly grabbed my checkbook and wrote him a bad check for a house. I didn't, but it got our tab paid."

Charles interrupted, "Virgil, anything useful?"

"They don't have Blue Hawaiis at that restaurant, although—"

Charles said, "Virg—"

"I know, I know," Virgil interrupted Charles's interruption. "Everyone there loved Clarence, but even after they said Terrell talked to each of them about Clarence's death, no one said much about Terrell. Hell, he was dead, too.

"The party was for Clarence," Charles said.

Virgil looked out the window before turning to Charles. "How many times did someone say Sol Legare was a tight-knit community? Don't answer, Charles. It was several. If that's true, why so little talk about someone who was murdered out there less than a week ago?"

It was a good question, one for which I had no answer. "Charles, what did you learn?"

"Clarence's favorite singers were Aretha Franklin and Bob Marley."

Wasn't it only seconds ago Charles was on Virgil's case for mentioning things that weren't related to the death of the three men?

Virgil said, "Charles, what's that have to do with the murders?"

I stifled a giggle while keeping my eyes on the road.

"Nothing, it popped in my head. Let's see, we didn't know it before, but Sandra was out on Mosquito in the early fifties when Elijah was killed. She was quite a charmer back in the day."

"And she dated Elijah," Virgil added.

Charles said, "Not really a date. Met him one time, and that was in the pavilion to dance. Not a date in my book."

"That's all she admitted to," Virgil said. "She was sitting with her husband when she said it. Since he swept her off her feet a few months after that, I figured she didn't spend much time talking to him about Elijah."

"Chris," Charles said, "what'd you learn?"

"You've already covered most of it."

Charles said, "Most?"

I told them about my encounter with Andrew Delaney.

Charles said, "You were gone so long I thought you left us."

Virgil said, "Do you think Andrew was right about the killer or killers being at the restaurant?"

"Don't know. It makes sense, but that doesn't narrow it down much."

I let Charles off at his apartment; did the same for Virgil.

I pulled in my drive and repeated what I'd told Virgil about not knowing if the killer was in Island Breeze. What I did know, it was my fault Terrell wasn't there.

———

"Thought I'd find you here," Charles said as he lumbered up the steps to the second level of the Folly Beach Fishing Pier. I figured it was his cane tapping on the steps before I saw or heard him.

"Why?"

He wore a long-sleeve, purple T-shirt with Carroll Saints on the front, tan shorts, red tennis shoes, and his summer Tilley. He bent at the waist, put his hands on his knees, and then waved for me to move over.

He sat beside me on the picnic table then pointed to his chest. "It's Carroll College in Helena, Montana. Knew you'd be interested."

"I asked why, not what."

"Why what?"

Why did I even ask, I wondered? "Why did you know I'd be here?"

He rubbed his chin. "Let's see, you weren't at the Dog, Amber said you hadn't been in. You weren't home, or if you were, you were either dead or didn't want to talk to me. Neither option struck my fancy. Then it came to me in a moment of brilliance. Where else would you be if you wanted to think, ponder something, or just hang out to pretend you were thinking when you were snoozing?" He waved his hand around. "Here you are."

For the second time, I wondered why I asked.

"Did any other insightful nuggets come to you in that moment of brilliance?"

"Nary a one. I figured you'd have one or two to share after last night's visit to the Breeze."

Charles was more intuitive and sensitive than he'd like others to believe. Additionally, after him knowing me more than a decade, he knew my moods.

"I was thinking about Terrell, how he'd be alive if I hadn't let him go on and on about finding the person who killed Elijah and Clarence."

Charles removed his Tilley, set it beside him, and wiped perspiration off his brow. He watched two men untangling their fishing lines at the edge of the lower deck, then glanced over at me. "Knew that's what you'd be pondering."

"How'd you know that?"

"Hey, I don't call myself a detective for nothing. That's the way you are. After we left there last night, I could tell it was bothering you. Don't ask why. I knew because it was also bothering me. It didn't bother me enough to keep me awake all night, like I bet it did you."

I started to deny it. No need to lie to my friend. "You caught me."

On the railing behind us two white and black seagulls were squawking, probably laughing at our discussion.

"Know what I figured out, didn't have to stay up all night to do it?"

I probably would regret asking, but he was going to tell me anyway. "What?"

"Terrell's death is not your fault. It's not."

"Maybe, but—"

"No but. Let me finish."

I nodded for him to continue.

"Did you encourage him to nose into their deaths?" He held his hand in front of my face, palm facing me. "No, you didn't. Clarence was Terrell's friend. He'd known him his entire life, looked up to him, was a father figure to him. His death hit Terrell hard. Hard enough to do everything he could to find out who killed him. Could you have stopped him if you tried? No."

"I could've tried."

"Sure, you could have, but you would've failed. I saw that in Terrell's eyes when we met him behind Rita's. Remember, then we were only talking about finding who killed Elijah sixty something years ago, a man Terrell never met. He was going to get involved because his grandpa knew Elijah. Think how much it had to be tearing his inside out when Clarence was killed."

"True, but—"

He pointed his cane at me. "Want to know something else I remembered about that meeting?"

"Of course."

"I heard you tell him without mincing words that whoever killed Elijah wouldn't hesitate to harm anyone trying to dig up the truth after the skeleton was dug up. I also know you enough to know even though I didn't hear you, I bet that wasn't the only time you told him."

Crap, he was good. "I did warn him again after Clarence was killed."

Charles held out both arms. "See, more proof it wasn't your fault."

"You may be right, but it doesn't make me feel better."

"Know what would?"

I took a deep breath, glanced at the seagulls continuing their conversation, then turned to Charles. "Catching the person who killed him."

Charles smiled. "Finally, you got something right."

Chapter Thirty

Charles had decided over the years that some of our best thinking came when we were walking and talking; therefore, a walk on the beach would be our best chance of figuring out who killed Terrell, Clarence, and possibly Elijah. I had serious doubts, but the temperature was mild, and we were graced with a blue sky peeking through puffy white clouds. This was the perfect combination for a walk on the beach, something we'd done many times.

Sundays in mid-September were not normally the busiest days on the beach, but you wouldn't know it today. It seemed every square inch of sand was occupied by vacationers of all ages, locals on their daily walk weaving around carefully to not kick sand on the outsiders, kids doing their seagull imitations by flapping their arms while squealing. There were several surfers plus two paddle boarders avoiding the crowded beach by staying a hundred or so yards offshore. I didn't know if we could solve any murders, but the feel of the beach, seeing hundreds of folks and hearing their enthusiastic voices about being on Folly buoyed my spirits.

Before we'd made our way to the steps leading from the Pier to the beach, Charles stopped three times to talk to men fishing off the structure, twice to pet three dogs accompanying their owners. While my spirits were lifted, I knew we couldn't have a serious conversation when surrounded by hundreds of people who'd gathered in front of the Pier or the Tides Hotel, so I motioned for us to head east where there were fewer distractions.

We'd gone a couple hundred yards before either of us spoke.

Charles broke the silence. "Do you think the same person killed all three guys?"

"Makes the most sense. Elijah's body turns up. Clarence made it known to everyone who'd listen he was going to find out who killed him. And don't forget, Terrell left me the message saying he thought he knew who killed both men."

"Couldn't there still be more than one person doing the killing? Terrell said he thought he knew who it was. He could've been wrong; heck, even if he was right, someone else could have shot him."

"You're right, but it makes more sense one person did it all."

"If true, the person is probably in his eighties."

"Yes."

"How many people who live on or near Sol Legare are that old?"

"Several, I suspect. Many of the residents have been there generations, lots of older folks are still around. Also remember, the killer could live anywhere."

"True, but if he lived far away, he probably wouldn't have known about Clarence or Terrell trying to find him."

We passed a group of five couples sitting in folding chairs arranged in a circle. Six of the chairs had orange backs with VOLS in large white letters. Charles pointed his cane their direction. "Want to yell Roll Tide Roll?"

"How many of them can you outrun?" I asked the master topic changer.

He glanced back at the group. "Zero."

"Then, no."

He shrugged. "Who've we met in their eighties from Sol Legare or nearby?"

I said, "The guy who's going to build your house. Then there's Jamal Kingsly, Sandra and Robert Graves, umm. I guess that's all."

"What about your buddy the triple-K guy?"

"Andrew Delaney. He could've killed Clarence and Terrell, but he's in his sixties so wouldn't have been old enough to have shot Elijah. What would be his motive?"

"Did you forget the KKK part?" He snapped his fingers. "Or, one of his relatives, one still alive, killed Elijah and Andrew killed the other two who were getting close to figuring it out before they revealed a family member as the killer."

"He's a suspect, but I doubt he did it."

"How about anyone you've met when I wasn't around?"

"Can't think of anyone."

"Okay, now we have a suspect list, what next?"

"Think back to last night. The place was packed. Other than those at our table, how many other people did you see who could've been in their eighties or older?"

Charles stopped, closed his eyes, and shook his head. "A half dozen, maybe more."

"The killer could've been any of them. Plus, Terrell told me there were a few others he needed to talk to who would've been in that age range."

Charles smiled. "Chris, the other day I was talking to Benny Hilton, he's a big golfer. Said he'd rather golf than eat. I don't believe it since he weighs about five pounds less than a papa elephant. Anyway, I ran into Benny in front of the Crab Shack when he started jabbering about playing the Country Club of Charleston the day before. He was laughing at Shannon, don't know his last name, who's one of his playing partners. You know Benny, don't you?"

"No. Your point is?"

"Touchy today, aren't we?"

"Charles."

"Okay. Benny said whenever Shannon hit a ball into the rough, something he does a lot according to Benny, he drives on the cart path through the rough. He expects his ball to always be sitting there waiting for him. He never thinks it could be somewhere in the rough where there isn't a path."

"The point of the story?"

"The point is we don't know any of those other senior citizens who were at Clarence's party last night, so we have to start our search by the cart path."

"With the suspects we know."

"You're catching on. After I teach you how to be a good detective, maybe I'll teach you golf."

From earlier conversations, I knew Charles had never played golf, nor indicated he'd wanted to start.

"For sake of argument, let's say one of the people we know

killed Elijah Duncan in the early1950s, buried him on Mosquito Beach, never to be found. If it's someone we know, he stayed in the area and remained under the radar until Clarence discovered the skeleton. Then Clarence took it upon himself to dig into the killing hoping he'd learn who killed Elijah."

"A fatal mistake," Charles added. "Then our new friend Terrell took it upon himself to see if he could learn who killed Elijah, simply because his grandpa told him about his friendship with the guy years before Terrell was born."

I nodded. "Then snooping into his friend Clarence's murder was Terrell's fatal mistake."

Our conversation had taken us across from the Folly Beach water tower. Charles pointed his cane at the structure standing taller than any surrounding building and asked if I was ready to head back. I was, so we pivoted to begin the long trek back.

"Okay," Charles said, "we don't know for certain, but the odds are both Clarence and Terrell were killed because they were getting close to learning who killed Elijah."

"I agree."

"To figure it all out, don't we need to know why Elijah was killed? Who'd he piss off enough to bump him off?"

"I don't remember exactly what each of them said about Elijah, but the overall feeling was he was a troublemaker. Even Al, his friend, called him a hell raiser. I think Jamal said something about his having a chip on his shoulder, Terrell hinted that his constant speaking out about African American rights caused problems for blacks. It got whites stirred up and put blacks in their sights. Don't forget Sandra knew Elijah, even danced with him. She could've known him better than the men."

Charles said "Those are pretty weak motives. There must be more. Know what I keep thinking about?"

"What?"

"I keep coming back to how quickly good old Eugene ended our two meetings when we brought up Elijah's name. That fella wants to sell me a house as much as he doesn't want to talk about Elijah."

"True."

"I'd put him at the top of our list. I'd bet others on Sol Legare would too. Eugene thinks folks there like him, but they don't. He took advantage of them with low wages when blacks couldn't speak out for their rights."

"Elijah did."

Charles stopped and said, "That's what got him killed."

Chapter Thirty-One

After the beach walk with Charles and still exhausted from last night's party at Island Breeze, I thought sleep would come quickly. Wrong. My eyes failed to stay closed while my mind kept drifting back to the murders.

I wasn't as confident as Charles about Eugene being the killer, but he was as good a suspect as any. So what? There was no evidence to indicate any of the people I'd met were responsible.

I felt I owed it to Terrell to see what I could do to help the police but realized how handicapped I was. In recent years, some of my friends and I had been lucky enough to help the police. The task was made easier because we knew Folly Beach, were familiar with many residents, plus we had connections with the police. People trusted us so they'd share things they wouldn't tell others.

I had none of those advantages when it came to Sol Legare Island and Mosquito Beach. I was an outsider. The men I knew best from there were dead. Even then, I didn't know them well. With Island Breeze being the center of the tight-knit community, it was the only place I could go without appearing to be nosing around.

With that working against me, why did I feel I had to do something? Wouldn't the easiest, possibly safest thing be to leave it to the police? Then, why was I tossing, turning, and thinking about what had happened on Mosquito Beach?

The answer came down to two words: Al and Terrell.

Al Washington is a friend, has been for years. He's a friend who'd sacrificed most of his eighty-two years, while raising nine adopted children, risking his life, and becoming a hero in the Korean conflict, and experiencing health problems that would've been the end of most people. Add to that, he's put up with Bob Howard for decades. That's suffering personified. Because Al is a friend, I feel an obligation to help him learn what happened to Elijah Duncan, the young man he knew in the 1950s.

It's three-thirty. Sleep, where are you?

I owe it to Terrell because, regardless of what Charles or anyone else says, I feel responsible for his death. I could've discouraged him more than I had. Would it have worked? Would it have prevented his death? I'll never know. What I know is I must do something.

Still no sleep.

Before Charles headed home, he wanted me to call Detective Callahan to tell him … tell him what? Charles, who seldom runs low on ideas, said I'd come up with something to tell the detective. He may seldom run low on ideas, but some aren't worth the energy it takes for him to share them. I told him this was one of those times. Callahan had already talked with many people about the deaths, including some if not all our "suspects." The Detective had the voicemail Terrell had left me. There wasn't anything else I knew that could be helpful. Of course, that didn't stop Charles from saying I should tell him about Eugene ending our conversations when Elijah's name came up.

I'd left Charles with, "I'll think about it."

And here I was, in the middle of the night, thinking about it, thinking about the other murders, then thinking about Al.

Sleep, please hurry.

A glance at the clock told me it was seven forty-five. I'd finally drifted off after sleepless hours trying to put my arms around the happenings on Mosquito Beach. As promised, I'd thought about Charles's suggestion for me to call Detective Callahan. I rejected it. There was nothing I could tell him he didn't know. I wanted to see if the detective had learned anything leading him closer to the killer, or killers, but knew it'd be foolish to ask. The next best thing would be to see if Chief LaMond had news. I tapped her number on my speed dial.

"Cindy, this—"

"Meet me, the Dog, twenty minutes."

I hated Caller ID. No need to respond, she was gone.

Fifteen minutes later, I found Cindy on the side patio sipping coffee.

A server saw me at the table and set an orange mug of coffee in front of me without me asking for any.

I took a sip and asked Cindy, "Why'd you hang up on me? How'd you know I'd meet you?"

"What else do old retired guys have to do at eight in the morning? Besides, I hung up in case someone was holding you for ransom and calling me to pay to get you released. I'd hate to tell them no way, Jose."

I deserved that after calling so early. "Good point."

She smiled. "I don't suppose you called to wish me happy Monday."

"I always want you to have a happy day, but there was something else I was wondering."

"Duh. Who would've guessed?"

"Charles, Al Washington, Virgil and I were at a party at Island Breeze Saturday."

"Who'd be desperate enough to invite you to a party?"

I explained it was Clarence Taylor's last wish.

She stared at me. "Clarence Taylor wanted a party after he was dead?"

I nodded. "He left a note saying he'd been to too many funerals, didn't want one for himself but wanted his friends to throw a party."

"And why were you, Charles, Al, and since I only know one Virgil, that the fourth was Virgil Debonnet, invited?"

I explained how Al had met Clarence, so he wanted to honor his life by attending. Virgil was more difficult to explain since he was relatively new to Folly and as far as Cindy knew, didn't know anyone on Sol Legare.

"Okay, now that I know you didn't call to invite me to the party, why'd you ruin my perfectly pleasant Monday?"

"I was wondering if Detective Callahan had any leads on the cases over there."

"So, instead of calling Detective Callahan who would've laughed you off the phone or threatened to have you arrested for nosing in his business, you called me."

I smiled. "Excellent summary."

"You think I don't have enough to do maintaining law

and order on this island where there are, oh, let's say, a zillion clowns who love to get drunk, throw beer bottles at vacationers peacefully walking down the street, drive a hundred miles an hour over the speed limit, see how many ways they can nearly drown in that big pond out there?" She pointed toward the Atlantic. "Do you think I have enough time to take care of all that, then add whatever is going on in the rest of Charleston County to my to-do list?"

"No one could do it better than you, Chief LaMond."

She rolled her eyes. "Go get me a refill while I sit here, soak up that praise, and pat myself on the back."

She was on the phone when I returned. I set her coffee in front of her then stepped off the patio to give her privacy. She motioned me back after ending the call.

"Detective Callahan says the coroner didn't find anything unusual on Terrell or Clarence's bodies, that is other than bullet holes. There were no unidentifiable prints in Terrell's house, and, of course, no witnesses to either shooting. The bullets were from the same gun, verifying what everyone suspected; the same person probably shot both men. There's no physical evidence the person who killed Terrell and Clarence is the person who killed Elijah Duncan. Callahan assumes it is. That's why he's interviewing everyone in the area old enough to kill all three."

"He told you all of that while I was getting your refill? I'm impressed."

"Callahan talks fast, doesn't beat around the bush like you do. He's like that guy on that old TV show that started with, "Dum—de-DUM-DUM.""

"*Dragnet.*"

"Yep. You geezers know all that worthless trivia."

She was kind enough to check with Callahan, so I ignored her insult. "Did he learn anything from the interviews?"

"He learned everyone loved Clarence, thought highly of Terrell."

"Someone didn't."

"Therein lies the problem. Now that I've done my good deed for the day, did you and your motley bunch of amateur detectives—I'm being generous calling you amateur, but couldn't come up with a word that meant less than amateur —learn anything at the party to help the real police?"

"Not really. Charles thinks it's Eugene Dillinger, he's a builder who lives over here."

"I know him. Seems like an okay guy although he's accumulated a passel of parking tickets. Why does Charles think it's him?"

I told her about our conversation at the house he was building, then at the empty lot. When I mentioned that we were there because Charles had told Eugene he was interested in a house, Cindy laughed so hard that coffee spewed out her nose. Fortunate for the Chief, I was the only witness.

She regained her composure then asked if that was all I had.

I nodded.

"I spend way more time than I should telling a handful of our locals not to jaywalk across Center Street. Telling them doesn't mean a thing. They're going to continue until one of them becomes road kill. I tell them anyway."

There was a point coming. I wondered if it would arrive before I finished my coffee. I motioned for her to continue.

"Whoever killed Clarence and Terrell is still out there. He has nothing to lose if he kills again. I'm telling you, and by extension, your friends, to be careful."

"Cindy—"

"I'm not telling you to leave it to the police. I'd be wasting my time. All I'm saying is be careful."

"Thank you for caring."

"Hell yeah, I care. Who'd buy my coffee if you were dead?"

Chapter Thirty-Two

I was crossing Center Street—yes, jaywalking—heading home from the Dog when a blue pickup pulled in a parking spot in front of me. Andrew Delaney stepped out wearing a black T-shirt and light-gray shorts.

"Well if it isn't my bleeding-heart liberal friend," he said with a smile.

Hadn't I denied that characterization when we talked at Loggerhead's? Regardless, I said, "Morning, Andrew."

"I apologize, I forgot your name."

"Chris."

"Chris, got it. I'm off today, so it's a good morning."

"You live out near Harris Teeter, don't you? What brings you to Folly?"

His gaze narrowed. "This is still a free country even though it's getting less free every day. I can be here if I want to be."

Wrong question!

"Whoa, I was simply making conversation. Didn't mean to offend you."

"Sorry to snap. I'm frustrated about what's happening to my country. Seems like I have to be careful about what I say, where I go, who I hang with, what I do with my own free time." He shook his head. "Don't get me started." He hesitated, looked at me, then chuckled. "Suppose I already got started. Sorry."

I didn't know what to say so I nodded like I knew what he was talking about.

"I came over to wake up my friend to see what he's doing. He's always telling me I should go surfing with him. He's off today and says he has an extra board. I thought I'd give it a go." He smiled. "Can you picture this beer-bellied body on a surfboard?"

I started to laugh but held back. I didn't want to get snapped at again for saying or doing the wrong thing. I said, "Looks like a good day for surfing."

I expected him to say he had to go so I could continue home. Instead, he pointed at the Tides Hotel. "They still sell Starbucks in there?"

I nodded.

"It'd be silly to wake my friend this early. Let me buy you coffee. I promise not to spill it on you, may not even lecture you about anything."

I had exceeded my coffee limit for the day but figured there must be something on his mind besides caffeine.

"Sure."

We entered the Tides and followed the corridor to Roasted, the hotel's coffeeshop.

Andrew looked around. "I've only been in here once." He looked out the large windows facing the ocean. "Great view."

I agreed as he stepped to the counter and asked what I wanted.

I wanted an explanation of why we were here. Instead, I said black coffee. He ordered two cups, paid, handed me mine. We moved to a small, round table in the center of the room. Other than the clerk, we were the only people in Roasted.

Andrew slowly sipped his drink, set the cup on the table, then said, "How well did you know Clarence Taylor?"

"Not well. I met him once when I took a friend to Mosquito Beach so he could see where he spent time in the 1950s."

"Oh, when I saw you at that party, I figured you two were friends."

"Why'd you want to know if we were friends?"

"I think I told you outside the party I'd known Clarence a long time. As unlikely as it was, we were sort of friends."

Something had been bothering me about Andrew from when we'd talked at Loggerhead's. Do I risk asking about it and getting coffee thrown in my face? Why not?

"If I remember correctly, when we met for the first time at Loggerhead's outside bar—"

He smiled and interrupted, "When I shared my beer with you?"

I returned the smile. "Yes. I asked if you heard about a murder on Sol Legare. You were vague when you said all you heard was that it was an old black man."

His smile vanished. "So?"

"A little later you asked where I'd met Clarence. You went on to say you may've worked with him at a landscape company."

Andrew shook his head. "I was hoping your memory wasn't that good. Yeah, I sort of lied."

Sort of lied, I thought. "Why?"

"I'd known you for what, thirty seconds? I didn't know if you were a cop or a crusader set out to blame white guys for everything bad happening to, umm, black people." He smiled. "Besides, I'd had a few too many, if you know what I mean. Hell, it's no telling what I said."

"I understand."

"Yes, I knew Clarence. Like I told you before, I didn't want to, but I liked him. When I saw you at his party, I thought you might have an idea who killed him."

"Did you know Terrell Jefferson?"

Andrew closed his eyes and then shook his head. "He that other black guy killed after Clarence was shot?"

"Yes. He was a good friend of Clarence, had known him most of his life."

"I heard a rumor the same person shot both guys."

"Yes."

Andrew looked in his coffee cup then at the ocean. "There's also a story going around the cops think the Klan did it."

"Is that possible?"

He looked up from his cup and glared at me. "If it was, would I have been asking you if you had an idea who killed them?"

The word no was not anywhere in there. "Not really."

"Look, Chris. Let me be honest. I'm a member of the Klan. I'm not ashamed of it. The guys I know in it don't like black people. Hell, they don't like brown people, or red people. But, killing those who don't look like us ain't something I condone. Neither do my friends. I can't speak for every Klansman, but I can speak for me and my buddies. None of us killed Clarence or that Terrell guy. Period." He swirled the coffee around in the cup. "I asked if you had any idea who killed him or them for two reasons. First, the last thing the Klan needs is to be accused of killing two black men in Charleston County. Second, Clarence was a friend."

"I understand. While I hardly knew him, he seemed like a nice guy."

"Let me ask you something else. Do you know if there was someone at the party named Jamal?"

"Jamal Kingsly?"

"Don't know for sure. If Clarence ever said his last name, I don't remember."

"Jamal Kingsly was a friend of Clarence. He was at the party."

"Thought it may be the man Clarence talked about but wasn't sure. I only saw the guy Clarence called Jamal twice. That was a bunch of years ago. I remembered him being heavy with a white beard. When I saw someone who looked like that go in, that name popped in my head."

"What'd Clarence say about him?"

"Said he was always reading books. Not much else I remember except once Clarence was telling me about growing up on Sol Legare, about the pavilion out there, and the fights he had with some of the other people." He chuckled. "Think it was always over gals."

"Do you think Jamal killed Clarence?"

Andrew shrugged. "Why not? Someone did. It sure as hell wasn't me. Chris, I'm being honest. It wasn't any of my friends."

I started to respond, when Andrew looked at his watch, gulped the last of his coffee, then said, "Time to go wake my buddy. As he'd say, waves are awaitin'."

I wished him luck surfing. I remained seated as he headed out.

Chapter Thirty-Three

"Okay, you got me," Charles said when I answered the phone. "Your car's at your house, but you ain't. You're not at the Dog, not on the Pier, not walking aimlessly down Center Street. Where are you?"

"Good morning, Charles. Nice day, isn't it?"

"You forget the question?"

"Did you forget to start the conversation with something a normal person might begin with, something civil, maybe even polite?"

"No. Where are you?"

Once again, I wondered why I tried to introduce Mr. Fowler to civility.

"The Tides, sitting in Roasted enjoying a cup of coffee, some peace and quiet. That is, I was until the phone rang."

"On my way."

Peace and quiet was ending soon.

Three people who appeared to be staying at the hotel came in the coffeeshop, ordering drinks, were looking at

Tides T-shirts, and picking through the Folly Beach post cards, when Charles bounded through the door. He looked at the vacationers then motioned me to follow as he exited as quickly as he'd arrived.

He didn't say anything until we'd walked up the steps leading to the Folly Pier.

He pointed to the far end of the structure. "We need to have a meeting of the Charles Detective Agency in our Atlantic office."

Over the years, Charles had given his business several names, and so had those of us who knew him. I leaned toward calling it imaginary, while others preferred names ranging from delusional to hilarious. I didn't recall him ever mentioning the Atlantic office. I didn't question him about it more than I was going to ask about the University of Florida long-sleeve T-shirt he was wearing.

Apparently, the imaginary office was on the upper level of the Pier. He sat on a picnic table facing the shore, took off his Tilley, set it beside him, and propped his cane against the table. I waited for him to call the meeting to order.

The wait was short.

"I spent hours last night thinking while you were wasting your time sleeping. Know what I figured out?"

"What?"

"Nothing."

"Wow!" I said. "To think, I wasted all that valuable thinking time asleep."

He glanced at me. "You making fun of me?"

"Yep."

He sighed. "I deserved it."

"Yep. If our meeting has started, might I ask what you were thinking about while I was asleep?"

He sighed again, shook his head, and said, "Did you forget we're trying to solve three murders?"

"Since you mention it every time we talk, I don't see how I could forget. I also don't see how we know enough to figure out anything."

He smiled. "That's why we're meeting. Let's talk about what we know, not what we don't."

"Good plan, Mr. Detective. No doubt that'll be easier than talking about what we don't know. You first."

"Terrell and Clarence were killed by the same person."

"Killed by the same gun," I said. "Not necessarily the same person."

"Close enough. We know, okay, not know but suspect they were killed by the same dude who offed Elijah back when we were in kindergarten."

"I agree."

"Finally," he said. "Now we're getting somewhere. Whoever it is has to be old."

"And, a current or former resident of the Sol Legare area since everyone says it's a small close-knit community. Outsiders would've had a hard time knowing all three men."

Charles rubbed his chin. "I got that far in my last-night pondering."

He also had gotten that far when we last talked.

"That all you have?"

"Close, but not all. Motive becomes the big bugaboo in figuring it out. We think the reason the person killed Clarence and Terrell was because they were snooping around trying to catch the killer."

I added, "Don't forget, Terrell thought he knew."

"So, if true, it's probably someone he talked to. Someone who decided freedom meant more than getting locked up and decided to kill Terrell after he'd already bumped off Clarence. That means it's someone among the living since I doubt Terrell talked to the ghost of whoever killed Elijah."

"True."

"That's where my figuring ran into a dead end. Three dead ends." He tapped me on the leg. "Now I'll turn the agenda over to you. Who are your most-likely suspects?"

"Your good buddy and your future home builder Eugene Dillinger, Jamal Kingsly, Robert Graves, and then I would guess a handful or more other people who either live on Sol Legare or nearby who would be old enough to have killed Elijah."

"Don't forget Robert's wife."

"And Sandra. Plus, I wouldn't rule out Andrew Delaney."

"I'm not great at math, but if my cyphering is correct, he's not old enough to have killed Elijah."

"He isn't, but he could've shot the other two. Want to know why I was at Roasted when you called?"

"Hiding from me?"

I sighed then shared my conversation with Andrew.

"Let me see if I have this right. He told you neither he nor his friends killed anyone, so you think he did it. Why?"

"I doubt he did, but it struck me strange how much he went out of his way to deny it. Also, he brought Jamal into the conversation hinting he may have something to do with the murders."

"Okay, I'll put Andrew on the B list of suspects. Could he be right about Jamal?"

"We don't know any of them well enough to do more than guess. We know Jamal has a temper. Terrell even apologized to me after Jamal went on a mini-rant about Elijah when he said Elijah had been causing trouble for the black community by pushing hard for equal rights." I paused then remembered something else about Elijah. "The first time I met Jamal he said the skeleton was probably some old-timer who died whose family didn't have enough money to have a proper funeral. He also said the murder was ancient history. I had the impression he didn't want to talk about it."

"Didn't Jamal say he thought Elijah ran off?"

"Yes."

"When we were talking to him, he said he'd put money on the body being Elijah. That'd be a safe bet if he killed him."

"The more everyone learned about the skeleton the more they were convinced it was Elijah."

"Yet, the only proof, if you can call it that, is those fancy shoes."

"Shoes, age of skeleton, how Elijah had disappeared," I said.

"Think Jamal killed all of them?"

"I don't know. I wouldn't rule him out."

"I'd put him on the A list, high up on it. At the top, I still come back to slick Eugene. When we were at that house on East Ashley talking about the skeleton, he said it was probably some old bum, that it was ancient history."

"That's not much different than what Jamal said. Why do you put him above Jamal?"

Charles looked at the Tides, glanced at three surfers off to our left, before saying, "He's sleazy. You said he wasn't liked by the folks on Sol Legare. Back around Elijah's time, Eugene hired a lot of guys from out there and underpaid them. Didn't you say that the only reason they put up with him then and now was because he hired guys from there?"

"Yes, but—"

"Hold on," he interrupted, "there's more. Remember how quick he wanted to get away from us whenever I mentioned the murders?" He snapped his fingers. "Chris, remember when we were at Clarence's party, and I believe it was Jamal who asked Eugene if Elijah had worked for him back in the day?"

"Eugene said something like he had for a while."

"Yes, Eugene then said we weren't at the party to talk about Elijah then changed the subject. That's Eugene changing the subject every time Elijah's name popped up."

"When we were touring Eugene's construction project, he said he didn't know who the skeleton belonged to."

"Then changed the subject. That's all he said about Clarence but remember at the party he said Terrell came to his construction site to ask what Eugene knew about Elijah."

"Eugene said he told him he had no idea who killed either man. That's hardly a confession."

"I'll give you that," Charles said then looked toward the shore. "Remember what he also said?"

"No."

"Terrell was at the house for a half hour. How long do you think it takes to say you don't know who killed either man?"

"Not that long."

"I repeat," Charles said, "Eugene is suspect number one."

"What about Robert?"

"Other than being old enough, what reason would he have?"

"I don't think he did, but he's the only other person we know who's old enough to have killed Elijah."

Charles picked up his Tilley and waved it in my face. "Wrong, wannabe detective. Don't forget Sandra."

"Okay, what motive would Robert or Sandra have?"

"Didn't they say Elijah dated Sandra. Jealousy has to be right up there on the list of reasons to kill someone."

"She said he met her once at the pavilion where they danced. That was it. And, she said Robert wasn't in the picture until months later."

"Swept her off her feet. Did it enter your mind that Robert could've killed Elijah, so it'd be easier to sweep her?"

"That's a possibility," I said, more to get Charles to move along rather than it making sense since Robert and Sandra didn't know each other at the time.

"Glad you agree. He's on my list," Charles said as he scribbled an imaginary word in the bench with an imaginary pencil. "He's sharing equal billing with Sandra."

"What's her motive?"

"Heck, who knows. Maybe Elijah wasn't satisfied with one night of dancing. She thought one night was enough, so when he kept pursuing her, she ended his courtin' with a bullet."

"Going back to your golf ball near the cart path story, the only suspects we've talked about are people we've met. There could be others." I kept coming back to what Terrell had said about Charles and I being outsiders.

"Think it's time for you to call your favorite police chief and tell her what we know. She'll pick out the best parts and share them with Detective Callahan. He can put it all together. *Voila.* We've helped the cops catch another killer." He clapped then pointed to the pocket holding my phone. "Meeting adjourned."

The meeting may've adjourned, but that didn't stop Charles from insisting I call Cindy. That was the only thing I could do to get Charles off my back, so I picked up the phone, punched in her number.

I was rewarded with voicemail. Since I didn't know what I could tell her that'd be helpful, I breathed a sigh of relief and left a message for her to call when she got a spare minute. Charles huffed as if Cindy intentionally ignored my call. Her phone had caller ID, so he could've been right, but I didn't share that thought.

He stared at the phone, then turned to me. "How long do you think it'll be before she calls?"

"Charles, I don't—"

"I know, I know," he interrupted. "You don't know and don't want to sit here waiting until she calls. Call me after you talk to her."

I promised I would. Our after-meeting discussion ended when he headed off the Pier, his cane tapping on the wooden surface with each step.

Chapter Thirty-Four

Spare minutes were few and far between for Folly's Director of Public Safety, so I wasn't surprised she hadn't returned my call. The only calls I received between leaving the message and nine-thirty that night were two from Charles asking if the Chief had responded. His calls weren't as irritating as robo-calls telling me that the IRS was going to knock down my front door in the next two hours if I didn't call immediately, but they weren't far off.

The phone rang at ten o'clock and to my surprise it wasn't Charles. It also wasn't Cindy.

"Chris, this is Al. I hope I didn't call too late."

I told him he hadn't and started to ask if he was okay until I remembered how he'd said I didn't have to ask each time he called.

"I've been giving a lot of thought to what's happening on Mosquito. Do you think you could spare a few minutes for this old man to talk about it?"

"Of course. What's on your mind?"

"Chris, umm, I hate to ask, but could we talk in person? I ain't my best when talking on the phone."

I chuckled. "Me either. Want me to come to the bar tomorrow?"

"Tomorrow's a light day. None of the suppliers are scheduled to stop by. I figure Bob can handle whatever happens, so I told him I was taking the day off."

"What'd he say?"

Al laughed. "He said he wasn't giving me a paid day off. I told him he wasn't paying me when I was there. He grumbled about me starting a damned greeters union, then added before he knew it, I'd be demanding a salary for doing nothing but sitting by the door."

"I'll meet you at your house unless you're afraid you may get fired from your nonpaying job."

"Sounds like a plan, my friend, yes it does."

We agreed on a time then I headed to bed without hearing from the Chief, another call from Charles, or the IRS.

———

After a quick stop at Bert's for coffee and a Danish, I was on my way to Al's when Cindy called.

"Please tell me you called to take Larry and me to Halls Chophouse for a steak dinner."

Halls was one of Charleston's finer restaurants.

"Sorry, Cindy, reservations were last night. You didn't call back, so I cancelled."

"I didn't get to be Folly's head police honchette by believing all the crap some of our fine citizens or vacationers hurl at me. Why'd you call?"

I spent the next ten minutes telling her what Charles and

I'd talked about. She mostly listened, listened between overblown sighs, a couple of giggles, a handful of profanities. In the middle of one of her profanity-laced tirades, I missed the turn to Al's house and had to go around the block to get back on track.

Cindy never got off track. She ended the call with a simple question. "In all those words did you say anything that could help the police, you know, the people trained to investigate murders, learn who killed any or all of the men?"

I admitted if there was anything, I didn't know what.

Cindy ended the call; I ended my wayward drive. The parking space in front of the house where I'd parked the last two times wasn't available, so I drove around the corner before finding a space.

Spoiled Rotten announced my arrival. The Rottweiler's barks weren't as hostile as they'd been during my first visit, although I wasn't ready to risk life or limb by going over to pet him.

I knocked three times before Al opened the door. He was barefoot, wearing navy blue pajama bottoms, and a thin, white tank-top undershirt.

He stepped on the porch, said hi to his neighbor's dog, waved me in, then said, "From the sound of his barks, Spoiled Rotten likes you."

"I'm glad."

"Up for coffee?" Al said, then shuffled to the back of the house before I answered.

I followed. The kitchen was spotless, much neater than the rooms we passed along the way. A chrome and black Hamilton Beach coffeemaker and two white mugs were the only things on the counter. He'd planned for my visit. Al poured me a cup, refilled his, before taking a seat on the opposite side of the small table.

"Hope you don't mind my clothes. You caught me in my lounging duds. You don't know how good it feels for this old man not to have to get dressed on my day off."

I told him I did know as he took a sip and stared in his mug.

"I appreciate you coming over, I truly do. I know it's out of your way."

"Glad to come."

"Nobody mentioned it at the party, so I was wondering if there was a funeral for Terrell."

"Sorry, I thought I told you. He told his neighbor when he died, he wanted to be cremated with no funeral service like his friend Clarence. He said he was going to put it in his will, but, as you know, he was killed long before his time. He didn't have a will. The neighbor told the police and the coroner what Terrell wanted. He didn't have any known next-of-kin, so they honored it."

"I've got it in my will I want a funeral, want a chance for everyone who knew me to take a look in my coffin, see me smilin'." He laughed. "Maybe not Bob, but everyone else."

He was kidding about Bob.

He took another sip then turned serious. "That wasn't the reason I asked you over. I suppose you're wondering why."

I smiled. "It crossed my mind."

"Mr. Chris, I don't have many years left to look forward to, so I spend most of my idle time looking back." He chuckled. "I'm not talking about looking back at yesterday or the day before when Bob's fighting with his customers, days where I'm having to listen to Conway Twitty on Bob's jukebox. I'm talking back to the days when I was full of energy, enthusiasm, learning my way around the world. I've told you before some of my best memories are of the times I was out on Mosquito, yes they were."

I nodded, again.

"Anyway, a lot of those memories came back to me when I thought about you and me talking to Clarence when we were out there looking to where the old pavilion used to be. More memories flooded back at Clarence's party."

"You appeared to have a good time."

"My hearing ain't as good as it once was. There were a lot of folks out back making noise." He smiled. "That ain't counting Aretha Franklin and Bob Marley booming over the speakers. I didn't hear everything said, no I didn't."

"I didn't either."

Al took another sip, set his mug on the table, gazed in it, then looked at me. "Chris, before I start telling you something, remember I'm recalling something that happened sixty-five years ago. My memory could be playing tricks. And, heaven forbid, I couldn't raise my right hand and swear on a Bible what I'm saying is the truth, the whole truth, nothing but the truth. No, I couldn't."

"It was a long time ago, so I understand."

"At Clarence's party, Sandra was talking to Jamal. They were sitting at the other end of the table, so I couldn't hear what they were saying. Truth be told, I wasn't trying to listen because I knew it was too loud to hear them. I was sitting there staring at Eugene and for a moment I drifted back to 1953, yes I did." He closed his eyes and slowly nodded. "One Saturday night, a scorcher as I recall, I was in the pavilion talking to Elijah. See it clear as day. Then....Chris, forgive this old man, here's where it gets fuzzy. Elijah looked up the road, said something about having to talk to a man. He told me to wait in the pavilion. He walked in the direction of a man leaning against a car, an old black Dodge, as I recall." Al stopped and looked at my mug. "Let me get you more coffee."

I started to say I was fine, when he stood, grabbed my mug, and headed to the coffeemaker.

"Want a cookie? I've got Oreos."

"No thanks."

I didn't know where the story was going, but Al was in no hurry to get there.

"While I wouldn't swear on a Bible about it, I'd almost swear to you that Elijah went to talk to Eugene."

"That was decades ago. What makes you think it was Eugene?"

He shook his head. "First, the man was white. You've heard me say there weren't many whites on Mosquito in those days. My eyesight was better then, so I know the man was thin and stood straight as a flagpole. I noticed the same thing about Eugene the other night."

"Did you get a clear look at his face?"

"Not clear. It was dark, but I got a quick look when a car drove by. Headlights hit the man and Elijah."

"Did Elijah come back to the pavilion after talking to the man?"

"Before he left to talk to the man, he was in a great mood. We'd had a few beers. I remember him laughing, having a gay old time. When he came back, he brought a dark cloud with him."

"Did you ask about it?"

"I don't know for certain, but I can't imagine not being

curious and asking him, especially since his mood shifted so much."

"Did he seem angry?"

Al shook his head. "Angry, no. Chris, my gut said he was scared."

"Al, do you think Eugene killed Elijah?"

"I only saw Elijah one more time after that. Must've been the next Saturday. I can't tell you anything he said but can tell you one thing. He wasn't the same Elijah I knew before." He shook his head again. "Do I think Eugene killed my friend? Don't know if he did or didn't. I'll tell you what I do know. My friend was spooked by something Eugene said, he sure was."

"Do you remember anything Elijah said before that night about Eugene? Did he ever mention wanting to work on one of Eugene's construction crews, or anything about other people he knew working for Eugene?"

Al looked back down in his mug then closed his eyes like he was trying to relive the past.

"Don't recall him saying anything about Eugene, but he often spoke about white men taking advantage of Negroes. That was one thing that got him pissed more than anything else he talked about."

"Did he talk about specific, umm, white men?"

"That was a long time ago. If he did, I don't recall. Sorry."

"No reason to be sorry, Al. I'm just trying to figure it out."

He smiled. "Good luck with that."

"Would you mind if I told Detective Callahan what you remembered?"

"Don't guess it'd hurt, although I'd hate to get Eugene in trouble if my memory is wrong." He shook his head. "A lot's gone on in this old head since way back then. No telling how far off I could be."

"If Eugene is innocent, he'll be okay."

"Mr. Chris, I reckon I didn't ask you over for you to do nothing. Do what you think is best."

Chapter Thirty-Five

I thought about calling Detective Callahan when I got home but decided to get it out of the way. I pulled over and dialed his number before leaving Charleston. He answered on the second ring and I told him who I was.

"How may I be of assistance, Mr. Landrum?" he said in a tone the warmth of an iceberg.

I shared what Al told me about thinking he saw Elijah with Eugene; how he felt that his friend was afraid of the builder.

Callahan paused when I finished. I wondered if he was still on the phone.

Finally, he said, "Mr. Landrum, I hope you appreciate how patient I've been with your interference, your theories over the years. Chief LaMond thinks highly of you, and you've occasionally garnered information before we were able to."

"Chief LaMond is a good friend. She's told me on more than one occasion you're an excellent detective."

"Neither here nor there. I appreciate you thinking what

Mr., umm, Washington told you was important. My problem is he's talking about something that occurred before I was born. Let me ask you, do you think you could identify someone you saw two years ago? How about one year?"

"It depends, I suppose, on how well I knew the person."

"Okay, I'll give you that. But what about someone you saw thirty, forty, fifty or more years ago? How well did Mr. Washington know this Eugene Dillinger?"

"Detective, I get your point. Al had only met Eugene a time or two."

"He saw someone across a dark parking lot, and thinks he remembers who it was? Give me a break. It's not possible."

"You don't know Al like I do. He has an excellent memory. He wouldn't have said anything unless he was certain. Besides, the person he remembers seeing was white, a rare sight on Mosquito Beach in those days."

"Let's assume for sake of argument your friend is right, that he saw Eugene Dillinger talking to Elijah Duncan. What's there to say he killed him?"

"Nothing from that brief encounter."

"Correct. We're now faced with no evidence from all those years ago. There wasn't even a missing-person report. There was no reason for the police to look for Elijah. As I suspect you know, I've talked to several Sol Legare residents old enough to remember Mr. Duncan. When he disappeared the thoughts on what happened to him ranged from him running off with a preacher's daughter, him just running off, to him being killed by the Klan. Nothing specific, little the police at the time could've followed up on."

"But—"

"Let me continue, Mr. Landrum. Considering all that, we're still not certain the remains are Mr. Duncan. The time of death is consistent with his disappearance, the bones are of a black male approximately Mr. Duncan's age. From everyone I talked to who was around Sol Legare in 1953, Mr. Duncan wore shoes like those found with the remains. I don't think anyone doubts that the skeleton belongs to Mr. Duncan, but no proof can and probably ever will be found."

"It appears the recent murders of Clarence Taylor and Terrell Jefferson are related to Mr. Duncan's murder. Wouldn't you agree?"

"It makes sense, but again, other than both men taking a strong interest in learning who killed Mr. Duncan, there's nothing tying them together."

"My understanding is they were doing more than taking, as you say, a strong interest. They were talking to everyone who was around in those days, and don't forget, the voice-mail Terrell left me saying he knew who killed both Clarence and Elijah."

"Mr. Landrum, did you forget your friend Chief LaMond said I'm a good detective? The murders of Terrell Jefferson and Clarence Taylor are mine to solve. They're not the only homicides on my plate, but they're at the top. I appreciate you sharing what you consider important information about the death of Elijah Duncan. Now let me share something that's important. The deaths are a matter for the police. Step aside, let us do our job. Do you understand?"

I told him I understood. I didn't tell him I'd step aside.

———

I started the next morning with a pack of mini-donuts, coffee from Bert's, and a nagging feeling I'd let Al down. I'd shared his recollections with Detective Callahan yet knew Al wasn't certain he'd seen his friend talking to Eugene. Even if Al was one hundred percent correct when he saw Elijah talking to someone, there was no proof Eugene killed Al's friend. Unless someone confessed to murdering Elijah Duncan, it'd remain unsolved. Terrell thought he knew who killed both Elijah and Clarence. Now he's dead.

That got me wondering what Terrell could've possibly learned to lead him to the conclusion he knew the identity of the killer. He wasn't alive in the 1950s, so it couldn't have been anything he had direct knowledge of. He'd heard stories about Elijah from his grandfather but when he talked to me, he'd never said anything about his grandfather knowing what'd happened. I assumed he'd learned something from one or more of the old-timers he'd talked with.

Even if Terrell was right, how could that help? As he hadn't hesitated pointing out, I was an outsider to the Sol Legare community. What excuse would I have for nosing around?

The phone interrupted as I was working hard figuring out nothing. I didn't recognize the number.

"Is this Chris Landrum," said a vaguely familiar voice.

I said it was.

"This is Jamal Kingsly from over on Sol Legare. Did I catch you at a bad time?"

"Hi, Jamal. No, it's fine."

"You gave me your number when you were at Clarence's party. I hope it's okay to call."

"Sure."

"Good. I'm calling to let you know a few of us were talking last night about the party we had for Clarence and wanted to do the same for Terrell. Him and Clarence were good friends, so we were feeling bad about having a big

shindig for Clarence but nothing for Terrell. The last time I
talked to Terrell, he said some nice things about you and your
friends Charles and, umm, Vernon, so we wanted to invite all
of you. I only had your number."

"His name's Virgil. I think it's a kind gesture. When?"

"Tonight. Sorry about the late notice. We only decided last
night. If you think you can be here, could you ask the other
guys?"

I told him I'd love to be there and would ask the others.
He told me what time, then again apologized for the late
notice.

My first call was to Charles, who took approximately a
nanosecond to say he'd go. Virgil took a little longer.

"Hey, Chris. Guess where I am?"

And I thought I only had to play this game with Charles.

"Zurich, Switzerland."

"You been drinking?"

"No. Where are you?"

"On the Pier watching—wow! There goes two. Almost
jumped plum out of the water."

I sighed. "Dolphins?"

"No, mermaids." He laughed. "Just kidding. Been out
here an hour watching a flock, herd, or whatever you call a
bunch of dolphins horsing around, no, dolphining around
close to the Pier. Boy, are they cool."

"A pod."

Charles would be proud of me for knowing that bit of
trivia.

"Huh?"

"A group of dolphins is called a pod."

"Silly name. Anyway, you should be here. They're
fantastic."

"I was talking to Jamal from over on Sol Legare. He told me about a party tonight for Terrell and wanted to see if you, Charles, and I wanted to attend."

"Tonight? That's almost here. I'll have to check my social calendar. Also need to see how much longer this pod—still think it's a silly name—will be swimming around." He hesitated then continued, "Whoops, where'd they go? Umm, guess I'm available. What time?"

I told him and he said he'd see me then, before saying he was walking to the other side of the structure to see if the pod was over there. I didn't wait for an update.

Jamal hadn't mentioned Al, but I'd invite him anyway. I wasn't as lucky with Al. He said he'd love to go, but this was one of the bar's busiest nights. He'd told Bob he'd work. He asked me to let him know how the party goes and told me to say hi to his new friends.

I hung up and stared at the phone. "Thank you, Jamal." I now had a reason to be nosing around.

Chapter Thirty-Six

On the way to Island Breeze, I told Charles and Virgil what Al had said about possibly seeing Elijah talking to Eugene.

"Holy, moly," Virgil said from the back seat. "Does Al have a photographic memory?"

Charles said, "Eidetic imagery."

Virgil leaned between the front seats. "Huh?"

"The name for photographic memory is eidetic imagery," said the walking, talking trivia collector.

"Porpoise pods, eidetic whatever. Do you guys sit around reading the encyclopedia?"

Charles turned to Virgil. "Chris doesn't read anything deeper than road signs. I'll admit to reading most of the encyclopedia. Skipped the x words. Virgil, did you know the word mosquito in Spanish means little fly?"

"The encyclopedia translates Spanish?"

"Nope. Aquilino at Snapper Jacks told me. Since we're headed to Mosquito Beach, thought it'd be a good nugget to know."

In a transition that made sense to Virgil, he said, "So, did Al really remember something he saw on a dark night a million years ago?"

I said, "Unlikely, although knowing Al, I wouldn't rule it out."

Virgil said, "If Eugene is there, are you going to ask about it?"

"Not unless it makes sense in the conversation," I said.

Charles's silence told me he wasn't saying no.

The parking areas around the restaurant weren't nearly as full as they'd been during Clarence's party. His event was on a Saturday which could've made some of the difference. With the temperature in the upper eighties, I hoped those gathered for Terrell were inside rather than on the back patio.

We were in luck. In a large room off to the left, Jamal was carrying drinks to two tables that'd been pulled together. The man we'd been talking about possibly being seen with Elijah was at the table. Sandra and Robert Graves were watching a man I didn't know play pinballs on one of the two machines in the other corner. Jamal set the drinks on the table and told Sandra and Robert where they were.

Eugene saw us. "Welcome. Jamal said he invited you. We hoped you'd come."

I think he'd have a different opinion if he knew one of my reasons for being there.

Sandra and Robert returned to the table then grabbed their beers like they thought someone might take them. Jamal was breathing heavily as he shook our hands. He offered to go to the bar to get us drinks. I told him to sit while I went. Charles was already talking to the Sandra and Robert, so Virgil accompanied me.

The lady who'd been behind the bar during my previous

visits got us a beer and two white wines. We headed back to the table where there were four vacant chairs so I wondered who else might be joining us.

Jamal said, "Charles was telling us Al couldn't make it. He seems like such a nice man. Sorry he's missing it."

"He is, too," I said.

"I've invited three or four others, but it's iffy if they'll show. Having this on a weeknight probably wasn't a good idea. Youngsters have jobs, you know."

Coming from Jamal, that probably meant guys under seventy.

Eugene said, "Some of us older guys also have to work."

"The rich get richer," Jamal said with a faux smile.

If it bothered Eugene, it didn't show. He turned to Charles, "Talked to your financial advisor yet? The lot's going to go quick. I've already shown it to three couples."

"Got an appointment next week," Charles said. "I'll let you know when I learn something."

Virgil, the man who knew Terrell less than anyone at the table, ignored their conversation, lifted his wine glass, and said, "I'm sure Terrell will know it's the thought that counts. Let's toast to our friend. I didn't know him well but could see he was a fine gentleman with a big heart."

Each of the four people who knew Terrell longer than we three newcomers combined, graciously lifted their bottles to toast. Sandra thanked Jamal for pulling the event together then agreed with Virgil that Terrell would be pleased.

The sounds of Aretha Franklin singing "Spanish Harlem" was playing, but not as loud as it had been on my previous visits. Tonight, I could hear everyone at the table.

"Anything new on what happened to Terrell?" Charles said, not wasting time digging for answers.

"If you mean, has anybody been arrested, not that I know about," Jamal said.

Charles said, "I wonder if the police have suspects."

Sandra took a sip, pointed her bottle at Jamal then said, "I doubt anyone over here shot him. Terrell had a temper and worked on Folly. It's no telling who he may've pissed off."

Robert put his arm around Sandra and said, "That police detective, what's his name?"

"Callahan," Sandra said.

"Yeah, Callahan came to the house to talk about Terrell, but mostly he was interested in what we remembered about Elijah Duncan." He smiled. "Think it was because we're old, old enough to have known Elijah."

Jamal said, "He talked to me, too. Don't know why he cared about something from the '50s when poor Clarence, now Terrell have been murdered, all within a mile of this here spot." He waved his arm around the room.

Eugene added, "He came to my house. We had a pleasant talk, but he didn't tell me anything I didn't already know."

I didn't remind him the detective wasn't there to tell him anything, but the other way around.

Virgil leaned closer to the table. "He probably thinks the same person killed all three."

Jamal looked at Sandra who glanced at Robert who said, "Can't imagine how a killing that many years ago could've been made by the same person."

"Me either," Jamal said.

Sandra added, "No way."

Eugene took another sip and didn't say anything.

"How well did you all know Elijah?" Virgil asked.

Each shared memories and opinions which could be summed up with they didn't know him well. They agreed he was a troublemaker, a spiffy dresser, and disappeared. Sandra repeated the part about him meeting her once at the pavilion to share a few dances. They didn't say anything we didn't know.

Charles turned to me, "Weren't you saying Al told you he thinks he remembers Elijah talking to," Charles turned to Eugene, "Gosh, I guess it was you Eugene."

They don't call Charles subtle for nothing.

I smiled. "That's right. Al was talking about how much fun he had out here after he got out of the service. Said those were some of the best years of his life. Anyway, he thought he remembered a night he was talking to Elijah when his friend saw someone in the parking area he wanted to talk to. He thought it was you, Eugene."

Eugene looked around the table then focused on me. "If Al remembers something like that, he's got a better memory than me. Crap, I can't remember who I talked to last week, much less, what, sixty-something years ago."

I smiled. "He wasn't certain either, but I've known Al a long time. I've never known him to be wrong, at least not wrong about something important."

Eugene returned my smile. "I don't remember, but it could've happened. Elijah was out here nearly every time I ventured over. I wasn't here often, but I'm sure we talked."

"That makes sense," I said.

Thankfully, Charles didn't mention what I'd said about Al thinking Elijah was scared after talking to Eugene.

"Sandra," Virgil said, "you think it was someone from Folly who shot Terrell. That makes sense. Guys, any of you have other ideas who might've done it?"

Robert said, "I agree with Sandra."

Sandra chuckled. "Wise man."

"I know what side my bread's buttered on."

Virgil said, "Other than being a wise man, and I agree with that, why do you think it's someone from Folly?"

"I don't know people on Folly like I know guys around here," Robert said, "I can't speak about them getting along with Terrell. I know he was liked by everyone here. Since the police say the same gun shot Clarence and Terrell, it couldn't have been anyone I know. Clarence wasn't only liked, he was loved by everyone."

Charles, Virgil, please don't say, All but one.

"I agree with Sandra and Robert," Jamal said. "I don't know about it being someone from Folly. It could be. I don't know many folks there. All I'm certain of, it wasn't anyone here."

"Enough murder talk," Robert said. "Next round is on me while we talk about the good stuff we know about our friend Terrell."

No one argued, especially about Robert buying the next round.

One more round later, this one paid by Eugene, you would've thought from listening to Robert, Sandra, Eugene, and Jamal that Clarence and Terrell were candidates for sainthood. Stories of acts of kindness from the two dominated the conversation. I didn't know either man nearly as well as they did but couldn't find reason to argue with their conclusions. I also couldn't find any hints one of them may've been responsible for either death. I liked the group. On one level I was relieved no one at the table struck me as a murderer. On the other hand, that left me with no clue who may've ended the two, probably three lives.

After several beers, the conversation took a turn that I would've preferred to avoid. Virgil told the locals that

Charles and I, along with his assistance, had helped the police catch the person responsible for the plane crash that took two lives. Jamal said he remembered the crash but hadn't kept up with stories about what happened. Eugene said he'd heard more than Jamal remembered; primarily because he lived on Folly he also casually knew the survivors. He asked how we knew so much about the crash to help the police. Charles gave an abbreviated—abbreviated for Charles—version of what'd happened. Virgil chimed in with his contribution that took a murderer off the street. Robert and Sandra appeared more interested in their drinks and music from the sound system. I'd hoped Jamal and Eugene followed their lead.

The party broke up when Jamal announced his hemorrhoids were acting up from sitting too long. That was clearly a party-ending revelation. We took the hint. Eugene, Jamal, and Robert settled their checks, and Jamal thanked us for coming.

Aretha Franklin escorted us out of the restaurant with her rendition of "Natural Woman."

Chapter Thirty-Seven

During my near seven decades on earth I've received thousands of telephone calls. Of those calls, I couldn't recall a single one coming at six a.m. bringing good news. That's why when my phone jarred me awake, I took a deep breath and feared the worst before answering.

The name Tanesa Washington appeared on the screen. I'd met Al's daughter several times over the years, then when Al had experienced serious health problems, we had daily contact.

"Chris, this is Tanesa. Did I wake you?"

I lied. "No."

"Good. Dad said you're an early bird. He made me wait to call."

Al didn't want me to ask how he was every time he called, but he wasn't calling.

"Is he okay?"

"He will be. Around three this morning, his neighbor's dog awakened her when it wouldn't stop barking and scratching at the window. The neighbor saw smoke coming from Dad's second-floor window. She called 911 before running next door and pounding on his door. It took Dad a long time to answer. She thought he was dead." Tanesa sighed. "He finally answered. Dad's got more lives than a cat."

"You sure he's okay?"

"The neighbor rushed him to the hospital before the fire trucks arrived. He told them in the ER he was fine, that his daughter worked there. I wasn't on-duty, but the nurse knows me and called. Dad wasn't about to spend another minute at the hospital, so I rushed over to bring him to my condo. I gave him something to help him sleep. He's shook, his asthma is acting up, but he's stable." She chuckled. "Before he fell asleep, he wanted me to call you. I asked why. He said, and this is dad for you, he wanted to know about the party you went to last night."

"Do you want me to come over?"

"He'd like that."

"When would be a good time?"

"He's never slept more than a few hours a night in his life, so I suspect he'll be awake by noon. I have to be at work at one, so why don't you stop by around twelve-thirty. I'll let you in?"

I said I'd be there then asked how much fire damage there was.

"There's a firehouse fewer than five blocks from his house, so they got there quickly. Most of the fire damage was limited to the second floor, but there's a lot of water downstairs."

"They know what caused it?"

"If they do, they didn't tell me. I was only there for a minute before picking him up at the hospital. I heard one of the firefighters say they needed to call an arson investigator. I don't know if that's standard procedure or if they suspected something."

Something told me it wasn't standard procedure, but I didn't tell Tanesa.

————

I drove by Al's house on the way to Tanesa's condo. A red Ford Explorer with a Charleston Fire Department Fire Marshall logo on the door was parked in the drive. From a previous encounter with the Fire Marshall Division, I knew it investigated suspicious fires, which reinforced my hunch it wasn't accidental. The fire had burned through part of the roof. Two of the upstairs window frames were flame blackened. It could've been worse, much worse.

Tanesa lives in an up-scale condo development overlooking the Ashley River and adjacent to the Bristol Marina. The building is less than a mile from Al's house and within walking distance to her hospital. The contrast between Al's wood-frame, ninety-year-old house and Tanesa's three-story, brick and glass modern condo building was night and day. I rode to the third floor in the quietest elevator I'd ever been in.

Tanesa greeted me with a smile and a hug. Her bloodshot eyes told me she'd had little sleep, something she was used to considering her erratic hours as an emergency room doctor.

"Thanks for coming. Dad already asked me three times since he got up when you were getting here."

I whispered, "How's he doing?"

"I hear you talking about me in there," came a voice from my left.

Tanesa laughed. "That answer your question? He's in the kitchen. Want coffee?"

I told her that sounded good then followed her through the immaculate condo. The dark, hardwood floors in the entry and living room opened to the white kitchen floor, most likely some Italian, aka expensive, tile.

Al was seated at a small, round table and gripping a mug. He wore blue pajamas. He smiled when he saw me, but not nearly as big as Tanesa's smile when she'd greeted me. Tanesa poured me a cup as I sat. She said she had to get dressed for work and left us to talk. I glanced at the granite countertops and stainless-steel appliances mentally contrasting them to Al's kitchen.

"How do you feel?"

"Chris, know what I'm looking forward to when I'm stretched out there in my coffin?"

I couldn't imagine looking forward to anything. "What?"

He chuckled. "You won't walk in, look at my wax-looking face, and say, 'How do you feel?'"

I smiled. "You're not in a coffin yet, so how do you feel?"

He shook his head. "And Tanesa invited you over. That gal's going to be the death of me yet." He put a hand in front of my face. "Okay, I'm tired, sore all over from having to move so fast getting out of the house. I'm pissed. Chris, I've lived in that house since the beginning of time. It's paid for. I can't imagine living anywhere else. Now it's … I don't know how it is."

"I drove by it on the way over. It looks like the damage was contained on the second floor. I think it can be repaired."

"Whew," he said. "Tanesa said it didn't look too bad, but I figured she was soft-pedaling it so I wouldn't worry. I figured with it being old and all wood, it'd be burnt to the ground."

"It'll be as good as new."

"It hasn't been as good as new since Indians roamed the neighborhood, but it's my house, my home. Tanesa said I can stay here as long as I want." He hesitated then looked at the door to the living room before lowering his voice. "She has it in her mind for me to live here the rest of my days. Chris, it ain't going to happen. I want, no, need to get back to my place as soon as I can."

"I understand. What happened?"

"Wish I knew. I went to bed like I always do around midnight. Was slow to go to sleep, but finally did. Next thing I remember was a horrible pounding on the front door. I opened my eyes, thought I smelled smoke. Figured I was dreaming. The pounding continued. I realized the smoke was real. It took me a long time to get moving, gets longer each day, I'm afraid. I managed to get to the door to see my next-door neighbor standing there in a bathrobe, pink curlers in her hair. That was a sight to behold, I tell you." He smiled, shook his head, then took a sip of coffee. "Chris, what's it like outside?"

"Nice, cooler than it's been. Why?"

He pointed to a door leading to the balcony. "Let's go out there. Since I wasn't sure I'd live to see today, I'd like to enjoy it."

He struggled getting out of the chair. I wanted to help, but knew he needed to do it on his own. He refilled his mug, slowly walked to a large glass-topped table on the patio and lowered himself in one of the four chairs around the table. He was out of breath after the short walk. I took the chair closest to him.

The view was fantastic. The marina was directly in front

of us and a large sailboat was maneuvering away from the dock.

"Your neighbor was at the door, then what?"

He looked at the sailboat, bit his lower lip, and said, "She told me what I finally figured out. The house was on fire. Seems Spoiled Rotten was barking up a storm. He woke her up. She looked out, saw smoke, then skedaddled over to save this old man. I've got to get to the store to buy the biggest bone they have for Spoiled Rotten. If it wasn't for him, you'd be looking in my coffin, not asking how I was, yes you would." He pointed his mug at me. "Tell you one more thing, Chris. If my bed hadn't been moved to the living room, I'd be in that coffin even if my neighbor knocked on the door. Not only did moving the bed downstairs save my knees and heart, it saved my life."

"Any idea what started the fire?"

"Chris, that's all I've been thinking about since I got here." He smiled. "Except when I was sleeping. That danged daughter of mine drugged me."

"You needed your sleep."

"Same thing she said. Now to what you asked. Didn't storm overnight so it wasn't lightning. Nothing electric is plugged in upstairs. I wasn't burning any candles upstairs so a mouse couldn't have knocked a candle over. Didn't even have a lantern up there so old Mrs. O'Leary's cow couldn't have kicked it."

His sense of humor was intact, thank goodness. "You don't know what could've started it."

He slowly shook his head.

I told him about the Fire Marshall's SUV at his house.

He tilted his head. "You don't think somebody did it on purpose, do you?"

"Don't know."

His hand trembled as he gripped the mug. "Suppose they'll figure out what happened." He glanced again at the sailboat then turned to me. "Didn't Tanesa tell you I wanted to hear about last night's party, not talk about the fire?"

I nodded.

"So, let's hear it."

Before I started, Tanesa came out, patted Al's arm, said she had to head to work, and asked if he needed anything before she left.

"Yes, my house fixed. A ride home."

"Afraid I can't do that, but I called your insurance agent. He's going to send an adjuster. He'll call me so I can meet him there."

Al said, "You don't need to meet him. I can do that, yes I can."

Tanesa patted his arm again. "Maybe so, but you're not going to. Doctor's orders."

He frowned at his daughter, the doctor. "More like prison guard orders."

She kissed the top of his head, leaned down, hugged me, before heading out.

"Al, you've raised a fantastic woman."

He beamed.

I told him everything I remembered about the party. He listened without moving. I couldn't tell if it was because he was exhausted or paying rapt attention to my fascinating description of events. He asked twice if I'd shared his condolences, how much he'd wanted to be there.

"Chris, I was wondering if you told Eugene I recalled seeing him talking to Elijah?"

"Yes. He said he didn't remember, but it could've been

him. They knew each other plus he'd been at the pavilion several times."

"Did you tell him Elijah was scared after talking to him?"

I smiled. "I left that part out."

"Did you tell him I wasn't certain it was him Elijah was talking to?"

"I think so."

"Good. It was a long time ago." He closed his eyes, then said, "Chris, I don't want to be antisocial, but think everything's getting to me. Maybe a nap would do me good."

"Anything I can do for you before I leave?"

"No. My prison guard fixed me a salad, put it in the frig for when I get hungry." He laughed. "Think I would've preferred normal prison food like bread and water instead of salad. Her heart's in the right place."

"Sure there's nothing I can do?"

"There's one other thing, it's a big one. Could you stop by the bar and tell Bob what happened? He expects me to be there later this afternoon. Don't think I'm up to it."

"Consider it done."

Chapter Thirty-Eight

"The damn dog did what?" Bob yelled.

Roy Acuff's "Wabash Cannonball" blared in the background.

"Flames coming out his roof!" Bob screamed.

The country legend managed to get in a few more words of his song.

"He's running around in his pajamas," Bob moaned.

Roy finished his classic. Silence came from the jukebox.

"Poor, poor old man," Bob broke the silence as he plopped his ample behind at his table. He put his hands over his face.

All I'd managed to say was Al's house had a fire in the middle of the night, his neighbor's dog alerted the neighbor who saw smoke and called 911, that Al was okay and staying at Tanesa's condo. Okay, I must've mentioned pajamas, but I didn't recall saying it. Fortunately, Al's was empty except for Bob and his cook, Lawrence, when I entered and attempted to tell the owner what'd happened.

"Mr. Chris, can I get you something to eat or drink?" Lawrence asked as I sat across from the bar's owner.

"Some water, if that's okay."

I knew Bob was shook because he didn't rant and rave about me not buying anything. That was a first, I might add.

Lawrence set a bottle of water in front of me then asked if I was okay, something that must've slipped Bob's mind. I said I was, Bob asked me to start from the beginning, not to leave anything out.

Johnny Cash's unmistakable bass-baritone voice shared "Love is a burning thing, and it makes a fiery ring." I held my breath waiting for Bob to react to the words from "Ring of Fire" with another rant.

Instead of an outburst, he said, "Tell me everything. I mean everything."

I began with Tanesa's call. The only time Bob interrupted was when I told him about the dog alerting the neighbor.

"The damned dog's named Spoiled Rotten?"

I told him that's what Al called it, it wasn't its real name. That satisfied him for the moment.

"Any idea what caused it?"

"No, when I passed it on the way to Tanesa's place, there was a Charleston Fire Department Fire Marshall vehicle in the drive. They'll determine cause."

Bob rubbed his chin. "I suppose it could've been anything. That house is as broken down as Al, and older. Maybe they'll have to tear it down so Al can move into something nice with a real bedroom on the first floor. The day he moved it downstairs to the living room, he was so embarrassed. He doesn't deserve embarrassment."

"I wouldn't bet on him moving anywhere. He said he's

moving back to that house. I mentioned Tanesa wants him to move in with her."

Willie Nelson's "My Hero's Have Always Been Cowboys" broke the background silence.

Bob looked at the jukebox like you'd look at someone who just slapped you in the face, then continued, "Chris, whatever my friend wants is what he needs to get. From my days in real estate I've accumulated enough tradespeople who owe me favors to get the house repaired, get it done fast. Al will never ask me to do it, so you'll have to let me know what it'll take. Thy will be done."

"He'll appreciate it. Something else, Bob, do you know anyone who had anything against Al?"

"You mean someone pissed enough to torch his house?"

"Yes."

"Hell, Chris. I'm the maddest person I've ever seen at Al, and I love him to death. No way anybody could be angry with him. Do you really think someone could've done it on purpose?"

"Al's convinced there wasn't anything on his second floor that could've started the fire."

"It sure as hell wasn't spontaneous combustion. Suppose we'll have to see what the fire department finds. Is there anything the poor man needs, other than his house?"

"I don't think so. Tanesa fixed a salad for when he gets hungry."

"A damned salad! That gal was smart enough to go to doctor school yet thinks a freakin' lettuce and other little green things scrunched together will make him feel better. Is she trying to kill him?"

I told him I didn't think so. I also didn't tell him that he may want to try more of those lettuce and other green things occasionally. I'd already heard enough of Bob's rants for one day.

He pushed his way out of his booth then yelled, "Lawrence, fix me two cheeseburgers to go, throw in an order of fries, no, make that two! I've got to go on a mercy mission to save my friend from drying up and blowing away after eating a damned salad. While I'm gone, drag some customers in here, make them spend money. Tell them that unless they do, I'll have to fire my cook."

Clearly, my conversation with Bob was over. He had a more important mission. I didn't want to stand in his way.

Patsy Cline's "I Fall To Pieces" was playing as I left.

———

The sun had slipped behind the marsh before I finished two slices of pizza I picked up at Woody's Pizza on the way home. Bob's tirade plus my poor eating habits kept me from ordering a Greek salad to go with the pizza.

I moved from the kitchen to the front porch to watch the early evening stream of traffic and to reflect on the day. I didn't know Al as well as I did the bar's new owner, but from my many conversations with him and the way his former customers treated him, I agreed with Bob about no one disliking him enough to burn his house, especially with him in it. I also knew Al enough to know when he said there was nothing on the second floor to start the fire, there was no doubt in his mine. Of course, it could've been ancient wiring in the wall.

I interrupted reflecting to call Charles to tell him about the fire. I was surprised when he didn't go through his usual griping about me not calling him as soon as I heard about the near disaster. Charles knew about Al's health issues, so was quick to ask how he was doing. I assured him he was okay, or as okay as one could be under the circumstances. Charles transitioned to asking what started the fire, to which I gave the same answer I shared with Bob. Unlike Bob, it wasn't good enough.

"You mean you haven't called the arson inspector demanding the cause?"

"Tell you what, Charles. Let me find their number so you can pester the people at the fire department."

"So, you'll let me know the cause as soon as you hang up from the fire folks?"

Why do I even try with Charles?

"I'll make a call. I'll let you know if I learn anything."

"Good," he said, then hung up.

I told him I'd make a call but didn't say it'd be to the County Fire Marshall.

Instead of saying something normal like hello, Cindy LaMond answered with, "Guess what I'm having for supper? Hold it, don't guess, I don't have all night. I'm having a Stouffer's Chicken TV dinner I cooked all by myself because Larry's in Columbia at an incredibly fascinating, his words, hardware store trade show. Know what else I'm having? I'm having a wonderful, peaceful time eating while enjoying the silence." She sighed. "You're going to screw it up, aren't you?"

"Good evening, Cindy. I didn't mean to interrupt your delightful meal."

"Smart ass."

I chuckled. "Yep. Want me to call after you finish your culinary creation?"

"You've already ruined my peaceful respite. Go ahead, ruin it more!"

I told her about the fire. She interrupted to ask how Al was holding up. I shared everything I knew about his condition.

"Why do I have a tickle in my gut telling me there's more to this call than telling me about the fire?"

"You're way too wise, Chief."

"Tell that to the Mayor."

"He knows how good you are."

"Okay, Mr. Charm, what do you want?"

"You're so well connected, so well respected, I thought you could contact the Fire Marshall's Office to see if they know the cause."

"Do you think it was intentionally set?"

I told her Al's thoughts on why it couldn't have been accidental.

"Do you know how many fires there are each year caused by faulty wiring—wiring the homeowners swore was fine and couldn't be the reason their houses were turned to charcoal briquettes?"

"How many?"

"Hell if I know but it's a bunch. Crap, that's why accidents are called accidents."

"You're right."

"Aren't I always?" She laughed. "Don't answer that. I'll call in the morning, will let you know."

"You're an angel."

"Always right, angelic. Think I'll order business cards with that on it."

"Add modest."

"Smart ass."

Chapter Thirty-Nine

"Hello," was all I said in the phone before Cindy took over.

"If fortunetelling wasn't illegal on Folly, I'd recommend you open a shop to read palms, leaves, shiny yard globes people stick in their garden, the people who think those round things aren't as stupid looking as everyone else does, or whatever else those quacks read before taking their naïve customer's bucks."

"Good morning, Cindy. Care to enlighten me as to what you're talking about?"

"Arson."

"You sure?"

"Unless Al accidentally stuck a ten-foot ladder behind his house, climbed up it on his rickety legs, threw a gas-filled bottle with a burning piece of cloth sticking out through his upstairs window, yes. The brilliant investigator using all his training cyphered it was arson."

The house wasn't air-conditioned. The windows had been

propped open when I visited, so it would've been easy to do what Cindy described. What I didn't know was why.

"Did the investigator learn anything from the Molotov cocktail?"

"If you mean did he find a scorched, signed *Thinking of You* note attached to it, no. Actually, he didn't find anything important. The bottle was generic. The ladder was stolen from a house two doors away. The owner said the last time he saw the ladder it was parked beside his garage. The investigator figured whoever was on it was scared off by the rotten dog."

"Spoiled Rotten."

"What ever. That leads back to who and why? You sure Bob or Al didn't know anyone who'd want to harm Al?"

"That's what they said. I don't know anyone who had anything against him, but someone did."

"Duh, Sherlock," Cindy said. "You're nearly as smart as the arson investigator."

I heard someone talking in the background and Cindy said she had to go. Something about if it was okay with me, she had to go make Folly safer. She added, "You know Folly, the place where I have jurisdiction."

I thanked her for calling then wished her well making my island safer.

The call left me with a headache plus an unanswered question: Why would someone want to kill Al?

He'd spent a lifetime thinking of others. He and his wife had sacrificed more than anyone should be expected to while adopting and raising their children. He'd been a war hero. From everything I knew, he was generous, kind, harmless. By putting up with Bob for all so many years without killing him, showed he wouldn't harm anyone. So again, why'd someone want to kill him?

I didn't have an answer, but knew there was one question I could answer, and that was who I'd better tell about the arson.

"Good morning, Charles."

"It's another fine day in paradise," he said, almost laughing out he words.

I was pleased he was in such a good mood, but also surprised by his early morning enthusiasm.

"What're you so happy about?"

"What's not to be happy about? I'm sitting at the Dog, sipping coffee I didn't have to fix myself, talking to the lovely, charming, talented Amber. Thanks for calling to check on my happiness."

"In addition to that, there's something else I need to tell you. I just got off the phone with Cindy. She—"

"So," he interrupted, "you on your way?"

I smiled. "Yes."

"Hurry, you're already late."

Ten minutes later I headed to Charles's table when Marc Salmon waved for me to stop at the table where he was sitting with his fellow council member Houston.

Marc looked around to see if anyone was listening. Then asked me to join them for a minute. I was curious, so I took the vacant chair. Marc looked around again, leaned closer to me, and said, "Remember when you were asking what I knew about Eugene Dillinger?"

"Of course."

"I heard something yesterday. Don't know if it has anything to do with the killings on Sol Legare, but figured you'd want to know."

Amber set a mug of coffee in front of me. I thanked her, while Marc looked around the room once more.

"I didn't hear it firsthand so it may not be exactly the way it happened, but his foreman told me Eugene was out at the house he's building on East Ashley. He threatened to kill one of his workers."

"Was he serious?"

"Don't know. Rumor is he has a short fuse, flies off the handle without much provocation. Apparently, he'd told one of his Mexican workers to do something with a window they were installing. The next day Eugene got to the house and whatever it was hadn't been done the way he wanted. He grabbed the worker by the arm then read him the riot act about not doing whatever it was he was supposed to do. Said if it happened again he'd kill the guy." Marc smiled. "Want to hear the funny part?"

I couldn't imagine what'd be funny about the story. I told him yes.

"Eugene lambasted the wrong man. The guy who was supposed to do whatever wasn't even at the house. Eugene told the guy who told me the story to him all Mexicans looked alike."

I still didn't see the humor in it but smiled to not disappoint Marc. I added, "That's interesting."

"Yeah. The foreman said he thought Eugene was mad enough to harm his worker, don't know about killing him. Thought you'd want to know since you're trying to figure out who killed those guys on Sol Legare. Sounds like it could be Eugene."

"That's interesting, Marc. Thanks for sharing."

"Doing my civic duty. Public service is what I'm about."

Behind spreading gossip, I thought, but kept it to myself.

"I appreciate it, Marc."

Houston spoke for the first time. "Chris, you'd better get over to the table with Charles. He looks like he's about ready to lasso you and drag you over."

I thanked both for letting me interrupt their conversation, took my mug, and prepared to be interrogated by Charles.

"It's about time you got here. My coffee's almost cold."

He was in a better mood on the phone.

Amber appeared, kissed the top of my head, then said, "Glad to see you at the right table."

"Nice to see someone's happy to see me."

She smiled.

Charles said, "I ain't about to kiss your bald head, but I'm happy to see you."

Amber ignored him, a talent she's used countless times to maintain her sanity. She asked if I wanted something to eat. I told her French toast, she faked shock, then left to put in the order.

Charles took another sip before saying, "Two questions, you got off the phone with Cindy, and?"

"She called to—"

"You ain't heard question two. What could've been so important that you parked your butt over there for what, an hour, instead of landing where you are now?"

I told him what Marc had shared.

"See, I told you he killed those guys."

All I saw was Eugene had a temper, had trouble recognizing one man from another. I told Charles it was possible, but I wasn't convinced. He mumbled something as he changed the subject to what Cindy wanted. I told him the arson investigator's findings. He asked the same question I'd asked myself, "Who'd want to harm Al?"

I said I didn't know.

"I do. Eugene."

"Because?"

"Because of what Marc just told you. Your memory slipping?"

"Connect the dots for me."

"Okay, Al was partying with Elijah at the pavilion when Elijah saw Eugene. He went to talk to him. Elijah came back scared. Right?"

I nodded.

"I told Al's story at Terrell's party the other night, you know, the one about Elijah seeing Eugene and talking to him."

"Charles, I heard you tell the story, remember?"

"Making sure. Anyway, I figure Eugene was worried about what Elijah may've told Al, so he started the fire to kill poor Al."

"That's quite a stretch."

"Not really," Charles said while he tapped his fingers on the table. "Eugene killed Elijah. After the bones popped up, Clarence and then Terrell started asking questions. Questions that led them to Eugene which led them to getting themselves dead. Al's the only person left who may know who did it."

I said, "Even though Al doesn't know more than he's already said, Eugene doesn't know that. As far as he knows, Elijah told him what got him so scared of Eugene. Now Al's put two and two together and figured Eugene is the killer. A good reason to want to get rid of Al."

"You're catching on junior member of my detective agency. With that figured out, what're we going to do about it?"

"Detective Callahan knows Al's idea about Elijah talking to Eugene, then quickly discarded it as ancient history."

"But he doesn't know about the fire," Charles said. "He stared at my phone like it'd call the detective if Charles wished it to.

He didn't have to wait for a miracle, I called and got Detective Callahan's voicemail. If I hadn't, Charles would've never let me enjoy my breakfast that Amber slipped in front of me while I was calling. I left Callahan a brief message about what happened to Al. I also suggested he may want to verify the cause of the fire with the Fire Marshall's Office.

My semi-peaceful breakfast ended after sharing with Charles a second time how Al's house looked after the fire; in excruciating detail, what Tanesa's condo looked like; and finally, a second time, that Spoiled Rotten was unhurt by either the arsonist or the fire. He'd milked me for everything I knew before saying he had to deliver a package for the surf shop.

He picked up the check and left the restaurant leaving me in shock.

Chapter Forty

On the walk home, I kept thinking something Marc said was important. I tried to replay our conversation and was so focused on it I nearly collided with Virgil walking the opposite direction.

"Sorry, Virgil. I was daydreaming."

"No apology necessary. I spend most of my wake hours daydreaming. I probably do the same when I'm sleeping." He chuckled. "Suppose that'd be nightdreaming. Glad I ran into you, or you ran into me. Got a few minutes?"

I nodded.

He pointed to a bench in front of the Sand Dollar Social Club. "Care to join me in my office?"

We crossed Ashley Avenue to commandeer the bench. He watched the traffic light change from red to green, or I assumed that's what he was doing since I couldn't see his eyes hidden by his ever-present sunglasses. He turned to me. "Chris, you know I'm not as good a detective as you and

Charles, but something's been bothering me about what happened to Terrell."

He hesitated and waited for me to say something. I wasn't about to respond to his detective comment, so I jumped right to, "What's bothering you?"

"Remember when we were at Terrell's house?"

"Yes."

"He was doing a fine job fixing up the place. Anyway, remember that big box in the middle of his kitchen?"

"A new stove."

"Not just any stove, a Wolf stove. I had one like it back when I was rich."

"I remember you telling Terrell. What about it?"

"I'm not certain, but I seem to recall him saying it got there that morning. I asked if he needed help installing it."

"That's what he said. What's bothering you about it?"

Virgil leaned back on the bench, again staring, or so I thought, at the light change colors. Once the excitement subsided over watching green turn to yellow, he leaned forward. "Chris, this is where I'm putting on my detective-in-waiting hat." He pretended to put a hat on. "Remember when we were at the party for Clarence?"

"Of course."

"Someone mentioned Terrell's new stove. Remember who?"

"No. There's a lot I didn't hear that night. It was noisy, the sound system was turned up. You were sitting at the other end of the table, as I recall. Why?"

He looked at his resoled Gucci shoes and said, "It seems to my way of thinking whoever mentioned the stove had to be in Virgil's house after we were there, or the person wouldn't know about it."

"You think the person who mentioned the stove is the killer?"

Virgil nodded.

"You don't recall who said it?"

"No sir, but it narrows it down to Sandra, Robert, Jamal, and Eugene. In my amateur detective brain that's pretty good whittling down the suspects."

"I agree."

"There's hope for me yet in this detective racket. Why not call Charles? See if he remembers?"

Add Virgil to the people who think I'm their personal secretary, or more politically correct, administrative assistant. Either way, he had a valid point.

The phone rang several times before an out-of-breath Charles answered. "I'm on my bike. Hang on a sec, let me pull over."

I hung on. It was way more then a second, but I didn't do what he would've done. I waited without telling him he was taking too long.

"Whew," he said, "Dude has me delivering a humongous box to a house out by the County Park. I'm getting too old for tooling around on my bike." He took a deep breath. "Did you call to see what I was delivering?"

"No. Got a question. When we were at the party for Clarence, do you remember anyone mentioning Terrell's new stove?"

"His stove? That's one of the stupidest questions you've called to ask. What's that got to do with anything?"

"It may tell us the identity of the killer."

"I already told you, it's Eugene."

"Humor me. Do you remember the conversation about the stove?"

"Not really. I suppose it was Sandra Graves. She'd know more about stoves than anyone else there." I heard what sounded like him snapping his fingers. "Tell you what I do remember. When you and I were talking to Terrell behind Rita's, he said he'd talked to a few old-timers about Elijah's murder. He said he still had to talk to Robert and Sandra. Maybe they came to his house and saw the stove."

"Maybe," I said with little conviction.

"Have you checked with Al? He might remember."

"That's my next call. Have fun with your delivery."

I told Virgil what Charles said before calling Al. For the second time this morning, I received a voicemail rather than a live voice. I asked Al to give me a call when he had a chance.

"Well, that's the pits," Virgil said.

I agreed. Before Virgil headed to his apartment, I said I'd let him know what Al had to say.

It was late afternoon before Al returned my call. He said he'd hung around Tanesa's condo as long as he could. He added something about it being so clean, neat, and new he felt he was in a spaceship from the future. He couldn't wait to get back home, his comfortable old shoe. Since moving home was out of the question, he'd convinced Bob to help him escape from the spaceship. He was at Al's keeping the peace between owner and customers.

"Al, I've got a question. Remember when we were at Island Breeze at the party for Clarence?"

"I'm afraid I do remember it. Sad. Clarence seemed like such a nice man."

"Virgil remembers someone mentioning the new stove Terrell got for his house. He didn't remember who said it. Charles thinks it was Sandra Graves. Do you remember hearing anything about it?"

I heard Hank Williams's nasal sounding baritone voice singing "I'm So Lonesome I Could Cry" in the background and a customer moaning. It was good that Al was there to mediate debates about music, race relations, or just Bob being Bob.

"Sure do," Al said. "Don't tell him I said this, but Charles got it wrong. Right family, wrong person. Robert mentioned the stove. I remember because Wolf is a fine stove. I was surprised Terrell got himself one. Why?"

As soon as he said it, I remembered what Marc told me in the Dog that had eluded me earlier. When he shared the story about Eugene's temper, he added that Marc's source said that Eugene said all Mexican workers looked alike to him.

"Al, let me ask you one more question."

"Chris, at my age, you're pushing your luck."

"This one's harder. Back in 1953, when you said Elijah left you at the pavilion to talk to a man and returned scared, is it possible that Elijah went to talk to was Robert, not Eugene?"

There was a long pause. All I heard was Patsy Cline singing "Sweet Dreams." Al finally said, "Chris, in those days, segregation was still a big thing. I doubt there were a handful of white folks who ventured out to Mosquito. Robert and Eugene were two of them. Before you just asked me, I'd swear it was Eugene talking to Elijah, honest to God, I would. I hate being wrong, but you might be right. Robert and Eugene were both skinny, about the same height. It could've been Robert, yes it could've."

"Al, that was a long time ago. It would've been easy to mistake the two men. It was dark, he was far away."

"And white," Al added.

"Yes."

"Are you saying Robert killed my friend, and the other two men?"

"I think so."

"You going to tell the police?"

"I'm calling them as soon as I hang up."

"Then go. I'm sorry to accuse the wrong person."

"No reason to be sorry. You may've solved the murders."

I didn't have to make the call. My phone rang, and I saw CCSO on the screen. This time I knew what it stood for.

"Mr. Landrum, this is Detective Callahan returning your call. What can I do for you?"

The tone of his voice made it sound more like, "Why are you pestering me?"

I thanked him for calling, then hesitated. Where do I begin? Do I tell him about the fire at Al's or what I learned in the last fifteen minutes?

"Detective, I called to tell you about a fire at Al Washington's house. The Fire Marshall's Office determined it was arson, and—"

"Mr. Landrum," he interrupted, "what's that have to do with me?"

"Maybe nothing but let me tell you what I learned this afternoon." I shared everything that Virgil had reminded me about and the confirmation from Al that it could've been Robert that he saw talking with Elijah all those years ago.

"Mr. Landrum, if I was getting this from any Tom, Dick, or Harry I'd jot down the information then file it in that round container beside my desk, or in a file cabinet across the room that's stuffed with everything from thirty-year-old parking tickets to empty cheese cracker packages."

"But—"

"Hang on, I'm not done. Your Director of Public Safety

thinks a lot of you, says it an embarrassing number of times. To show how well our offices can cooperate—rare I understand—I'm going to get Robert and Sandra's address and take a ride out to their house to ask a few questions."

"Thank you."

"Don't get all excited. All I have to confront them with is ancient history and talk about some sort of fancy stove I've never heard of."

"Will you let me know what happens?"

"Don't push it. I'd talk longer but I need to go on a wild-goose chase."

I gave a sigh of relief as I poured a glass of wine and settled in my living-room chair while staring at a mindless television sit-com.

Chapter Forty-One

I was awakened from a nap I didn't know I was taking by a loud drug commercial on TV. It was almost nine o'clock, so I must've been asleep thirty minutes or so. The next sound I heard didn't come from the television, but from someone knocking on the door. I was still groggy as I reached the door. My sleepy eyes were suddenly jarred awake when I saw Robert Graves, wearing a black T-shirt, black slacks, a River-Dogs ball cap, and holding a black matte, semi-automatic Glock handgun I couldn't help notice was pointed at my stomach.

I tried to slam the door, but he'd put his foot between the door and its frame.

"May I come in?" he said as calmly as if he was selling Girl Scout cookies.

I didn't see an option. "Sure."

I must not have moved quickly enough. He shoved the gun in my stomach. I took three steps back. He stepped in, slammed and locked the door.

"These old bones ain't what they used to be," he said. "Shall we sit?"

Again, I didn't see I had a choice. I motioned him to the chair in the corner while I took my recliner.

He surprised me by saying, "Where's Al Washington?"

"How would I know?"

"Because I hear your buddies think you know everything. You think I haven't noticed you and your friends nosing around Island Breeze? So, cut the bull, where is he?"

I glanced around to see what might be nearby to use as a weapon. All that was handy was my cellphone, no competition for a handgun.

I shrugged. "I don't know where he is. As you know, his house was torched. Speaking of his house, why'd you decide to kill my friend with a fire rather than a gun like you did the other three men?" I pointed at the Glock that hadn't wavered from pointing at me since he'd lowered himself in the chair.

"See, I was right about you knowing too much. You and especially Washington."

"You don't have any reason to leave me alive, so how about feeding my curiosity before you move on?"

"Why would I do that?"

"I figure you'd want to tell someone other than Sandra about it."

"Why do you think she knows?"

"Does she?"

"Maybe, maybe not. What're your questions?"

"Let's begin with why you killed Elijah Duncan."

He lowered the gun a couple of inches, but not enough for me to reach him before I'd regret trying.

He shook his head. "Elijah, Elijah. You heard the stories how he was a troublemaker and stirred up all sorts of rifts about equal rights. I didn't have anything against that, in fact, I agreed with him. I saw how blacks were treated in those days. Like dogs at times." He shook his head again.

The Glock swayed along with his head. Could I get to him now? It was as if he heard my thoughts. He leveled the gun at me.

"You also heard Elijah and Sandra met once in the pavilion. It was scandalous in those days."

"Wasn't that months before you met her?"

"Yes, their date at the pavilion was nearly three months before we met. Huh, if that ended it, Elijah might still be alive." He chuckled. "If he hadn't already died of old age."

"They dated after that night?"

"Dated, no, but he didn't stop trying. There were several lovely gals around then, yet damned Elijah wouldn't give up on Sandra." He shook his head. The pistol didn't shake. "By that time I'd met her, and thought she was the prettiest young lady I'd ever seen. We'd gone out a couple of times before she told me about how Elijah kept trying to get her to go out with him. Don't think anybody else knew."

"What happened?"

Robert closed his eyes. I pushed out of the chair. His eyes popped open. He stood and moved a couple more feet away from me.

"Sit!"

I sat. He remained standing.

"Thought you wanted to know what happened."

"I do."

Instead of returning to the chair, he walked behind me, then to the doorway to the kitchen.

"I confronted him out at the end of Mosquito. It was turning dark. Know what he did?"

I shrugged.

"He laughed at me. All I could see was those bright-white teeth and heard him laughing."

"You shot him," I said, and pointed to his handgun.

He nodded. "Not with this. I had an old cowboy six-shooter I bought off a man who probably stole it. I looked around afraid someone saw or heard what'd happened. No one did. I dragged him behind a big-old tree, got a shovel out of the trunk." He smiled. "Dad always told me to carry one in there. Said I'd never know when I'd need it. Smart man. Anyway, I buried Elijah twenty feet from where he took his last breath."

"Did you tell Sandra?"

My phone rang before he answered. He jumped like a cannon had gone off behind him. I reached for the phone.

"Wouldn't do that if I was you."

I pulled my hand back but saw that the call was from the CCSO. It rang five more times before kicking over to voicemail.

"No," Robert said.

"You didn't tell Sandra?"

"Not a word. I walked around on eggshells the next couple of weeks. Then I started hearing the rumors, best news I could've got. Did I know Elijah left the area? Did I know he was killed by the KKK? Or my favorite, did I know he ran off with some preacher's daughter? I could breathe again. A year later, Sandra and I tied the knot. We've lived happily ever after." He pointed the gun at the floor, blinked twice. "Lived happily until his damned bones jumped up in front of Clarence."

My phone dinged indicating I'd received a message. Robert jerked up from the chair again and pointed the gun at the phone like he was going to shoot it. I thought I was scared and nervous. It appeared Robert had me beat. And, he had the gun.

"I can understand why you killed Elijah, but why Clarence? All he did was stumble on the bones."

He moved the gun to the other hand. "I hated that. Old Clarence was a good man. I really liked him, I really did."

You had a funny way of showing it, I thought. "What happened?"

He glanced back at my phone like he was still considering shooting it. "Of all the people out that way, it had to be Clarence finding the bones."

My phone rang once more. This time Robert pushed out of the chair, grabbed the phone, mouthed *Charles*, and switched off the ringer. He lowered the gun, and I started to dive for it, until he raised the weapon again. It ran through my head that if he heard the phone one more time, he'd go berserk.

He was breathing heavily. I gave a silent prayer this would be a good time for his heart to give out.

It didn't.

Robert said, "Three days before Clarence met an untimely end, he ran into Sandra at Harris Teeter asking if she knew who killed Elijah. She told him of course not, but when she told me about it that night, she said he didn't believe her. I asked how she knew. She said she just did. The next day I went to his house, found him in the yard, said I was there to talk about Elijah. The old coot grinned like he knew I'd done it."

"Did he accuse you?"

"No, but he was going to. I'm certain." He smiled for the

first time since he'd arrived. "Now, he can't." He burst into laughter.

Unless I did something soon, I'd be joining Elijah and Clarence. But, what?

"Why kill Terrell?"

"Loose end, my friend. Terrell looked up to Clarence, saw him as a father figure, or so I heard. Terrell told everyone he had to avenge Clarence's murder. He was a lot younger than most of us, full of energy, full of using it to catch the killer." He shook his head. "To catch me. The police weren't doing much. I know they figured whoever killed Elijah was long gone or was dead, besides, they didn't have any evidence. The gun I used got swallowed up by the deep blue sea decades ago. There was no way for the cops to figure it out. None of that was going to stop Terrell, especially after Clarence's death. He'd talked a little to Sandra and me. He wanted to talk more. I went to his house to see how I could help. He met me at the door looking like he'd seen the devil. I figured maybe he had. Somehow, he knew it was me, or had a serious hunch it was. I invited myself in like I did here." He smiled showing no humor. "The boy was doing a good job fixing up the old house. New stuff everywhere. I hated messing it up with his blood. Oh well, he didn't have to clean it up."

"How did he know it was—"

"Enough chit chat. One more time, where's Al Washington?"

"Why do you need him?"

"Next to you, he's the last loose end."

I wondered why he wasn't considering Virgil or Charles loose ends but didn't dare mention their names.

His phone rang. He nearly collapsed. He looked at the screen, answered and said, "Hi, Sandra. What's up?"

He listened a few seconds. "You're kidding. How long ago did he leave?"

He looked at the ceiling and closed his eyes.

I took two quick steps, swatted his arm away that held the gun, then rammed my head in his stomach. He stumbled over the chair, dropped the phone, then tried to pivot so the gun faced me.

I grabbed for his arm holding the gun. I missed. He twisted toward me. I grabbed for it again. His knees buckled. I rammed him a second time. His head hit the floor, the gun slid out of his reach.

I lunged for the weapon. Robert tripped me before I reached it. I turned toward him as he swung at my head. I ducked. His age finally took its toll. He fell and grabbed his chest. I slid over to the gun, grabbed it, and pointed it at the eighty-five-year-old man gasping for breath.

My phone was six feet away. It seemed like miles. I scooted over, punched in 911, told the dispatcher to send the police and an ambulance. I remained on the floor outside Robert's reach until I heard sirens approaching. He hadn't moved since hitting the floor.

When I heard the first patrol car stop in my drive, I pulled myself up with the door handle to greet Officer Bishop, accompanied by a steady stream of first responders. Bishop was kind enough to help me to my chair without making me feel like an old man or an invalid.

An hour later, I'd shared my story with Bishop, Chief LaMond, and a detective I didn't know from the Sheriff's Office. Robert Graves was alive when he left my living room on a stretcher. Barely alive, according to one of the EMTs.

After everyone was gone, I remembered the voicemail message and tapped on the icon.

"Mr. Landrum, this is Detective Callahan. I just left the Graves's house. Robert wasn't home. Sandra claimed she didn't know where he was. I started asking her about the fire at Al Washington's house, then about the deaths of the three men on Sol Legare. She said it'd be wise if she didn't say anything else and called an attorney. I don't think you have anything to worry about, but I wanted to let you know Robert was out there somewhere. You might want to be careful until we find him."

I laughed, pushed out of the chair, and headed to the kitchen for another glass of wine.

Epilogue

The smell of fresh paint mixed with a faint aroma of burnt wood greeted Charles, Virgil, and me as we entered Al's house. It'd been seven weeks since the mystery of the three murders on Sol Legare was solved in my living room. It'd been two weeks since Bob's makeshift crew of carpenters, painters, and roofers had restored Al's house to, in his words, a better condition than it had been in since the Revolutionary War. Al wasn't prone to exaggerate, but I suspected that was one of those times.

Tanesa saw us and rushed to greet her Dad's guests to the housewarming party, or as Bob called it, "house cooling party." He didn't think warming was a good word to use after the fire. Written invitations weren't sent, so he could call it anything he wanted.

Tanesa wore a light-blue blouse, tan slacks, and a smile. She kissed each of us on the cheek then thanked us for coming. Charles said nothing could've kept us away. She said the house was too small to hold everyone, that the other guests were in the back yard. As we walked though the house, I agreed with Al. The restoration was impressive. The walls had a new coat of paint and felt fresh. His former living room, now his bedroom, had new furniture that wasn't there on my previous visit. A fifty-five-inch flat screen television was on a low stand opposite the bed. Something told me that Bob was responsible.

Fortunately, the temperature was mild. The high humidity that'd blanked the area the last two weeks was only a memory.

A makeshift bar was near the back fence. A college-age man wearing a white waiter's coat was behind the bar handing a beer to someone I didn't recognize. Two other men who looked vaguely familiar were waiting behind the one being served. If I wasn't mistaken, they were regulars at Al's. I'd wager Bob also deserved credit for the bar and bartender.

Al was seated in a kitchen chair beside the steps leading from the kitchen to the yard. He was patting Spoiled Rotten that had one paw firmly placed on Al's thigh. He saw me and tried to push the dog's paw off his leg. He failed. I told him not to stand. I thanked him for inviting us.

He introduced me to Gertrude, the dog's owner, who said it was nice meeting me, before adding that she needed to get home to take some "God awful" pills.

Al then gave me his full attention. "Mr. Chris, you've got to be kidding. Don't tell me not to stand. I owe you a stand, a salute, and a bow. You've given this old man peace knowing who killed my friend. I'm sorry you nearly died doing it."

"The house looks great," I said, changing the subject.

"Better than I deserve," he said and smiled.

"That's for damned sure," Bob said from behind me. He

patted me on the back before he grinned at Al. "Just kidding, friend."

Al smiled.

Charles and Virgil joined us and thanked Al for inviting them.

Two more people arrived before Al responded.

Jamal and Eugene looked around like they were at the wrong party. I went to greet them. I thanked them for coming and escorted them to Al.

Jamal said, "Eugene made me. I don't get this far from home unless I'm kidnapped."

Al said, "Jamal, you're welcome at my humble abode any time you want to venture over."

"My friend, I appreciate that. I just might take you up on it. My house is always open to you."

Charles butted in the middle of the conversation. "Anything new on Robert and Sandra?"

Jamal said, "I don't know all the legal stuff, but after Robert got out of the hospital, he got moved to a medical unit until his trial. That's a nice way to say a prison hospital. Old Sandra got herself a different lawyer than Robert's. She's claiming she don't know anything about anything. I'm figuring a jury ain't going to buy it."

Virgil joined the group. "Enough lawyer, jail, and killing talk. I know I'm a newcomer to this group, but unless I'm mistaken, this is a party. So, let's party."

Tanesa helped Al to his feet then clinked two glasses together. We all turned to our host.

"Ladies, gentlemen, and Spoiled Rotten," Al said. "I propose a toast to my good friend Bob Howard who made my burned house the showplace of the neighborhood, and—"

Bob interrupted, "You'll be getting the damned bill, old man."

Al rolled his eyes. "As I was saying, a toast to Bob. A toast to Terrell Jefferson and Clarence Taylor who gave their lives for the truth. And, especially let's toast to my long-gone friend Elijah Duncan. His life wasn't given in vain. Finally, let's raise our glasses to Mosquito Beach for she will always be with us."

About the Author

Bill Noel is the best-selling author of twenty-one novels in the popular Folly Beach Mystery series. The award-winning novelist is also a fine arts photographer and lives in Louisville, Kentucky, with his wife, Susan, and his off-kilter imagination.

Learn more about the series and the author by visiting www. billnoel.com.

Made in the USA
Middletown, DE
20 July 2022

69749333R00176